'I'm nothing like
normally chase.

'What?' he asked gently.

'Plain,' she choked out. 'Ordinary. Boring.'

'I've never been bored with you, Amanda, and I don't think there's anything ordinary about you.'

Amanda sighed, not wanting to continue this conversation with him. Josh was rich and dangerous and absolutely gorgeous. She'd seen him in the society pages, photographed with some of the world's most beautiful women hanging on to his arm. She'd spent more time than she should have looking over those photos, wondering about his life.

Fantasising about him. She was not the kind of woman he dated, not the kind he should notice. 'Josh—' she began.

'Careful. I'll think you're fishing for compliments.'

'I'm not. I know what kind of woman I am.'

'You don't have a clue, Amanda. Did you ever stop to think that maybe you don't know me as well as you think you do, either?'

Dear Reader,

Welcome to March's Sensations™.

Linda Turner leads off the line-up with another of her popular McBride stories, where *The Best Man*, Sheriff Nick Kincaid, is looking for an upgrade to groom. Moreover, there are two more strong, mysterious lawmen in the offerings from favourite Intrigue™ writer Amanda Stevens (*Obsessed!*) and wonderful new recruit Linda Winstead Jones (*Every Little Thing*).

There's classic Sensation drama and excitement in *Cinderella and the Spy* by Sally Tyler Hayes and *Family on the Run* by Margaret Watson, where some rather sexy secret agents do their very best to capture the bad guys and keep their ladies safe!

Finally, award-winning Ruth Wind returns to a familiar setting to give us a story of a heroine who's transformed by weight loss, although Robert Martinez always thought she was beautiful!

Enjoy them all and come back to us again next month for the best in romantic suspense,

The Editors

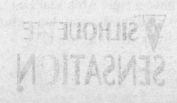

Cinderella and
the Spy

SALLY TYLER HAYES

™ SILHOUETTE
SENSATION®

*First published in Great Britain 2001
Silhouette Books, Eton House, 18-24 Paradise Road,
Richmond, Surrey TW9 1SR*

© Teresa Hill 2000

ISBN 0 373 27071 2

18-0301

*Printed and bound in Spain
by Litografia Rosés S.A., Barcelona*

SALLY TYLER HAYES

lives in South Carolina with her husband, son and daughter. A former journalist for a South Carolina newspaper, she fondly remembers that her decision to write and explore the frontiers of romance came at about the same time she discovered in school that she'd never be able to join the crew of the *Starship Enterprise*.

Happy and proud to be a stay-home mum, she is thrilled to be living her lifelong dream of writing romances.

To my sister, Angie Sears, soon to be
Angie Sears, RN—
I'm very proud of you.

Prologue

"Give me a minute with her," Joshua Carter said, waving off the virtual army of men who accompanied him to the modest, two-story home on a quiet street near Washington, D.C.

One of the military intelligence officers protested, but thankfully the two grim-faced FBI agents and the FBI evidence team behind them, as well as the other agent from Josh's own office, stayed quiet. They'd come in three cars—a damned caravan—to pick up one woman.

"She's not going anywhere," Josh said, tired from lack of sleep and absolutely hating his job at the moment. "Surround the damned house if you want, but there's no reason to scare her half to death by all of us showing up at the door at once. And I'd better not see anybody pull a weapon."

He didn't wait for their agreement. People were too edgy this morning, and there were too many jurisdictional problems involved. He charged ahead, intent on making this as easy for her as he could, because he didn't think she was guilty of anything.

He would shield her as best he could. Normally he'd have the power to do much more, but this wasn't just Division One's mess. All of Washington was in on this one. He was expecting the damned CIA at any minute.

Josh rapped on the door. It swung open, revealing a woman in a thick terry cloth robe, clutching the sides together with a hand at her chest. Her long, dark hair fell to her shoulders in a loose, quietly sexy mess of curls and shimmering lights. Her soft lips, totally free of any adornment, formed the barest hint of a smile, and her pretty brown eyes widened in wary surprise.

"Josh? What are you doing here?"

Josh moved to the left, hoping to block her view of the three cars parked out front and the huddle of agents he'd left in his tracks, and he reminded himself he had a job to do.

"I need to come inside, Amanda."

He didn't wait for her consent, just pushed his way through the doorway. She backed up immediately, looking wary, and he closed the door firmly, wondering how long he could keep everyone else out.

Her eyes got so big, spiky lashes a mile long not enough to shield them now, and she was scared. Already she was scared. He took her cold, trembling hands in his and held on tight. If she fainted on him, he didn't want her to fall down. Then he glanced down at the ring she wore on the third finger of her left hand. He'd always hated the sight of Rob Jansen's ring on her finger. Even though there was nothing between him and Amanda Wainwright and likely never would be, he still hated that ring.

He took a breath and said, "Rob died this morning."

"What?"

"He died," Josh repeated. "I'm sorry."

She tightened her grip on his hands, and then tilted her head to the right, as if that might be enough to change her view of the world or maybe the words he'd said.

"I don't…I don't understand."

She stared at him for the longest time, and slowly her expression started to crumble. Her bottom lip trembled. She bit it to make it stop. Tears filled her eyes, overflowed and ran in rivulets down her pale cheeks. Her lashes came down, and every dab of color left her face. She gasped once, then again, and then she made the sound of a woman in awful, physical pain.

He pulled her into his arms, bringing her to a place he'd never thought to have her again. If there was a shred of decency in his body, he wouldn't have noticed how it felt to have her so close. The citrusy smell of her hair. The softness of her cheek. Was that baby lotion on her skin? He certainly shouldn't be aware of how little she had on beneath the robe, that her breasts were pressed against his chest, her arms wound tightly around his shoulders.

But then Joshua Carter had never taken a woman in his arms and felt absolutely nothing. He simply didn't have it in him. He was a connoisseur of women, and there'd never been one quite like Amanda. He hurt for her now. He would have gladly borne the pain she felt himself to spare her, and he really could have killed Rob Jansen for dragging her into the middle of this mess.

Finally her sobs quieted. She backed away and looked up at him with wet, sad eyes. "He had an accident?"

"We're not sure. His heart stopped. It looks like a seizure of some sort."

"He had asthma. He could control it most all the time, but—"

"It may have been related to his asthma." Or it could well have been murder, something Josh wasn't ready to tell her. He settled for a vague "It'll be a few days before we know for sure."

"I just...I can't believe it."

"I know," he said gently, giving her a weary smile, thinking about taking her in his arms again, wishing there was time but knowing there wasn't. "I'm afraid there's more, Amanda. It looks like Rob was doing some things he shouldn't have been doing."

Guileless, tear-stained eyes stared back at him. "What?"

"There are people outside. I'm sorry, but I have to let them in. I'd give you some time if I could, but it's out of my hands."

"I...I don't understand."

"I know. Just tell us what you know, Amanda, that's all you have to do, and everything will be fine, I promise."

He moved quickly then, opening the door. A team of men fanned out across the room, the technicians donning gloves and bringing their equipment.

Nodding toward them, Josh said, "They're going to search the house."

"Sir?" A red-faced colonel, still upset about being kept out of the house initially, cut in, "Did you advise Ms. Wainwright of her rights?"

"Rights?" Amanda repeated, close to panic now, looking back to Josh.

"I haven't advised her of anything," Josh said, "except the fact that her fiancé is dead."

Amanda edged closer to Josh. "What does he mean, 'rights'?"

"We have to ask you some questions. You need to get dressed and come with us."

"I don't understand," she said again.

She'd be saying that again and again, Josh suspected, before they were done. "I know," he said again. "This is about Doc."

"Doc?"

Josh nodded grimly. Doc was a federal agent, a colleague of theirs, and this was deadly serious.

"Amanda, we think Rob was involved in Doc's murder, and we have to ask you some questions. You have to come with us. Now."

Chapter 1

One year later

Joshua Carter sat in his car across from her house. He hadn't been here since the day he told her Rob Jansen was a traitor, a murderer and that he was dead. Josh doubted she would be glad to see him, but he couldn't stay away any longer.

Taking a breath to steady what were normally rock-solid nerves, he approached the house and rapped on her door. "Amanda," he called out in a voice that sounded strangely harsh to his own ears. "It's Josh."

He tried to prepared himself for the sight of her, which somehow always managed to suck the breath from his lungs. He hadn't seen her in eight long weeks. Without meaning to, he'd kept track of the days. Like some lovesick kid.

Lovesick?

Josh laughed wryly. He wasn't in love with her. He

didn't do love. He merely found himself in the decidedly uncomfortable and unusual position of being obsessed with her.

They worked in the same office. Within minutes of returning to the office after a long mission, he'd be searching the room for her. If he didn't see her, he'd start asking, with practiced casualness, "Where's Amanda?" He wondered whether anyone saw through the act and if they were enjoying it. Joshua Carter, the consummate ladies' man, obsessed with a woman he would likely never have.

Looking up, he saw her through the door. Her eyes got so big he thought he might drown in them. He felt immensely better, just seeing her face.

"Open the door, Amanda."

The door swung open finally, giving him a good look at her. On a normal day the sight of her could nearly bring him to his knees. But seeing her like this—her body covered in soft, loose-fitting, cream-colored things that might have been pajamas, her eyes huge and dark and wet with tears—was painful, staggeringly so.

She looked so fragile and small, as if a stiff breeze could carry her away. There were dark smudges under her eyes. Her face looked painfully thin and pale, the only color a flush in her cheeks, which he attributed to her embarrassment that he'd found her like this.

She wasn't the most beautiful woman he'd ever met, but it was her face he saw every night before he drifted off to sleep. She was the one who haunted his dreams, whose taste he still remembered from a single, long-ago, stolen kiss, and he worried about her, almost every bit as much as he ached to make her his, to wipe the sadness from her face, if only she would let him.

Her hair was brown, shot through with bits of red when it hit the light just right. She had piled it on her head, which only made him want to pull out all the pins and take it down. Still, the style had its advantages; it showed off the curve at the back of her neck. Her nape. He found that spot utterly enticing, found himself wanting to press his lips to that spot, to see just how soft and sensitive it was. He liked the way bits of her hair always managed to escape from all the pins, little curls hanging down her neck, curls she sometimes tucked behind her ears, that sometimes curled in a tiny circle against her collarbone and her throat. Which made him want to have his mouth all over her neck.

She had big, innocent-looking brown eyes, spiky, thick lashes and a wide, generous mouth, and there was something about her features, some balance to the bones in her face, her cheek, her jaw, her brow, her neck, that he found utterly compelling at times. She'd turn her face at a certain angle, and one of those sweet, tentative half smiles would come across her face, and he'd be struck by how absolutely perfect her face was. Wide, guileless eyes, soft, generous lips, soft, pink cheeks. There were moments when she looked absolutely stunning.

Damn.

Josh, a man who prided himself on perfect control, had to turn his head away for a second to steady himself. His chest hurt, as if someone had it in a vise, and then he remembered—breathe. The message finally got through his pitifully muddled brain, and the pressure eased.

He forced a careless smile across his face and said, "I don't suppose you're going to invite me in?"

She hastily wiped away tears. "Josh, it's late."

"I know. But I just got back into town this evening," he explained. "Heard you had a rough day." Actually, he'd heard she looked as fragile as she had in the days immediately following Rob Jansen's death, and that had scared him.

She stiffened, folded her arms across her chest, the movement drawing his eyes to the soft curves of her breasts, unrestrained inside the folds of the oversize top. Dog that he was, he looked for another moment before turning his head away yet again.

"Josh."

There was impatience, irritation, bone-deep fatigue and maybe something else in her voice. Desperation? Need? That was the main reason he'd come. It was a long time until morning, and she would need someone tonight.

Although she'd been cleared today of any lingering suspicions anyone might have had about her involvement in the scandal that had rocked Division One, she'd been forced to relive the whole thing in her testimony before the Board of Inquiry. Josh was worried about all the questions she'd faced, all those nasty, old memories that might have been dredged up. And maybe a part of him was thinking about someone else entirely, a woman he'd let down so completely, so very long ago, because he simply hadn't understood how bad things were for her.

So no matter how much Amanda might think she wanted to be alone tonight, Josh wasn't going to let her.

"I thought we'd take a drive," he said, struggling for something they could do, someplace they could go. He didn't think she needed to be in this house tonight, knew he shouldn't be here alone with her.

"A drive?" She gaped at him.

Keeping her off balance was probably a good idea. She might not accept a normal show of sympathy or of support from him, but if he could keep it light, keep surprising her, she might let him help.

"You know…in a car. I have a fabulous after-hours car," he bragged, shoving his hands into the front pockets of his pants so he wouldn't touch her. "A '65 Jag, dark-green, butter-colored leather interior. Convertible, of course. Runs like the wind. Not a scratch on it. What do you say?''

She frowned at him. "You didn't happen to get hit on the head while you were in Rome, did you?"

"Paris." He flashed a smile, wishing she was indeed keeping tabs on him. "I was in Paris." A particularly frustrating experience. He hadn't found what he was looking for, and it had kept him away from her.

"Fine, Paris." She nodded impatiently. "Josh, I don't think this is the time…"

"It's the perfect time," he insisted, pushing his hands deeper into his pockets and purposely not gentling his wry tone. "What else are you going to do, Amanda? Sit here alone in the dark and cry?"

Her chin came up at that, and if she'd been about to shed another tear, she wouldn't dare do it now. Good. He wasn't ready to handle her tears, although before the night was over, he would find a way to do that, too. If she needed to cry, he wasn't going to let her do that alone, either.

"Hey, are you hungry?" he added.

She closed her eyes, no doubt looked for patience. "No."

"I am. I've had nothing but airline cuisine all day, and I don't have to tell you what I think of that."

He brushed past her and walked into the kitchen. He dug into her refrigerator, finding a deli bag full of roast beef. Not the kind of thing he normally fed his women, but it would do. He rifled through her kitchen until he found the makings of an adequate sandwich. Amanda watched, her arms crossed in front of her, her back rigid, but she'd given in. He could feel it.

"Grab a sweater," he said. "If I get going too fast with the top down, you'll get cold."

"*If* you drive too fast?"

That nearly won him a smile. Josh felt the pressure inside his chest ease. He could do this for her. He could help. "Okay, *because* I drive too fast, you'll get cold, even with the heat cranked up."

"You turn the heat on? So you can put the top down?"

He strove for impatience, a touch of arrogance, knowing he couldn't afford to be too kind. She would know he was up to something. "You've never owned a convertible, have you?"

"No."

"It's a damned shame." He shook his head. "Every woman should own a convertible, at least once in her life."

"I'll keep that in mind."

"And you'll understand why before we're through," he assured her. "Grab a sweater. And some shoes."

"Josh, I was ready for bed. These are my pajamas."

Closing his eyes, he nearly sliced off his thumb, instead of the tomato. He didn't need to know she was standing there in her pajamas, didn't need to imagine her climbing into a bed.

"They'll do," he claimed, "If you were rich, you'd have paid ten times more for them and worn them to fancy parties. Grab a sweater, Amanda. Dinner's almost ready. We need to get going."

"Josh—"

"I won't give up." He turned back to her. "You know that about me. I never give up."

She crossed her arms in front of her and frowned. "Like a two-year-old, right?"

He ignored that. "Scared to be alone with me, Amanda?"

"No," she insisted.

"Then come on. We have places to go. Things to see."

She looked tired, he thought. So tired. But he doubted she'd be able to sleep, even if he was willing to leave her here alone, which he wasn't.

Miraculously she abandoned all protests, grabbed her things, took one long, lingering look around her house, then followed him into the night.

"Can you believe it?" he said, showing off the car. "Looked like a rusty old can when I found it. Took me six years to get it into this kind of shape."

"I have trouble believing your attention span could last six minutes, much less six years," she quipped.

Josh glared at her and opened the passenger door, helping her inside. "This is a masterpiece," he protested. "A precision-tuned piece of art."

"I get it," she claimed. "This is about Bond."

"Bond?"

"James Bond," she answered. "I'm sure when you were a little boy, you had serious James Bond fantasies."

He winked at her. "It's no fantasy, Amanda. I am a spy."

And he was. The agency for which he worked was technically a part of the Commerce Department, housed in an incredibly bland-looking, four-story brick building in Georgetown under the name Linguistic Services, Inc. If anyone asked, he was a translator, and his office did indeed house experts fluent in more than a dozen languages who hired themselves out to high-ranking diplomats and Americans doing business abroad. But it was all a cover for a top secret counter-terrorism organization called Division One.

For the longest time, he'd loved his job, been in perfect control. But not anymore. Not with her.

Josh cranked the engine and sped off toward the Washington Beltway, across the Potomac and into Maryland, then south, to the bay. Amanda sat beside him as he bragged about the car's sound system, then tuned in his favorite rock station. The announcer made some silly quip about the station playing "oldies."

"*Old?* Can you believe this?" he complained. "Rock and roll will never be old."

"This stuff was actually popular when you were a kid?" she said innocently.

"A kid?" He nearly choked. "I'm thirty. Thirty is not old."

"Don't worry, Josh. To be old, you have to grow up first. You're in no danger."

She laughed a bit, and even if she was putting him down, it was worth it. Josh glanced over to find her hunched down against her seat, her sweater pulled tight around her, her hair fluttering in the wind. She tilted her head back to look at the stars. He felt a little better about kidnapping her this way.

"Still cold? I'll put the top up if you like," he offered.

"No. You know you've got me hooked now."

He'd counted on that—the cool air rushing at her, the car shooting through the blackness, the music loud and evoking all sorts of memories, the sky spread out like a blanket of diamonds overhead. There was something incredibly soothing about driving too fast in the dark with the top down.

It was nearly an hour later before he said, "So...want to tell me about the hearing?"

"What's left that you don't already know?"

He did know almost everything. He'd been beside her a year ago when she'd been questioned as if she was a criminal and her house had been searched. Days later, Josh had been back with more devastating news. They'd found her fiancé's partner in crime—Martin Tanner—Josh and

Amanda's boss at Division One. She'd been Tanner's secretary, which only fueled speculation that she was somehow involved. Two men closest to her, Josh thought, both of them liars, traitors. She probably despised all men right now.

Josh frowned. She hadn't particularly liked him before any of this mess. As she'd so often pointed out to him, she wasn't his kind of woman; he wasn't her kind of man. Which should have made it easy for him to forget all about her, something he'd never quite managed to do. If there was a shred of decency left inside him, he would leave her to find some nice, sweet, utterly safe man who'd make her his wife and be the father of her children. Someone who'd buy her a brick house in the suburbs and a damned minivan and a membership at the country club. Someone who could offer her an absolutely ordinary life, the kind he was sure she craved.

She would find someone else. He would have to sit right here and watch. He would stay quiet and smile politely, as if he didn't have a care in the world, while she came to belong to some other man, some eminently more suitable man.

The hell he would.

He couldn't leave her alone right now, and he couldn't stop wanting her. So something was going to happen between them. It was inevitable. He'd made himself a deal—he'd stayed away, given her time to put her life back together, to find someone else, to be happy, and she hadn't done it. She was every bit as alone and unhappy today as she had been a year ago, and Josh was sick of it.

He could help her now. He could show her how to enjoy life again. First they had to get past the hard stuff.

"I never believed you were a part of it, Amanda. Not from the very beginning."

"Really?" she said, pinning him with a disbelieving stare.

"I was just doing my job," Josh insisted. "I tried—"

He broke off. He'd tried to go as easy as he could. But a man had died. A friend of theirs. He had a duty to uphold. Despite what she thought of him, it was a duty he didn't take lightly. He wouldn't disregard it, no matter what he might feel for one devastated woman caught up in the middle of it.

But he didn't want to argue, and he wasn't here to defend his conduct in the investigation. He settled for adding, "I'm sorry if I made it harder for you because it was me asking all those questions."

She brushed off his apology. "It wasn't your fault, Josh. None of it."

"It wasn't yours, either," he insisted. "The Board of Inquiry just made it official. They cleared you today. The whole mess is over. It's time to put it behind you."

Josh was going to help.

Tonight, he would tell her he wanted to be her friend. She would probably laugh in his face, but he'd do it anyway. He would keep coming back until she believed him, until she trusted him just a little bit, and somehow he'd find a way to keep his hands off her. First he had to get her to talk to him.

"You can tell me about Rob," Josh said, gritting his teeth at the thought of her ex-fiancé.

"Josh, I try not to think about him at all or about how stupid I was—"

"It wasn't you, Amanda—"

"—because I loved him," she rushed on, color blooming in her cheeks and shame in her eyes, as if she'd confessed the worst kind of sin.

Josh frowned. He reached for her hand and held it. "I know. Took me a while but I finally figured that out."

He remembered every moment of that night he'd finally understood she did indeed love her fiancé. A night he'd reached for her and kissed her, thinking of nothing but what he needed, what he wanted. And he thought it was the ultimate irony that he, who'd so carelessly worked his way through woman after woman and scarcely ever been denied anyone he wanted, should find himself falling for her this way, wanting her now, at the worst possible time.

"Did you?" She hunkered down in her seat against the rush of the wind. "I loved him, Josh. Do you even know what that means? I thought I was going to spend the rest of my life with him. I thought I was being so careful, that I'd made a good choice. I respected him. I thought he was kind and understanding and gentle and patient, and that we wanted the same things out of life. And it was a lie. Every bit of it was a lie."

"He used you." Josh's hands clenched into fists on the steering wheel.

"That doesn't make it any easier."

And there was nothing Josh could say to that. They drove in silence. At nearly three in the morning he pulled into a little beach community in Maryland near Point Lookout, which jutted out into the widest part of Chesapeake Bay. At a deserted parking lot near a deserted beach he pulled a blanket from the trunk, grabbed the sandwiches he'd made and took off onto the soft, brown sand.

Reluctantly Amanda followed.

"We're going to picnic on the beach in the middle of the night?"

"You have no sense of adventure," he complained as he spread out the blanket and started digging into the cooler he'd packed.

"I'm not hungry, Josh."

"Really? When was the last time you ate?"

She considered that for a moment. He could tell the minute she remembered her last meal. She sat down beside him, and they ate. Josh listened to the wind, watched the play of light from the moon on the darkness of the water, the specks of light in the distance from the boats and houses along the shoreline. When he finally turned to her, he was pleased to note that she had eaten her entire sandwich.

"Not hungry, huh?"

"Okay. You were right. You always have to be right, don't you? And you have this annoying habit of always getting what you want."

"Not always," he said, trying to force a lightness to the words that he didn't feel.

"Josh, what are you trying to do tonight? Why did you bring me here?"

There was no stalling any longer. Staring off into the distance, he said, "Is it so hard to believe I want to help you? That I want to be your friend?"

"Yes. Josh, please, just take me home and leave me alone."

"I can't."

"Why not?"

"Because I can't."

"And what about me? What about what I want? What I need?" She glared at him. "God, this is just like you. So caught up in what you want, or what you think you want, that you don't give a damn about anyone else."

"That's not true." He took her stubborn chin in his hand, forcing her to look at him. "You taught me that lesson, and I promise, I learned it well."

She turned her head away. "Don't."

"I'm sorry I hurt you," he said. "That I made you uncomfortable that night. I just didn't understand, Amanda. I haven't had a lot of experience with women like you. But

I'm sorry, and I honestly and truly want to help you now, if you'll just let me.''

"Don't, Josh. Please, don't. If that's honestly what this is about—helping me—I appreciate it. Really, I do. But don't.''

He shook his head and went right on, just like she said he always did. "I know what you think of me.''

"Do you?''

"Selfish? Conceited? Irresponsible? Immature? You can stop me anytime, Amanda.''

"But you're doing so well," she said.

He could smile, even then. "I know I'm not your favorite person. Not going to stop me there, either?''

She shook her head back and forth.

"Let me help you through this, Amanda.''

"Why?''

"Because it's been a bad day, and I'm here. Because I care about you. I promise you, I am capable of caring about a woman in a way that has nothing to do with sex.''

"That's truly admirable, Josh.''

He laughed out loud, because he loved sparring with her, loved the way she cut him to the quick. "Look, the truth is I heard about the hearing today. I heard it was a little rough, and I was worried about you. That's it. I thought you'd need a friend. We could be friends, Amanda. If you could forgive me.''

"Forgive you?''

"For that kiss.''

She scrunched up her face and covered it with both her hands. "I don't want to talk about kissing you.''

Josh watched as her hair fell in a dark curtain that hid her face, and he itched to take his hand and smooth it back into place. He'd always suspected she thought of that kiss as some heinous crime, and he supposed to her it was. So often when she looked at him, he saw the guilt in her eyes, guilt that was rightfully his. They could settle that tonight, too.

He'd spent months wanting a taste of her—wanting much more than that in fact. And one night, at a party for a retiring colleague, not long *before* her fiancé died, he'd found her outside on a quiet terrace in the moonlight, looking more beautiful than he'd ever seen her. She seemed quiet and maybe a little sad. He'd tried to cheer her up, had flirted outrageously with her and once he'd coaxed a smile across her pretty face, he'd simply leaned down and taken that kiss.

Just one.

One too brief taste of her, and as stupid as it sounded, he could have sworn the ground moved beneath his feet that night, that the entire Earth shook with the force of one frustratingly brief kiss.

He'd been stunned.

She'd been horrified.

She'd never taken anything he'd said to her seriously, complaining that he flirted with every woman he met, and he supposed he did. He liked women, liked teasing them, liked making them smile, and he'd never quite seen the crime in that.

Amanda had always dismissed him totally as nothing but a flirt, and after that kiss, she thought he was pure scum. Because, as he'd discovered too late and much to his surprise, she was a woman to whom fidelity and loyalty were much more than obscure concepts.

She'd pulled away from him almost instantly, her eyes blazing and the color high in her cheeks, and told him she was engaged, that it might not mean anything to him, but it certainly did to her. And then she'd brought up fidelity, offering to define the term for him, just in case it wasn't even in his vocabulary.

He understood the concept; he'd just never found a woman who lived it. He hadn't understood at all, until it was too late, just how different she was. He'd thought women like her simply didn't exist anymore, that they were simply a myth.

She took her vows quite seriously, and she'd promised herself to Rob Jansen, which meant she didn't do anything with another man. And she saw kissing Josh as an absolute crime.

"You didn't kiss me. I kissed you. Once. A year ago. It was just one little kiss, Amanda," he said carefully, his tone purposely light, because he didn't think she'd believe him if he told her how much it had meant to him.

She still looked horrified by what she'd done.

"Do you have any idea how many women I've kissed?" he tried, figuring she'd damn him for that remark as well, but he'd rather have her angry at him than feeling guilty about her own actions, which really amounted to nothing but waiting maybe a half a second before she pushed him away from her. And maybe enjoying the kiss itself. He did think she enjoyed it, which would have made it even worse in her eyes. She hadn't known then that Rob Jansen was an absolute jerk, that he'd done nothing but use her, but Josh had never liked the man and had always thought he was absolutely wrong for Amanda.

It in no way excused the way Josh had grabbed her and kissed her, but there it was. He'd done it. He couldn't take it back now, just like he couldn't change the kind of man he'd been in the past.

"Engaged women, Josh? Just how many of them have you kissed?" she asked. "What am I saying? You wouldn't stop with a kiss."

"No, I seldom do," he admitted, digging himself even deeper. Grimly, he took it from her, accepted it. Because he deserved it for the way he'd chosen to live his life and for what little he'd shown her of himself.

But because he wanted a chance with her, he mounted a paltry defense. *"Before,"* he admitted. "I can't say I haven't done that. But it was *before*—"

"Before what?" she asked.

The best answer he could come up with was *before you.* It wasn't something he could tell her right now, wasn't something he was ready to examine in great detail himself. But he was afraid the answer was most definitely about her. *Before* he saw himself through her eyes. She thought he was careless with women, that he was selfish and indulged himself like a child. She thought there was something very wrong with the way he lived his life.

He'd been amused for the briefest of times by her whole attitude, and then he'd thought about trying to explain his life to her or the women he saw. They were so unlike her. They didn't want a long-lasting relationship any more than he did. They lived for the moment, and they didn't truly care about him, only the pleasure their time with him would bring.

Somehow just thinking about it had left him feeling a little tired and strangely alone and empty. She'd opened his eyes, made him think about the way he was living his life, and he found he wasn't comfortable with what he saw.

"Go ahead, Josh," she said. "Explain it to me."

"I don't think I could," he said carefully.

Because Josh wasn't the same man anymore. She'd changed him in some elemental way, maybe from that first kiss. He was still fumbling around and trying to fully understand it all, and obviously, there was no way he could explain it to her when he didn't even understand it himself yet. It was something about who she was, something tied up in the reason he couldn't quite forget about her after that one kiss, couldn't stop wanting her.

"We can analyze me another time, okay? Let's talk about you. Let it go, Amanda," he said. "All of it. Not just me and one little kiss. Everything with you and Rob. Everything with Tanner. You haven't done anything wrong. Nothing that happened was your fault."

"No?" she said bitterly. "Do you think Rob came after me by accident? Because he had any genuine feelings for me? He came after me because of who I was. Because I was Tanner's secretary. And I never suspected a thing."

"No one did. Not for a long, long time."

"You did," she said. "You stopped them both. You and Dan and the others."

"Not until it was nearly too late," he said bitterly. "Believe me, I have as many regrets about that as you do. But it wasn't your fault."

"You don't know that. You can't possibly know."

"I know what I see with my own two eyes. As blind as you think I am to anyone else's wants or needs, there are times when I notice what's going on around me." Particularly when it came to her. "All you did was trust the wrong man. Don't beat yourself up for trusting him, Amanda. Or for loving him."

God, he hoped she didn't still love him.

"You're one of the kindest women I know," he said. "Loyal. Trusting. Generous to a fault."

"Naïve," she added. "Stupidly naïve. Criminally naïve."

"There's no criminal statue for naïveté," he pointed out.

"Maybe there should be."

"You couldn't have stopped this," he insisted. "You

were an innocent bystander, and you're going to put this behind you.''

"I'm trying, Josh. I'm trying my best, I swear." Her composure started to crumble. There was a flash of hurt in her eyes, a trembling of her lips, a bewildered look on her face. "I just don't know how to do it."

"I do," he insisted. "I can help you, Amanda. Let me help."

"Why?"

"Because I want to. Because I'm concerned about you. Isn't that enough?"

"I'm not sure," she said, not even looking at him any longer.

Josh had a sinking feeling that he might not have done her any good bringing her here. He simply didn't have the words to make anything better.

Frowning, he got to his feet, put out a hand to pull her up, as well. "Come on. Let's take a walk."

They walked side by side, not touching, not speaking. The sand was soft, the wind cool and insistent, the tangy smell of the sea in the air. Birds were gliding across the surface of the water, diving into it at times, making all sorts of noises. But it was peaceful. He always felt the stress drain away, if not on the drive here, on the walks he sometimes took or in the sight of the rising sun.

Watching it climb into the sky, in this place where he could hear the wind, could feel it, could see for what looked like forever, had always given him the sensation that he could start over, wipe the slate clean with each new day. It was like being born again, everything made new, all things possible.

They paused, looking at streaks of golden light that seemed to radiate from the horizon line, growing more intense until the glow was nearly blinding. Moments later the sun appeared, rising like a ball of fire from the water.

"It is beautiful here," she said finally.

He nodded. This was what he'd wanted her to see, the magic he hoped she'd find.

"It's a whole new day. You can make it anything you want, Amanda. You can start all over again."

He didn't reach for her, though he wanted to badly. He waited. Maybe he was getting better at this waiting stuff. He waited until she leaned into his side and bent her head down low, until he felt her start to shake and knew she couldn't hold back her tears any longer. Then he took her within the circle of his arms and held her while she sobbed and shivered and hung on to him for dear life. Just as before, she felt like a puff of air in his arms, as fragile and elusive as a fairy. He worried he'd hurt her by holding her so tightly and felt totally inadequate when it came to easing her pain.

Normally, he charmed women, flattered them, made love to them, to expensive, moneyed, sophisticated women. Amanda was none of those things. She was sweet and innocent and lost, and he found himself in the ridiculous position of wanting her when her heart was breaking and she had no reason to trust any man, least of all him.

She pulled away from him to look up at him with sad, damp eyes, her lashes spiked together by tears, and soft trembling lips, and he wanted to devour her whole, right there on the spot. But he wanted something else, too. He wanted to make everything all better for her. Wanted to shield her, to protect her. To stand between her and the rest of the world, wanted the right to do that for her. He wanted her to like him, maybe even to respect him. To see that the image he presented to the world wasn't all there was to him.

Looking embarrassed and self-conscious, she dried her cheeks and tucked her hair behind her ears. He pulled out a handkerchief and mopped up what was left of her tears. "Better?"

She nodded. "I'm sorry."

"It's all right. You needed it."

"I guess I did. One last time." She sighed. "Every time I do this, I promise myself it's the last time."

"Hey, it was a bad day."

Amanda nodded once more, her breathing slowing. She offered him a watery smile, then stifled a yawn.

"Come on. You're exhausted." Josh put an arm around her shoulders and turned her back toward the car. "Time to get you home."

They packed their things, loaded up the car. Josh helped her recline her seat, then tucked a blanket around her. Five minutes later she was sleeping quietly beside him.

She woke on the outskirts of D.C. as the sun was beginning to get uncomfortably warm and asked if he'd mind stopping for some coffee. Josh pulled into the parking lot of a little coffee shop not far from his town house.

"I wanted to thank you," she said as he stopped the car. "For everything. And I'm sorry I fell apart that way."

He made it out to be nothing at all, when in truth it meant a great deal to him. How the hell did he tell her that? How did he make her understand? He wasn't fooling around here. She was important to him. Lately everything in his life seemed to be about her.

With a little groan Josh closed his eyes and leaned toward her. He let himself brush his lips against her forehead in what had to be the most chaste and most frustrating kiss he'd ever given any woman, and even that left her decidedly uneasy. He was moving too fast. With another groan,

Josh pulled away. He didn't even look at her as he made one last plea.

"We could be friends, Amanda. You could call me, just to have someone to talk to. We could just drive and drive and drive. Whatever it takes. Whatever helps."

"Josh..." He risked a glance toward her, already knowing what she was going to say, how she would look. All sad and lost again, maybe a little bit afraid. Why did he have to make her so afraid? "I don't think that would be a good idea."

Josh nodded, expecting that. All he wanted was a chance with her. They'd never really had a chance together. It was an uncomfortable feeling—thinking he might not be able to charm her into seeing things his way. That she might know him too well. That years of meaningless pleasure and indulging himself with women who, in the end, hadn't meant a thing to him might ruin any chance he had with her.

"Come on," he said to her, telling himself to get out of the damned car before he made it any worse. "Let's get some coffee and I'll take you home."

Chapter 2

Amanda was a little sleepy and way too relaxed when he made his move. His beautiful blue eyes closed. Minty aftershave filled her nostrils. A blast of heat radiated from his magnificent body as his warm, sensual mouth brushed the skin at her left temple. She braced herself as best she could, steeling herself for so much more, then somehow got lost in the feel of his mouth against her forehead. The touch was warm and soft, teasing, brief and somehow sexy as well. Only Josh, she thought, could kiss a woman's forehead and have her practically swooning.

He pulled away. She could breathe again. Almost. And when she opened her eyes, he was looking at her in that oddly unsettling way that always left her feeling uneasy and a little excited, a little scared.

Joshua Carter scared her to death.

Most men scared her to death right now. But especially him.

"We could be friends, Amanda," he said. "You could

call me, just to have someone to talk to. We could just drive and drive and drive. Whatever it takes. Whatever helps.''

He wanted to be her friend? She shook her head back and forth. ''Josh...''

He looked at her once more, a little zing of awareness shooting right through her, reminding her of all the reasons why he didn't mean that part about being friends. Or maybe he did, in his own way. Josh slept with his women friends; she was certain of that. And she wasn't going to sleep with him. She wasn't letting herself near any man.

Maybe in the next decade, she decided. Surely she would have wised up by then.

''I don't think that would be a good idea,'' she told him, hating that wimpy, breathless quality to her voice, the one that practically screamed *pushover!* Hating that part of her that wanted to cry and cling to him and feel sorry for herself for just a little bit longer. The part that wanted to let him be with her to keep her from feeling so absolutely and totally alone. Even knowing what he was, she was tempted to let him into her life, let him take charge for just a little while and take care of her.

Her entire life was in a shambles, and she couldn't quite figure out what to do about it. But she still had enough sense of self-preservation not to fall into his arms, at least not any more than she already had.

He sat there for a minute, looking much too intent and serious. But for once he didn't push. He came around to her side of the car, taking her hand and helping her out, as if they were pulling into the most elegant restaurant in town on a Saturday night and not a little coffee shop at seven o'clock in the morning with sand on their shoes and her hair a windblown mess. She took a deep, hopefully calming breath and tried to ignore the reality of her life at the moment. Her fiancé was dead, and before he died he'd betrayed her and everyone around her. Her boss was just as bad, and she'd trusted them both.

Stupid little Amanda, she thought. Naïve, trusting, gullible, foolish Amanda.

She hated that image of herself, hated it all the more because it was true. And she hated even letting Joshua Carter inside her house last night and taking off with him in this ridiculously expensive car of his and crying all over his impossibly broad shoulders before the night was done. She hated him seeing her for what she was—a sad, stupidly trusting woman grieving not so much for a man she'd lost but over the fact that he'd been so evil and made such an absolute fool of her.

And she absolutely hated the fact that once, a long time ago, Josh had kissed her and she'd liked it, a lot, even though she'd been engaged to another man at the time. She especially hated that even now, when she should have been so much stronger, so much smarter, so absolutely immune to any man's charms, that with every step they took, she was conscious of Josh's hand at the small of her back, in what could only be described as a light, ever-so-proper touch.

Of course, Josh managed to make it feel decidedly improper. Women positively hummed around him, glowed even. They nearly staggered under the potent spell of his considerable charms.

And he wanted to be her friend?

Amanda groaned.

"What?" he said, as he reached in front of her to get the door.

"Nothing," she insisted, closing her eyes.

She couldn't take much more of his I-want-to-be-your-friend routine. Much as she desperately needed a friend, it couldn't be him.

If only she didn't find him so utterly gorgeous. It took

her breath away, just to look at him. He was big and tall and very blond, his skin a permanent golden hue, and he just glowed. There was no other word for it. His features were absolute perfection; the bluest eyes, the darkest, most extravagant lashes and so very, very soft lips that were almost always stretched into a charming smile.

He was the fairy-tale prince, all golden and magical and absolutely out of reach to a woman like her. He was rich and very sophisticated and a beautiful dresser, and he made her feel as plain as she likely was. He made her feel like a too-innocent, too trustworthy, criminally naïve secretary from Kansas.

One who didn't believe in fairy tales at all anymore. Not after the last year of her life.

That should be the end of any ridiculous thoughts she might have about Joshua Carter.

They walked into the coffee shop. Amanda frowned, fatigue striking anew when she saw the vast array of choices available. She didn't want to have to choose, didn't want to think.

"Something wrong?" Josh, the ever-solicitous escort, asked.

"Why did coffee turn so complicated?" she said. "I just want caffeine. Enormous amounts of caffeine."

"Allow me," he said smoothly.

Amanda suspected most women allowed him anything, everything. He was a man used to getting what he wanted, and she knew the only reason he was interested in her was because for the most part, so far, she'd managed to resist him. Now she wished he would just go away and leave her to her misery and self-contempt.

Instead he gave her a staggering smile and a steaming jolt of caffeine. She sighed with sheer bliss at the first taste. When she glanced back at him, she found him staring again. At her mouth.

Did he ever turn it off? Or at least hit the dimmer switch?

"What?" she asked, fatigue, annoyance at herself and him creeping into her voice as he continued to stare.

He pointed with one long, elegant finger, at her upper lip. She swept the tip of her tongue past it, tasting sweet, silky remnants from her espresso. "Did I get it?"

He groaned and looked away.

"Josh?"

"You don't have any idea what you're doing to me, do you?"

She blinked up at him, noting the odd little catch in his smooth-as-silk voice, the way his mouth stretched into that tight line and the blast of heat in his eyes.

"I don't—" she began, as he groaned and reached for her.

"There's no way a woman in this day and age could be this innocent," he complained. "No damn way."

It sounded like a complaint. But his hands were gentle, his hold loose, his body blocking out the sight of everything else as his mouth once again came down to hers.

He wasn't going after her forehead this time, either, she realized, too late and too surprised to pull away. She made a mad gasp for air, felt his breath against her lips, smelled that wonderful scent he wore once again. This time his mouth settled against the corner of hers, against her upper lip, drawing it briefly and ever so gently into the cradle of his own lips. She didn't know lips could be so exquisitely soft, so gentle. She felt his tongue brush against her mouth, against the skin at the top of her mouth.

Froth, she thought, sheer giddiness creeping in. He tasted like froth. Like sweet, barely there bubbles of air and flavor. Having him touch her was like taking a monstrous hit of caffeine.

"Josh," she said, all breathless and helpless-sounding again, sternly reminding herself that he was like those little bubbles of froth, that the things he made her feel and believe were like that, too. It might seem like something, like it had a texture and a substance and a color. But touch it—reach out and try to grab it—and it simply disappeared into thin air. It was sheer nothing, and there was nothing to this silly game of Josh's, either.

Amanda watched warily as he backed away. He swore softly, his hands falling to his side, his shoulders rising and falling with every breath he took. He looked like a man who'd just run a marathon, she decided, except every perfect hair on his head was still in place. How did he manage that?

"What am I going to do with you?" he said, shaking his head, a bare hint of a smile on his handsome face.

"Nothing," she answered for him, surprise and amusement and sheer sexual bliss fading away. "Don't do anything with me, Josh. Please, don't."

Amanda was serious. At least, she told herself she was. She couldn't let herself get anywhere near him again.

"Last night…" she said. "I appreciate what you were trying to do. Honestly, I do. And it helped, Josh. I'm glad I wasn't alone. But let this be the end of it."

He backed up a step, his frown intensifying, and then he reached for her again. Amanda backed up herself that time, determined to be smarter, stronger.

"Please," she said.

He sighed. "All right. I'm sorry."

"I…uh. I need a minute, okay?"

Josh nodded grimly.

Amanda glanced around, spotted the ladies' room and fled.

At the sound of laughter behind him, Josh dragging his eyes away from the sight of the fleeing woman. He blinked, surprised to find himself in the middle of a quite ordinary coffee shop in Georgetown at an ungodly hour on a Saturday morning.

Yes, that's where he was. Kissing Amanda. Absolutely lost in Amanda and her all-too-innocent look. He could have been on top the Eiffel Tower or in the middle of a war zone for all he knew. He'd been that lost in her.

Great, he thought. *Smooth.* Joshua Carter was nothing if not smooth.

"You have the women begging now, Josh?" a man asked, the voice heavily accented, familiar, but one he couldn't quite place.

Josh turned around, working hard to keep his expression carefully blank, the odd sensation of being rocketed from one place and time to another shooting through his brain. He forced the corners of his mouth to spread wide into an easy smile, all the while his senses were screaming.

"Rudy?" He stuck his hand out. "What a surprise."

A damned nightmare was more like it.

Rudy Olivara was five-ten, with jet-black hair and a silly little mustache, a wicked gleam in his eyes and an Italian accent that got thicker the closer he came to a beautiful woman. He flitted across the continents from one rich man's playground to the next. At times in the past he'd actually been useful to Josh, and at other times Josh wondered if Rudy might slit his throat the next time they saw each other. The last time, in particular, Josh had wondered if Rudy knew exactly what Josh was doing.

Josh didn't want the man anywhere near Amanda.

"Never stop, do you, my friend?" Rudy asked.

"What?"

"The woman." Rudy grinned wickedly. "Most men are home in bed at this hour. Or, at least, in someone's bed. You're out after another one."

Josh said nothing. He wasn't discussing Amanda with Rudy.

"Or is this one left over from last night?"

"She's a friend," Josh said, glancing toward the back of the shop, where Amanda had disappeared, hoping she wouldn't come back anytime soon.

Rudy laughed again. "A distracting friend. You didn't even see me."

Josh smiled, while inside he was berating himself. Obviously he hadn't been aware of anything. If he had been thinking at all, he wouldn't have stopped here.

The place was close to his apartment, and he met people here from time to time. People like Rudy. He never should have brought Amanda here.

"I didn't know you were in town," Josh said.

"I just arrived. I haven't been in the States in a long time. The last few years... They have been difficult."

"Oh?" Josh said, feigning innocence.

"I ran into some trouble. Right after I saw you in Milan, in fact." Rudy's eyes narrowed, and he idly stroked a dangerous-looking scar on his jaw, a scar he hadn't had the last time Josh saw him. "Coincidence, I'm sure."

A bald-faced lie, Josh thought. Was Rudy on to him?

"But what does it matter?" Rudy said dismissively. "How was Paris?"

"Crowded," Josh said noncommittally, swearing inside. Rudy knew he'd been in Paris? Josh shouldn't be so surprised considering his current mission. Rudy was a middleman, someone who put people like the man Rudy believed Josh to be in touch with people selling certain illegal substances. In this case, the makings of a nuclear weapon. So, Rudy was going to be part of this.

"Ah." Rudy looked past Josh. "Here comes your most charming companion."

Josh turned to find Amanda by his side, Rudy looking at her as if she was a seven-course meal he might devour in one big gulp. Biting back a growl, Josh slid an arm around her waist and pulled her to his side, a direct, hands-off sign to Rudy.

Amanda tried to pull away, but Josh held her firmly.

Rudy wouldn't be dissuaded. "You will not even introduce me?"

"No, I wasn't going to."

Rudy laughed and held out his hand to Amanda. "My dear, I've never seen him so territorial where a woman is concerned. Good brandy, a fast car, but never a woman."

Mutely Amanda held out her hand, and Rudy bent at the waist, theatrically bringing her hand to his lips. Josh felt her tremble at the touch and tucked her more tightly against his side. She didn't object this time.

Rudy's eyes shone wickedly. "You must be someone very special. And since he is not going to do the honors, allow me. I am Rudy Olivara."

"Amanda Wainwright," she told him, ignoring the warning Josh shot her.

"You live here in the capital, Ms. Wainwright?"

"Yes," she said.

"And you and my friend...?"

"—have to go," Josh cut in. "Sorry. We're late."

"Of course," Rudy said.

Josh turned to leave. Amanda didn't, no doubt caught between his rudeness and her own good manners. Finally she said, "It was nice to meet you, Mr. Olivara."

"It was my pleasure, I assure you, my dear."

Josh turned, ready to hustle her out the door.

"You know," Rudy said, "I've taken a suite at the Drayton. I'm having a little dinner party next weekend. I'd love to have you both there."

Josh frowned. "Amanda's busy, I'm afraid. But I'd be happy to come."

"I'm so sorry to hear that, my dear. I hope you'll reconsider. Saturday night. Nine o'clock sharp. I'll set a place for you, my dear. Just in case.'' Rudy turned to Josh. ''I meant to ask. Did you happen to find what you were look-ing for in Paris?''

Josh swore silently, knowing what was coming. He'd known it all along. ''No,'' he admitted. ''I didn't.''

''I might be able to help you with that.'' Rudy grinned. ''You know, I like the idea of you being distracted, Josh. Saturday. Nine o'clock. Bring her.''

Josh swore and headed for the door. He dragged Amanda to the car and put her inside it, then took a long, careful look at the surrounding area, cursing himself for being so caught up in her he hadn't even noticed Rudy Olivara standing right there.

''What happened, Josh?'' Amanda was pale, her eyes wide. ''You're frightening me.''

''Not now.'' He pulled the Jag onto the street and started zigzagging left and right through the narrow streets of Georgetown. ''Buckle your seat belt.''

Her mouth dropped open. ''You think he's coming after us?''

''You should *always* buckle your seat belt, Amanda.''

''I don't want a traffic-safety lesson, Josh. I want an answer.''

''I don't know yet if anyone's coming after us, but if someone does, I want you buckled in.''

''I can't believe this,'' she said. ''You know him? Be-cause of work? Because of those trips you take where things get blown up and people get killed?''

''No one's getting blown up today,'' he promised rashly. ''It isn't Rudy's style.''

Neither was chasing them down in a car, but Josh didn't intend to take any more chances. Rudy liked knives, he'd heard. Occasionally a nice, odorless, tasteless poison, some-thing he could easily slip into someone's dinner.

''Oh, my God,'' Amanda said.

"It's all right," he claimed. "No one's following us. That was probably nothing more than a coincidence, seeing him there."

"You're worried," Amanda accused.

"I'm careful." Normally he was very, very careful. Maybe not with women, but for damned sure with his job. Who would have thought Rudy Olivara would have seen him in Paris? Maybe tailed him here? Josh was concerned that Olivara had seen him with Amanda.

"He's…what? A contact of yours?"

"Yes," Josh admitted.

"Does he know what you really do? Who you work for?"

"I hope to hell not," Josh said. Although running into Rudy here, on Josh's home turf…

"What was he doing?"

"Fishing would be my bet." But it was more than that. It was an invitation. More like a dare. Not to dinner, but to play a game. A very dangerous game. Rudy liked games. He'd implied that he could help Josh with that little problem in Paris. But the kicker was Rudy was also suspicious of Josh's true motives, his true loyalties, after that mess in Milan.

"He scared me. And he saw me with you, Josh. He knows my name."

"Amanda—"

"You're worried. I don't think I've ever seen you worried."

Then her memories of the days right after her fiancé's death weren't very clear, because he'd been plenty worried. About her. "Look," he said, "whatever happens, I can handle it."

He often conducted business with a woman by his side, beautiful, smart, dangerous women, women who were nothing like Amanda. Women he seldom worried about, seldom felt guilty over. This…this was totally different.

"Can you tell me about it?" Amanda said.

"I shouldn't, but…" He would. He needed her to understand how serious this was. "I saw him at a party in Italy a couple of years ago. I was working, trying to buy some uranium."

"Uranium?"

"A component in nuclear weapons. Rudy thinks my family fortune's gone. Or maybe it's just insufficient to meet my needs. I have very expensive tastes, you know? Or maybe he thinks I'm in this for the thrill of it. He thinks I make a little money on the side on the black market. Weapons trading."

"You?" She said it so innocently, with such astonishment.

Josh smiled gently. "What did you think I did on all those trips abroad, Amanda? Did you think I was there for the champagne and caviar?"

"I don't know. I guess I didn't think about it."

"My father's a diplomat, and he's filthy rich. I've lived all over the world. I know people—good and bad—all over the world, because of the way I grew up. And this image of me—the rich boy with so few responsibilities, with nothing to do but go from one party to the next? It's useful. It lets me move from place to place, to see all sorts of people without raising suspicions."

"You're telling me it's all the job? This life you lead? The women, the parties?"

He frowned. "I'm telling you it's useful to me—useful to the agency—for me to maintain that image."

"Josh—"

"Never mind," he said, impatience eating at him. "Believe what you like about me. The important part is that the last time I saw Rudy, he gave me some information.

He thought he was helping me buy uranium, and a few months later the uranium was gone. We intercepted it, and I'm worried somebody blamed Rudy... That scar on his face?''

"Yes?"

"He didn't have it the last time I saw him. I think he blames me for it.''

"But he just asked you to a dinner party.''

Josh nodded. "We're not a couple of thugs who hang out in dark alleys, Amanda. Rudy generally does business in a suit and tie, over things like dinner at the best hotel in town.''

"Oh," she said. "So he may just want to...sell you something else?''

"Maybe. Either that or...''

"What? What do you think he wants?''

"Well, if I were in his position...if I thought someone had double-crossed me and nearly gotten me killed in the process?''

"Yes?"

"I'd want to kill him.''

Amanda gasped.

"I just want you to be careful. Promise me that, Amanda. That you'll be watching, too. Just in case. "Let me know if anything out of the ordinary happens.''

"Like what?"

"If he tries to see you. To talk to you.''

Her jaw dropped. "You think Rudy might come after me?''

"No, I don't. I just want you to be careful.''

"Okay." She looked a bit dazed and confused. "What about you?''

"Worried about me? I'm flattered.''

She made a face. "Do you joke about everything?''

"Most things,'' he admitted.

"Well, I don't know how you can joke about this."

"It's my job, Amanda," he said, taking her hand in his, liking the idea immensely that she was worried about him. "I'm just doing my job."

Chapter 3

Nothing happened. By Monday morning Amanda had forgotten all about how frightened she'd been, and for the first time in months she felt curiously free of that whole mess with Rob.

Her only problem was Josh. She couldn't quite get her mind off him and how kind he'd been to her. Pushy, arrogantly sure that he knew what was best for her, but in the end basically kind. If she discounted the kisses—the amazingly unsettling one on her forehead and the frothy, almost-kiss at the coffee shop—she'd have said he was a perfect gentleman.

She still hadn't reconciled the image of Josh the playboy with Josh the agent who acted as an international arms dealer. She knew the agents at Division One had dangerous jobs; she just seldom saw evidence of it. For all the top-secret things that went on at the agency, Amanda's job was quite ordinary. She was a secretary. She answered the phone, made appointments, ran interference for her boss, kept him organized. Weapons dealers and uranium and people out for revenge were totally out of her league.

But it had been two days since she and Josh had run into Rudy, and nothing had happened. She felt fine.

Monday morning, as she locked the front door behind her, she turned around and nearly tripped over a huge vase of flowers left by her front door.

Startled, she jumped a bit, saw the huge bouquet in an ornate, cut-glass vase rolling back and forth on her porch, the water spilling out. She grabbed the vase, admiring the flowers and sniffing the obviously expensive arrangement. It had been a long time since anyone sent her flowers.

Josh, she thought. He wasn't done with her.

Irritated and flattered at the same time, Amanda opened the card. Oddly, there was no address or logo identifying the flower shop. Her address wasn't on the card, either. Just her name, handwritten in a large, flowing script. It wasn't Josh's handwriting, either, she realized. It was too legible to be his.

The first flicker of alarm trailed through her. Amanda removed the card, made of heavy, obviously expensive paper and scanned the message:

"Until Saturday. Rudy."

Amanda gasped, squeezing her eyes shut. Not that. Anything but that.

Rudy Olivara hadn't forgotten her. He'd gone to the trouble of finding out where she lived. She dropped the flowers, the vase breaking as it hit the steps, the flowers falling in a heap. She left the soggy mess on her porch, staring at it for a minute, stunned. She did remember to take the card with her. She shoved it into her purse and drove in a daze to Division One headquarters, praying she was wrong about this. Praying she had no reason to be afraid.

* * *

Dan Reese was in his office, along with his wife, Jamie, who also worked at Division One, and Josh. Amanda stammered about the flowers and handed over the card.

"Josh was just filling us in on what happened." Dan frowned at Josh. "Tell me who this guy is again?"

"Rudy Olivara." Josh stood in the corner, leaning carelessly and elegantly against the wall. "He's Italian. Nasty temper. Not as much money as he'd like everyone to think. Has a distant cousin who's a count. Used to be on the Grand Prix circuit. I've run into him five or six times over the years. He's been useful at times."

"Does he know it? How useful he's been to you?"

"Maybe." Josh shrugged. "I got something from him on that thing in Milan two years ago."

"Beirut, too," Jamie added. She was pregnant now, working strictly inside the office, but she and Josh had spent several years as partners.

"And he knew you'd just gotten back from Paris?" Dan asked.

"Yeah," Josh said.

"So Rudy saw the two of you at a coffee shop in Georgetown at seven o'clock on a Saturday morning..."

His voice trailing off, Dan looked to Amanda to finish the explanation. She blushed, stammered, no words coming out.

"Having coffee." Josh jumped in, his tone daring anyone to ask for more of an explanation than that.

Amanda groaned and thought about lies. If anyone was keeping score, would that one count? They had gone in there for coffee, had in fact purchased coffee. Amanda drank hers. But Rudy Olivara had found them in each other's arms, Josh licking the froth off Amanda's lips. From his reaction, Dan obviously knew there was more to this than either of them admitted, but he let it go at that.

"Do you think Olivara followed you here from Paris?" he asked Josh.

"It's possible," Josh conceded.

"Find out. Because, if he did follow you? If he blames you for what happened in Milan? If he knows what you really do—?"

Josh nodded. "This could get messy."

Messy? Amanda felt faint. She didn't want to be in any more messes. "So, what are we going to do?"

"You aren't going to do anything," Josh said. "You're done."

"Wait a minute," Dan said. "Rudy obviously wants Amanda there. You said he was insistent on that. Why?"

"Because he likes women. And—"

"And?" Jamie prompted, looking as if she was enjoying this.

Josh was fuming by then. "Because Rudy's decided I can't think straight when there's a woman around. I guess he wants every advantage he can get."

"I can't imagine why he'd think that," Jamie quipped.

Josh glared at her. "It's no problem. I'll give him what he wants. I'll take someone else. Who's in the office right now? Who's available?"

Amanda sank back into her chair, relieved. Josh could just take someone else. He could lick espresso off someone else's lips. It meant nothing to her.

She and Josh were done.

She was glad.

"Wait," Dan said. "This man has Amanda's full name. He went to the trouble of finding her address, maybe of hand delivering the flowers and the invitation. He wants her at that dinner."

"I'll tell him she dumped me," Josh said. "I'll tell him I found someone else. Oh, hell, it'll have been a whole week by then. He knows me. He'll believe that."

"But what if Olivara's interested specifically in Amanda? What if he knows about Rob Jansen. What if he thinks he can use her to get to you? Or all of us?''

''What?'' Amanda gasped. *Rob? Again?* It was a nightmare. One that never seemed to end. ''How could Rudy Olivara know about Rob?''

''We all know things we shouldn't,'' Jamie said. ''All the time.''

''He may know you work for us or he may not. But it's no secret Rob worked for the FBI. Or that the two of you were engaged. We can bet by now a lot of people know Rob was selling information. Rudy may think you were a part of it. He may think you have information you're willing to sell, too. And it probably piqued his interest to find you with Josh. Rudy might think he got lucky, that he wants to get to Josh, and that you'll be useful to him.'' Dan turned back to Josh. ''What did you find out about this dinner party?''

''He has a suite at the Drayton, booked a small dining room Saturday night for a party of sixteen.''

''Sixteen? At the Drayton? He's not going to try anything there,'' Dan said.

Josh hesitated, his gaze narrowing dangerously on his boss. ''No,'' he said, the tone clipped, final.

''No?'' Amanda asked. ''No, what?''

''We have to know what he's up to. How much he knows,'' Dan insisted.

''No,'' Josh said again.

''He knows where she lives. Do you think he's going to leave her alone if she simply doesn't show up at his dinner? You know better, Josh.''

''I know this isn't a job for someone like her. It's a job for an agent, and she's not an agent.''

''It's dinner,'' Dan said. ''We plant people in the hotel, get people on the wait staff. You'll be beside her the whole time. She'll be perfectly safe.''

Josh swore. "And if it turns into more than one dinner? What do we do with her then?"

"We deal with it at the time, if it happens."

Josh was obviously furious. Amanda was stunned. They wanted her to go to Rudy Olivara's dinner party?

"I really don't think this is a good idea," she said.

Dan ignored her and turned to Josh. "I don't like the idea of him knowing where she lives, either. You want to take care of that? Or should I get someone else?"

Josh groaned. "I'll handle it."

"It would be better if you did. We don't want to tip anybody off that anything out of the ordinary is going on."

Josh was still seething. Dan looked like a man who wasn't about to back down. Amanda was in a daze. She lost track of the conversation. Everyone got to their feet, and she did, too, realizing the meeting was over.

Dan looked at her, his face not quite as stern as usual, and said, "We'll talk later, all right? Try not to worry. We'll take good care of you."

It wasn't so long ago that she'd thought working at Division One was simply a grand adventure. The dangers inherent in what the agency actually did seemed far away. But one day, more than a year ago, three teams of agents—including Josh, Jamie, Dan and another friend of hers, Doc—were providing round-the-clock security for a mysterious government scientists' lab when everything changed. Doc died that night. Dan nearly did, and Amanda had been horrified when she found out that her fiancé, Rob, and her then-boss, Martin Tanner, were behind the whole plot to get the scientist, Alex Hathaway, and his newest innovation, a high-level form of plastic explosives. They'd nearly gotten away with it. If not for Josh and Dan and Jamie and a few others, they would have.

And in the aftermath, Rob had died. Tanner was in prison

and she was working for Dan, who was now running Division One.

Amanda found it hard to look at him, even now. More than a year after the shooting Rob helped arrange, he still walked with the aid of a black cane. She'd heard he probably always would, and she felt guilty every time she saw him, though he'd never given her any reason to think he blamed her for anything. And now he was trying to reassure her that he and the agency would protect her.

Amanda closed her eyes, the horror of the past year coming back yet again, her fears over what was happening now crowding in as well. It was dangerous here. She worked in a very dangerous place.

Josh took her by the arm, steering her into a small office and closing the door behind them. He led her to a love seat and pushed her down. He looked uncharacteristically somber as he sat down beside her, taking her hands in his.

"You're trembling," he said gently. "Cold?"

"No. Scared."

That was all it took. She watched mutely as he came closer and closer, invading her senses, pushing nearly everything else—even a good bit of the fear—away. She found herself enfolded ever so gently in his arms.

She knew the way his skin smelled, knew all about the heat of his body, the strength. She knew his arms could be exquisitely gentle and so could his hands. She knew how it felt to be cradled against that impressive chest, to hear every little beat of his heart, feel his warm breath against her ear. And when her world seemed to be spinning out of control, she welcomed the familiarity and the reassurance of his arms.

Josh, she thought, amazed. How could she ever be reassured by being close to Josh?

Amanda groaned, and his arms tightened around her. He had the embrace down to an art form, she realized, unable to help but snuggle closer. He was wearing a blazer in the softest wool, an immaculate white shirt and the same spicy aftershave he always wore. He always seemed so clean, so carefully put together, so absolutely perfect.

"I'm sorry," Josh said, his lips somewhere very near her right ear.

She shivered, from sheer pleasure this time, closed her eyes and gave herself up to the luxury of feeling momentarily safe and strangely content because she was in a man's arms. Just for a minute she told herself, she could stay here, could take every bit of reassurance he was offering. Just for a minute. If it made her weak, made her seem like a silly, scared female, she didn't really care. Josh already knew all those things about her. He'd seen her at her worst, and he probably didn't think a thing about taking a woman in his arms.

What had he said to her the other night at the beach? *It was just a kiss, Amanda. Do you have any idea how many women I've kissed?*

Hundreds, at the very least, she decided. Thousands, perhaps. Of course, she had no business thinking about kissing him. He was just trying to make her feel better, and she had more important things to worry about.

Like dinner with Rudy.

"I don't want to go to dinner," she said, the words muffled by the fact that she was snuggled against Josh's chest.

"I know."

She felt the words rumbling out of his chest. He was a tall man and so very solid. There was a lot of him to hang on to and something so different about being in his arms, as if he'd somehow chased away the awful loneliness that had dogged her the past few months. But there was more. It left her yearning for more. Of just this, she thought. Being held.

He kissed women all the time, but did he hold them, as

well? Just like this? Would he do this for her, if she asked? Just hold her? Could it be that simple? Josh, her friend? Holding her and reassuring her and chasing all the awful loneliness away?

He'd offered the other night, and she'd dismissed the idea without a second thought. But if friendship with Josh could be like this… Amanda buried her nose against the side of his neck, her skin against his, liking the sensation, liking everything about this. If she'd been a cat, she would have curled up in his lap and closed her eyes, purring while he lazily stroked her back.

Amanda laughed a bit, the image too ridiculous for words. She was losing it. Finally she'd cracked.

Josh pulled away slowly, carefully. "What's so funny?"

"Nothing," she insisted.

He wouldn't let it go. He never let anything go. "One minute I'm holding you, and you're so scared you're shaking. The next minute you're laughing? Tell me, Amanda. What did I do?"

"I was just thinking that you're too good at this."

"This?" he said, looking lost.

"At everything," she complained. "Everything to do with women."

He smiled then. "You liked it. You liked being in my arms."

"You could charge by the hour, Josh. Women would be lined up around the block."

He looked like the devil then. There was a twinkle in his eyes, a broad grin on his face. "You don't have to pay," he offered. "All you have to do is ask, and I'm yours. Whenever you need me."

"I'd have to wait my turn," she said.

Josh shook his head, undeterred. "There's no line, Amanda. There are no other women in my life right now. There haven't been for a while now."

"Yeah, right. I'm sure you've been a regular Boy Scout."

"I was a Boy Scout," he insisted. "I can build a fire with the best of 'em, and I tie an amazing knot."

He offered the latter with a positively wicked grin, showing a talent at turning any conversation at all to something sexual.

Fire? Knots? Amanda gaped at him, curiosity getting the better of her and overcoming any shyness or shock she might feel. She ended up blurting out, "You tie women up, don't you?"

He laughed sinfully. "Only if they ask nicely."

Her mouth fell open. It just hung there, no sound coming out, a fleeting image of Josh, a rope and a woman. A *smiling* woman. His women probably liked things like that.

Heat flooded her cheeks. She had never— She would never, not in a million years— But he just kept looking at her with those big, beautiful eyes of his, and he wasn't laughing anymore. She watched his shoulders moving up and down with the effort it took him to breathe. The air in the room changed entirely, the atmosphere suddenly charged.

Something was going to happen. She could feel it. She wanted it, too. She wouldn't have stopped it if she'd been given the chance.

Josh's golden head was sinking down to hers. His mouth… She knew all about his mouth. It was gentle and wicked and warm. His lips were soft, persuasive, and he tasted the way he had the other day. Sweet and oh, so hot, the connection of his mouth and hers like a jolt of sheer energy she couldn't begin to understand.

"You're going to be the death of me yet," he said, taking her mouth beneath his yet again.

She felt the shock of his tongue, drawing lazily along

her bottom lip, stroking, teasing, a leisurely exploration that had her trembling.

"It's all right," he said, moving closer, deeper. "Just give me a minute."

She'd give him hours. She was back in his arms, held more firmly than before, conscious now of the way her breasts were pressing against his chest, of the hard muscles of his thighs. She had her hands on his shoulders, felt steely strength there, determination as well. Amanda inched closer, her body coming to life, all kinds of achingly lonely places crying out for him.

He could fill her with heat and light, textures and sweet tastes. Sounds... She liked the little sounds he made, sounds of pure pleasure. She liked the way he seemed to be nibbling on her mouth, tasting, taking, always seeking more. His lips were firmly meshed with hers now, her mouth open beneath his, welcoming him, hardly able to get enough of him. His tongue brushed along her bottom lip, along her teeth, a slow, hot invasion of her space, her senses, and she liked it. She'd never been so totally blown away by a kiss, so lost in one. She didn't even think to end it, didn't want to. But he did. One minute he was devouring her and the next he was pulling away, holding her by her arms, keeping her firmly at arm's length.

They looked at each other for a moment, her mouth slightly open, her bottom lip trembling. She could still taste him, still smell that fresh, clean, intoxicating smell that was uniquely him, and she couldn't seem to move. She just blinked up at him, lost and dazed and dazzled by him.

As she always was when he touched her. The first time, she'd been absolutely shocked. That he'd done it. That she'd let him, at least for a moment. And that any single kiss could ever cause such havoc in a woman's body. Afterward, she'd trembled every time she'd thought of it. She'd hated herself for it every bit as much as she despised him, thinking it hadn't meant a damned thing to him and it had had her wondering if she was making a mistake with Rob. Because he'd never made her feel anything like that when he kissed her. And of course, she had been making a mistake with Rob. A huge one that had nothing to do with what she felt when she kissed him or Josh.

And the second time…the second time Josh kissed her at the coffee shop, she'd still been shocked. That it had felt so good. That he'd tasted so delicious. So wicked and so very sweet. So tempting. That nothing but the touch of his beautiful mouth could bring every nerve ending in her body to tingle.

And now, the third time…oh, it was every bit as good the third time, she realized with dismay. There was no denying it any longer, no escaping, it seemed. He could absolutely make the earth move with nothing but a kiss.

Josh didn't seem to have any more idea what to say than she did. The moment stretched out awkwardly, and in that instant he didn't look anything like the self-assured, utterly confident and in-control man she knew so well.

He didn't look as if he was teasing her, either, or playing with her, which she found even more unsettling than his kiss. He didn't look like a man who'd kissed thousands of women and forgotten them all.

He looked as though it meant something to him—kissing her. As though it had surprised him and pleased him and he wouldn't forget it for a long time to come. Amanda never would. She knew that, just as she knew with utter certainty that she was foolish in thinking there was anything special to him about kissing her.

"Oh, God," she groaned, stepping back and taking a much-needed breath. He was even more dangerous than she realized, his charm more lethal.

He had a gift, she decided, an ability to make every woman think she was something absolutely special. That it was different with her. He probably said that to women, she thought. *It's different with you. Special, with you.*

Amanda jumped to her feet. He rose, too, and she had to look him in the eye. He seemed wary of her now and a bit reserved.

"Do you want me to apologize for that, too?"

"What would be the point? You're not sorry."

He sighed, still looking a little lost. "I don't want to frighten you. Or make you uncomfortable."

Her chin came up a notch. She was a grown woman. She shouldn't be frightened by a kiss, and really that was all it had been. A kiss.

"I'm not scared," she boasted.

"Good," he said, some of that easy grace and charm coming back, the wicked grin. "Because the truth, Amanda, is that I have a hard time keeping my hands off you."

"You have a hard time keeping your hands off any woman, Josh."

"No, I don't. Granted, I don't try that often, because I like women. I like touching them. I like kissing them, and I never quite understood the point in denying myself the pleasure of a willing woman's company."

"Why would you deny yourself anything?"

He frowned. "You think there's something wrong with enjoying life, Amanda."

"I think you enjoy it enough for ten different men."

"Maybe I do." His mouth twitched with the effort not to smile as he suggested wickedly, "You think I'm easy. Is that what you're saying?"

"I know you're easy."

"I'm also very, very good," he boasted.

Flustered, wishing she'd never started this conversation in the first place, she headed for the door, "I'm sure you are, Josh. I'm just not interested."

He blocked her path, practically purred her name. "Amanda?"

"What?" She flushed and kept her eyes averted. She was way out of her league sparring with him.

"You shouldn't tell little white lies like that."

"Really?"

He nodded. She sensed the movement more than saw it, and her good sense was telling her something else. It was telling her to get out, to get away from him, while she still could.

"Come on," he whispered. "Look at me."

She took a breath, squared her shoulders and looked. He seemed bigger than life right then, taller, broader, even more blindingly gorgeous, almost god-like. Women worshipped him like one, falling at his feet, falling all over themselves for a kind word from him, a little smile, for the touch of his hands, and he was generous with all of those things. She knew. She'd seen him work a room before.

But it was just the two of them at the moment, his attentions focused entirely on her. He touched her again. His hand came up to the side of her face, his fingers spread wide, slipping into the ends of her hair, threading through it so he could wrap his fingers around the side of her head. His thumb brushed lightly across her cheek. She caught her breath as he stretched his thumb farther to the right, to her lips, tracing them with the pad of his thumb.

She wanted his mouth back, she realized, his lips, his tongue. She wanted him kissing her all over again, just like before. Because there was something intoxicating about the taste of him, the feel of him. Something addictive and highly potent and undeniably...right. It felt right to have him touch her.

No one had ever touched her like this. No one had ever made her feel like this.

Other men had kissed her, but they hadn't left her tossing

and turning restlessly in her bed, hadn't invaded her dreams and left her waking up trembling and imagining she could still feel their hands on her body. They hadn't created this strange, aching empty feeling to her body, this yearning, this awful need. She had dreamed about Josh, about this. She could swear that he knew it, too.

"Don't play with me, Josh," she begged.

"I'm not playing," he said roughly. "It's the truth. There are about a dozen different things I'd like to be doing with you right now. Believe me, it's a miracle I've managed to keep my hands off you for this long."

She stared up at him, unable to do anything else. He couldn't possibly be serious. He couldn't.

"Find someone else," she said, desperate to end this, no matter what it took. "There are thousands of women in this city. One's always been as good as another to you. Find someone else."

He glared at her. She'd never seen him utter so much as a sharp word to anyone, and now he looked as if he was about to explode. But he held his temper, much to her relief. He turned away and swore, softly, succinctly and cuttingly as he walked away, slamming the door behind him.

She flinched at the sound, couldn't tell if he was angry at himself or at her. She felt the ridiculous urge to apologize to him, had the odd sense that she'd hurt him with her words, but how could that be? Everything she said was true. He probably thought women were put on the planet for him to enjoy.

Well, Amanda wasn't having fun. Not at all. She was shaking, and her head was spinning, her lips quivering, the sweetly elusive taste of him lingering on her lips, and even now, she wanted more of him. She would likely dream of him again tonight. She would wake tossing and turning and still imagining his big, hard body next to hers. And he'd probably take her advice. Tonight, she'd be at home, feeling frustrated and lonely and dreaming of him, and he'd be with someone else.

Amanda closed her eyes, her head falling forward, something that felt suspiciously like pain—real, physical pain—shooting through her. She might lie to Josh about it, but there was no way she could lie to herself.

She absolutely hated the thought of him with another woman.

Chapter 4

"I'm not handling this well," Josh said.

Jamie had found him standing in the hallway outside his office and rescued him, dragging him into her own office and closing the door.

"You don't suppose my door slammed itself, do you?" he suggested.

"I think doors have been known to do that," she agreed.

"Amanda may have slammed it behind me."

"After she threw you out of your own office? I know she has a real vicious streak."

Josh frowned. He'd never felt so stupid in his entire life, never been so baffled by a woman. "It was either get myself out of there or strangle her."

"Oh?" Jamie looked absolutely enthralled.

"She thinks I'm pond scum," he complained.

"Imagine that."

"Do you have to enjoy it *this much?*" he complained.

She grinned. "I think so. It's such a novelty. I've never seen you in a bad mood."

"I have a right to be in a bad mood," he complained. "You don't know what she said to me."

Find someone else. He nearly growled. She could say that? Five seconds after he'd been devouring her with his mouth? Did she believe she wanted him to find another woman, and that he would? That he'd just pick someone and start in where he and Amanda had left off?

No way! Josh blew out a long, slow breath. He was sprawled in the corner of the love seat in Jamie's office, where he'd been hundreds of times before. They'd been partners for a couple of years. He was comfortable with her. Or with the woman she'd always been to this point. Ready to turn the conversation to anything but him and Amanda, Josh let his eyes rest on the rounded mound at her midsection.

"'Bout ready to pop?" he quipped.

Jamie frowned. "I can't believe women think you're charming."

"You know they do."

"Only because they don't know you as well as I do."

He grinned, ready for a fight. "Do all women get grouchy when they're pregnant?"

She picked up a cushion and threw it at him. He managed to duck in time, and soon they were both laughing like the old friends they were.

"Your husband's going to come charging in here any minute to see what we're up to," Josh said. "You know that, don't you?"

"He is not."

"Bet me," Josh boasted.

"He knows there was never anything between the two of us, and he knows how much you like needling him about thinking there ever was. It would be so much simpler if you both admitted you liked each other."

Josh ignored that. "You're really happy with this new life of yours?"

"As happy as anyone can be when she can't bend over to tie her own shoes."

He laughed and pressed his palm to the taut skin of her belly. "How's little Joshie today?"

"For the last time, we are not naming this baby after you."

"Just wait. You'll see," he teased. Then, before she could turn the subject back to him, he added, "You're really not coming back to work?"

"I'm not sure. I want to see how I feel after the baby comes."

Josh nodded toward her husband's office. "He wouldn't let you back out in the field, and I can't see you being happy sitting in front of a computer, plotting and planning, the way you've been doing the past few months."

"He's not my boss at home, Josh. Marriage doesn't work that way."

"You'd do anything Dan Reese asked," he insisted, still surprised by that. Jamie had been damned good at what she did, and he knew she'd enjoyed it. He couldn't imagine her giving all that up for a man. "You're going to sit in that big house in the 'burbs changing dirty diapers and going without sleep at night, your brain turning to mush? All for a man?"

It was unthinkable to him that someone like her would rearrange her life that way. Of course he had to admit she'd reached a point in time where she'd been absolutely miserable without Dan. Josh was absolutely certain the only problem was that sooner or later they'd be miserable together. Married people always found a way to be utterly miserable together.

Miserable apart, miserable together. That was what love did to people. Josh didn't want any part of it.

Jamie regarded him thoughtfully. "I worry about you."

"Why?" he said casually.

"Because you just don't get it. I used to think it was an act, an I'm-not-interested-in-settling-down, world-class playboy act. But it's worse than that. You just don't understand."

"Understand what?" he asked.

"Love. Commitment. Marriage. I would do anything for Dan. And he'd do the same thing for me. It's a two-way street, Josh. That's what makes it work. Dan doesn't order me around, and I don't blindly obey. I haven't rearranged my life to suit him."

"Yes, you have."

"We rearranged *our* lives to suit both of us," she insisted. "Josh, you're one of the smartest men I've ever known. How can you not get this? The job doesn't mean nearly as much to me as he does. Or our baby."

Josh frowned at her.

"All these years," Jamie asked. "You've never even come close to being in love?"

"God, no," he said, glad about that.

"Have you ever known anyone who was happily married?"

He shook his head.

"What about your parents?"

"Last I heard, they were still married."

"And do they love each other?" she asked.

"I wouldn't say that." Tolerated each other, at best. Tolerance that had given way to intolerance. To mutual disgust. Things had really deteriorated from there, and he didn't want to talk about it. There was no point. "Geez. Stop, okay? I'll talk about Amanda if you'll stop."

"Okay." Jamie looked perfectly happy. She'd gotten what she wanted.

"She's still hung up on Rob," he said, puzzled. "She's so sad. So lonely. And I...well, I..."

"You are going to burn in hell someday, Josh."

"Probably," he agreed. "But not for this."

"Don't toy with her."

"I'm not doing anything with her," he protested. "I may go to hell for what I'm *thinking* about Amanda, but not for anything I've actually done."

Josh willed himself not to look guilty. It wasn't a bald-faced lie. He didn't think a couple of kisses constituted a mortal sin, and he'd been a model of virtue around the woman for years. Okay, maybe not a *model* of virtue. He would never manage that in his life. But the worst he'd done was give her one, single, memorable kiss while she was engaged to another man.

"I'm worried about her," he said.

"You're serious?" Jamie crossed her arms and gave him an odd, speculative look. "You really care about her?"

"Of course I care about her."

"Not that 'she's a friend who's going through a rough time' kind of caring."

"She is going through a rough time," he insisted.

"I'm talking about her being special to you."

Josh frowned, his collar feeling uncomfortably tight again.

"Fine. I won't help you."

"Jamie! Help me. Please. I'm lost here," he said, the urgency of his tone giving him away. *Damn.* He didn't even know what he felt for the woman himself. How could he explain it to anyone else?

"She's so vulnerable right now," Jamie cautioned.

"Oh, hell, she's always been so damned vulnerable," he complained.

"She's never going to be able to hold her own with you."

"I know that," he admitted. "What do you want? A blood oath? I swear I won't hurt her."

"I don't think you ever set out to hurt anyone intentionally, Josh."

He hadn't, but that didn't mean he'd never hurt anyone. Even with the best of intentions it happened sometimes. Some women had trouble believing a man when he said he never stayed with any one woman for long. Josh meant it. He would tell Amanda that, right after he explained that he didn't care to go find anyone else for a quick roll in the sack right now. He didn't even want to think of the significance of that.

"She absolutely baffles me," he complained.

"Last year? When I was so crazy about Dan? When I was absolutely furious with him?" Jamie grinned. "He baffled me, absolutely and completely."

"I am not in love with her." It was ludicrous. Laughable. Joshua Carter, in love. Still, that reminded him of one more thing he wanted to know. "She hasn't been seeing anyone, has she?"

"I don't think so. It's too soon after this mess with Rob for her to be seriously involved with anyone."

"Oh, hell, I know that, too." He'd been waiting, after all. *Him* waiting for a woman. Waiting for something he didn't understand at all.

He'd never met a woman so thoroughly indifferent to him, and his ego had caught on to that right from the beginning. But this wasn't about his ego anymore. He thought of her when he shouldn't. He simply couldn't get her out of his mind. But none of that meant he was in love with her. None of that came close to love.

Misery, hurt, aggravation, anger, desertion, loneliness… *love*. No way Josh wanted anything to do with that.

Amanda wasn't handling this well. All the way home she thought someone was following her. Which was silly.

Rudy didn't need to follow her. He already knew where she lived. She turned onto her street, to the tiny house she and Rob bought together that she hadn't been able to afford on her own. She held her breath the whole way, waiting for disaster to strike, and what did she find? No sign of Rudy Olivara. She saw Josh's Jag instead.

"Oh, no," she sighed. Not now.

He was supposed to be out picking up willing women tonight, and she wasn't supposed to care. Not in the least. He could tie them up, using all those fancy Boy Scout knots, and she wouldn't so much as blush at the thought of the decadent things he would do with them. It didn't mean anything to her.

Frothy kisses and sunrises on the beach, a fabulous shoulder to lean upon, a blissfully strong embrace, a wicked grin—none of that should mean a thing to her, either.

Amanda sighed yet again, sitting in her car, afraid to get out and walk into her own house.

Chicken, she chided herself. She'd always been afraid of her own shadow, always despised herself for it. She'd always played it so safe, and where had it left her? Alone, heartbroken, pitied. Cringing, she wondered if Josh felt sorry for her, too. She'd absolutely hate that.

Amanda got out of the car, saw no sign of him. She put her key in the lock, expecting him to jump out of the shadows at any moment. He didn't, but the door wasn't locked. Sticking her head inside, she called out, "Josh?"

"In the kitchen," he said, as if there was nothing unusual about her coming home and finding him here.

Amanda didn't know what he was up to, but she had a feeling she wasn't going to like it. She could hear him whistling, and she smelled something, something indecently good and no doubt incredibly fattening. She found him standing over the stove, steam rising from the big skillet.

He didn't turn around, didn't so much as look at her. He kept whistling and stirring, relaxed and happy as always.

He was always so happy. She couldn't understand how anyone could be as happy as Josh. Maybe that's what a life of indulgence and privilege could do for a person.

Not fair, Amanda chided herself. He'd taken care of her the other night, when she'd been so alone, so broken-hearted. She had vague memories of him being kind, as well, in those nightmarish days after Rob died and all his awful secrets came out. So, obviously, Josh wasn't all bad. He just wasn't for her.

"What are you doing here?" she asked finally.

He grinned, glancing at her quickly, then turning back to his task. "Making dinner. You like veal?"

"I've never had veal."

"You'll like it. Promise."

She wanted to tell him not to promise her anything, not even something as simple as the fact that she'd like the meal he was preparing. She didn't want any promises from him, didn't want anything from him at all. She knew what he was, and she knew she couldn't have him in her life. She'd go to this dinner with the Italian arms dealer if she had to and be done with it. She'd go back to her nice, dull, careful little life. First, she had to get rid of Josh.

"What are you doing in my house?"

He kept right on stirring. "I told you. Cooking dinner."

"I didn't invite you."

"Amanda, if I waited for an invitation, it would never happen."

True enough. Which meant what? He would barge in uninvited? Insinuate himself in her life? Take over? She could see him doing just that. Steamrolling his way in, ignoring what she wanted, taking what he wanted instead.

Please, God, she hoped he'd gotten over that misguided notion that he wanted her.

"Josh? How did you get in here?"

"I picked the lock. I'm really good at that."

"Oh." She would add it to the list of his known talents.

"Not that it took much skill. A two-bit crook wouldn't need ten seconds to break in here. But don't worry. I've taken care of it. Someone's coming tomorrow to redo the locks."

"What?" she said, feeling that odd sensation of her life slipping out of control, taking an odd, unexpected turn, as it had a year ago, when Rob died and everything went so wrong.

"They're installing a security system, too. Don't worry. Dan's orders. Division One's picking up the tab."

Amanda suddenly felt a weakness in her knees. She pulled out a chair that had been tucked under the small table in the corner and sat down. "Why? Did Rudy do something? Has something happened already—"

"No." He finally turned to look at her. "Nothing like that."

"Then what? Why are you here?"

"I'm going to take care of you, Amanda," he said, quite sincerely.

"What?" Much as she liked the idea of someone looking out for her right now, it couldn't be Josh. She couldn't have him here, being charming, concerned, flirting with her, kissing her. She was every bit as weak and scared and needy as ever, and she was afraid she would do something utterly stupid. Like fall for him. Despite all that she knew about him.

"Rudy knows where you live," he said softly, patiently.

"I know." She wouldn't get a good night's sleep until this was all over.

"I'm not just doing this on a whim, Amanda. We traced

Rudy's whereabouts for the past week. He's been seen with…a contact of mine. Rudy's right in the middle of this, and he's here for a reason. Which means you and I have to be careful. Dan and I talked about it. I told him I'd take care of you. I promised."

"No," she said again.

"Yes. Get used to it, Amanda. Until this is settled, I'm moving in."

"No," she said.

Nothing else. Just *no*.

"Okay." Josh was prepared to compromise, to a point. "You can move in with me."

She laughed then, the sound bubbling out, scaring him a bit. She'd had a very bad day, after all. A bad weekend. A bad year. He settled his hands at the top of her arms, taking them in a strong, reassuring grip.

"Amanda, I know you don't want me here. I know what you think of me as a man. But this is work, and I promise you, I'm very good at my work. I take my responsibilities very seriously. I'm not going to let anything happen to you."

"You can't stay here," she said.

"Fine. Pack your bag. Whatever you'll need for the rest of the week. I'd rather have you at my place, anyway."

"You don't understand—"

"I do." He tightened his grip on her shoulders. "You don't want me here. I understand why. I'm telling you, you don't have a choice right now."

She stared at him, that soft bottom lip of hers trembling. He watched her work the muscle in her jaw, thinking of something to say and discarding it just as quickly. And he had an almost overwhelming urge to kiss her, just one more time. To take her mouth beneath his and press his lips against hers and kiss her soundly, until he held her limp and breathless in his arms, until she'd let him do anything he wanted with her. He could take all her fears away, could take her to the point where she could only think of one thing—*him.*

That would be taking unfair advantage of the situation, but Josh believed in taking every advantage offered to him. It was just the way he was.

He grinned at her. "It won't be so bad."

She put her hands against his chest and shoved him out of the way to stalk from one side of her kitchen to the next, nervous energy radiating from her.

"I don't believe you," she said. "You shoved your way into my house and dragged me away with you the other night. You made me talk about things I didn't want to talk about, because you think you know what's best for me and because, at the moment, you happen to think you want me. And while you're thinking of nothing but what you want, your friend Rudy sees us together and thinks there's something between us. And now I'm stuck in this awful mess? There's this awful man after me, and I can't even live in my own house. I'm getting paranoid, too. I could have sworn someone followed me home today—"

"Someone did, Amanda. Someone from the office," he said. "You don't think I'd let you be alone right now, with Rudy knowing where you live? Maybe even where you work?"

"You had someone follow me?"

"Of course I did. This is real, Amanda. The potential for danger is real. I'm sorry I dragged you into this. I'm sorry I tried to help you and made things worse. But I can't change what's happened. All I can do now is minimize the risks in any way I can. By having someone follow you home, checking your locks, arranging for a security system. The most important thing I can do is to never leave your side from this point on, until we resolve this mess with Rudy."

"Oh, no," she said.

"I'm sorry. That's the way it has to be."

Her face fell, her expression bleak. "Couldn't someone else—"

"Rudy thinks you and I are lovers," he explained. "He won't think a thing about me being here, or you being at my place."

"I could just leave," she said. "Couldn't I just leave?"

"Where would you go, Amanda?"

"I don't know. Home, maybe? Kansas. My parents' house?"

"And risk drawing them into danger, as well?"

She shuddered. He saw it, felt it, tightened his grip on her arms and fought the urge to pull her to him and wrap his arms around her. She'd liked it in his arms. She'd felt safe there. He knew it. She'd told him so.

"You think Rudy would take things that far?"

"I don't know," he said honestly. "I can tell you that even if you wanted to go, I wouldn't let you. Not by yourself."

"Oh, God," she said.

"I'm sorry if that scares you, but you have to be careful, and for now, you have to be with me."

"Oh, God," she said again.

"Look, if you're worried about something happening between the two of us…" Josh closed his eyes, squeezed her arms and then backed off, letting her go. He didn't like this. Didn't like it one bit. But he didn't see that he had a choice. He'd gotten her into this. It was his fault. "I'll back off."

"You don't know how to back off. And you're still playing with me."

"I'm not playing," he insisted. "I want you. Not anyone else. Just you."

"Josh—"

"I know. You don't believe me. Well, I don't suppose it matters for now. Because I've got work to do, and if you and I have to share the same house, we can do that. I can wait for the rest of it."

"The rest of what?" she said.

"You and me."

"Josh, there is no you and me."

"There will be," he said. "It'll be good, Amanda. I promise. You're still feeling a little uncertain because of Rob. You're still beating yourself up for trusting him, and you've forgotten all about enjoying life. But I can fix that. We could have a good time, you and I."

"You just want to go to bed with me," she said dryly.

"Is that an invitation?" He grinned, unable to help himself. It was, after all, his nature to flirt and he needed to lighten the mood. "Because, if it is—"

"You want to go to bed with every woman you meet."

"No, I don't."

"Josh—"

"Okay, with a lot of them. I admit it. It's not exactly a crime, Amanda."

"No, it's not that. It's just not the way I am. It's not the way I was raised, and it's not going to happen, Josh."

"Why not?"

"Because I don't want it to."

Josh weighed his options, not liking any of them but seeing no alternative. He had to make her a promise, a promise he would keep. Still, eventually she would be in his bed. He knew it.

"Sounds like we need to make a deal." He went back to the stove before he ruined their dinner and before he touched her again. "We can stay here or at my place. Your choice. But we're going to be living together for a few days.''

"That's a deal?''

"Hey, I'm letting you pick the place. Where do you want to stay?''

Amanda hesitated. "Does Rudy know where you live?''

"Maybe. Maybe not. He definitely knows where you live.''

"And you think we'd be safer at your apartment?''

"I know so. I'm on the fifteenth floor, and the whole place is wired.''

"Oh.''

She was giving in. He could feel it. "There are two bedrooms, Amanda. There's even a lock on the spare bedroom door.''

"Locked doors don't seem to give you much trouble.''

He grinned. "Barricade the door, if it makes you feel better.''

She frowned. "I'll think about it.''

"Fine,'' he said, the model of agreeability. He could back off, at least until he fed her, and let her think she had a choice. People tended to cooperate so much better when they thought they had a choice.

Still sounding wary, she asked, "What else do you think we need to do?''

"We drive to work together. We drive home together. You don't go anywhere, outside of the office or my apartment, without me. Just for a few days. You can stand my company for that long.''

"Okay. What else?''

"I won't touch you,'' he volunteered. He could do that, if he had to.

"Really?''

He turned around, one hip pressed against the kitchen counter as he eased his weight back against it, trying to look more relaxed than he felt. "Look." He held his arms up in front of him, palms flat, fingers spread wide. "No hands. Promise."

She frowned. "What about the rest of you?"

Josh cocked his head to the right and laughed. "What other parts are you worried about, Amanda?"

She blushed, a soft-pink flooding her cheeks. He studied her for a long moment, wondering one more time exactly what it was about her that he found so captivating.

She wasn't the most striking woman he'd ever met. There was nothing about her features that stood out in his mind. He had a bad habit of thinking of women as body parts, which were often the most interesting parts of the women he knew. He liked full, rounded breasts, curved in exactly the right way. Long legs in high heels and stockings. He liked hair he could touch, a woman who wasn't always worried about him mussing her up. He liked a soft, subtle scent, skirts that were just a tad too short. He liked soft, clingy clothes, not necessarily tight, but clothes that showed off a woman's shape, that fueled his imagination.

Amanda definitely fueled his imagination. There was something quietly pretty about her. Sweet. Innocent. *Real.* That was it, he supposed. Amanda was real. There was no pretense to her, nothing fussy or phony, either.

He looked up to find her looking at him, as well, had an inkling that she'd been every bit as caught up in studying him as he had in studying her. Josh grinned, thinking this was going to be just fine. And then he realized with a start that he had no idea where the conversation had gone or how long they'd been standing here staring at each other.

Something about him promising to keep his hands off her, he recalled. He could do that, he supposed. He could wait for *her* to come to *him.* The idea had infinite appeal. They would have days together, days and nights. There was a delicious intimacy to be found in sharing a confined space with a woman, when he wanted that level of intimacy. He seldom did. But right now he could hardly wait.

"What in the world are you thinking about?" she asked.

"That I can keep my hands off you if I have to." And then he remembered. They'd been talking body parts. "You didn't tell me, Amanda. What other parts are you worried about?"

She frowned, considered the point quite seriously. "Your mouth," she said. "Your lips. Are you going to keep your lips to yourself, Josh?"

He opened his mouth to answer her, to say something smart, something a bit wicked. But he was still caught up in the sight of her, still thinking of all sorts of things he'd like to do with her. Unbidden came an image of him holding up his hands in mock surrender, but leaning over her, touching her with nothing but his mouth, his lips, his tongue, kissing all those places he longed to kiss. He could see himself teasing her, keeping his word of sorts, could hear himself saying, *Just my mouth, Amanda. Nothing but my mouth.*

"What are you thinking?" she said, sounding way too innocent, bewildered even.

Desire slammed through him. Josh turned around, too quickly, not watching what he was doing, catching the handle of the skillet, nearly upsetting it and its contents. As it was he had to reach for it any way he could. He grabbed the broad, rounded bowl of the skillet and managed to put it to rights. It settled against the stove with a bang, only a little of the contents splattering out onto his forearm, his fingertips singed from their contact with heated metal.

"Oh, no," Amanda said, at his side in an instant.

Josh swore. He was never clumsy.

"Here." She grabbed him by the arm and tugged him over to the sink, turning on cold water and shoving his hand under it. "Try this."

"It's not that bad," he reassured her. "It's better, just with the water."

Still, she held his hand in place, her body soft and yielding, his hard and hurting just thinking about her, about his mouth on her.

She'd looked at him as if she had no idea what he was thinking. She was a sheltered, small-town girl from Kansas, and he wondered just how conventional her experiences had been. How did nice boys from Kansas handle themselves in the sack with a woman like her? Were the lights always out, the covers pulled up over both of them, so there was nothing at all to see? Had they rushed her, so intent on getting from point A to point B that no one had ever lingered over her body? Exploring? Lips trailing over every inch of that delicate, soft skin of hers?

Would she be shocked if she knew what he'd like to do? Explore her with nothing but his mouth? Tasting, teasing, tormenting? It would take hours to do it the way he wanted.

"Damn," Josh said.

"I know," she sympathized. "You should have just let it go, Josh. We could have found something else for dinner."

Josh laughed a bit. She honestly didn't have a clue, although when she crowded in beside him to inspect his hand, she came dangerously close to finding out exactly the direction his thoughts had taken. He was hard as a rock. Even the pain in his hand hadn't distracted him enough to change that.

"I'm all right, Amanda," he said, thinking it would be a good idea right now if she stopped touching him, especially since he hadn't gotten her moved into his apartment yet. He didn't want to shock her, and he had a feeling the effect she had on his body would indeed shock innocent little Amanda.

"We need to get something on those burns before they blister," she said, shoving his hand back under the water.

Now that she mentioned it, it did hurt. He stood, unprotesting, with his hand under the water while she fussed around him, gathering a bit of ice in a bowl, filling it with water, sitting him at the table and putting his hand in the blessedly cool water.

"Better?" she asked.

"Yes. Thanks."

She foraged through her cabinets for first-aid supplies. She took this so seriously, worked so intently over his hand and his arm. He found it utterly appealing in the end, Amanda taking care of him. He didn't remember having anyone fuss over him so. Certainly not his mother, not even the no-nonsense nanny, particularly over such a meaningless injury. He liked having her do it, in a way that had nothing to do with the little sexual thrill that came from having her close. She had kind hands, every bit as soft and as gentle as he imagined, hands that slathered his with salve and bandaged with gauze.

Josh didn't normally turn to a woman for niceness, for kindness, for caring. Not that he dated unkind women. Kindness simply wasn't an issue. Caring wasn't. Gentleness…well, that could be nice, at times, but he preferred a bit of an adventurous streak, of aggression, a woman who knew exactly what she wanted and how to get it.

So he found himself baffled by Amanda once again, by that odd little tug in the region of his heart when she tried so earnestly to help him. He didn't even protest that she'd gotten carried away. His job had the potential to be very dangerous, and he'd been lucky over the years. But still, there had been times when he'd been hurt much worse than this. Burned fingertips were nothing.

"There," she said. "All done."

"Thank you."

She smiled up at him, seeming more at ease than she ever had with him. That was worth a few singed fingers, he supposed.

"I guess we should eat dinner. Especially after all you suffered to save it."

"Sure," he said, getting to his feet.

"No, you sit. I'll take care of it."

Josh sat, trying to get his head screwed on the right way once again. She wasn't touching him any longer. The pain in his hand settled down to a hard, pulsing ache. There was no more odd tugging at his heart from the sight of her worried face. He was focused, sure of what he wanted, needed. Everything would be fine.

He had days, after all. Days to bring her around to his way of thinking. He could do that, even with no hands, no kisses. He would enjoy the challenge, just as he intended to enjoy every bit of her. She would feel better. She'd smile, laugh, and when it was all over between them, he would leave.

There, he thought, relaxing a bit. He had everything figured out.

The phone rang. He thought about stopping her, cautioning her, but she grabbed it on the first ring. He saw her recoil. Then she said warily, "Mr. Olivara."

Josh was beside her in an instant, his arm around her back as he pulled her against his side. She sank against him, with a death grip on the phone.

"Rudy," she said. Then lied badly, "I'm fine."

Josh told himself that it wasn't such a bad thing having her scared. It would make her more careful, make her listen to him and do what he said. He needed her to do that so he could keep her safe.

She thanked Rudy for the flowers, then she turned into Josh's arms, her head nestled against his chest. He stroked her hair, trying to reassure her.

"Yes," she said. "I'll do my best to make it to dinner."

Josh took the phone from her trembling hand. "Rudy, we were just sitting down to dinner right now. You can talk to Amanda on Saturday, all right?"

Rudy more or less agreed. Josh was marginally polite, then hung up.

Amanda was trembling badly and clinging to him. "I'm sorry," she said.

"It's all right." In truth, it was no hardship at all to hold her this way. He just wished she had come into his arms for an entirely different reason.

"I hate this. And he scares me, Josh. He scares me so much."

"I know, Amanda." He stroked her hair again, liking the feel of her snuggled against him. "But you're going to be fine. You're going to be with me."

She looked so sad, so overwhelmed.

"Come home with me, Amanda. Let me take care of you until this is over."

"All right," she said, slipping out of his arms, looking dazed and uncertain and a bit embarrassed. "I'm sorry."

Josh grinned. "Why?"

She shrugged uneasily, looking up at him. "I, uh—"

"No hands?" he guessed.

She nodded.

"Sorry. It's going to take some getting used to. I tend to be a hands-on kind of guy."

"I know, and…I'm not complaining. Not about that. It was…nice."

Nice, he thought, trying not to grimace. He didn't think *nice* was the word that came to mind when women usually thought of him.

"And it wasn't your fault, anyway," Amanda offered. "It was me."

"No problem. You were frightened. If you need me, you

come to me. I'll be right here. Otherwise, I won't touch you.''

''Okay. Thank you.''

Josh shoved his hands into his pockets and stood there. She sighed, looking tired and worn and scared. Damn, she still looked scared.

He would keep her safe and keep his hands off her, and Rudy would go back to Italy. After that Amanda would know Josh better, trust him. She would have come to depend on him. Anything could happen then.

Chapter 5

Amanda woke the next morning to the slow, silky slide of truly expensive linens against her skin, feeling a bit like a character in a fairy tale who'd opened her eyes and found herself in an entirely different world. A dangerous man knew where she lived, had her phone number, was stalking her with flowers and invitations to dinner, and Josh—who had to be the most dangerous man she'd ever met—wasn't going to let her out of his sight for the next week.

Amanda still wasn't sure how it happened. She'd heard Rudy's voice on the phone, and the next thing she knew, she had her face buried against Josh's chest, his arms wrapped securely around her. There was nowhere on earth she'd rather have been in that moment. She would have followed him anywhere.

And he'd brought her here to his apartment. All done in rich, brown leather, the walls a warm buttery-cream with dark-green accents, there was a subtle air of money to the place. He had a few paintings—probably obscenely expensive but admittedly pleasant to look at—an eclectic music collection and a sound system that had to cost more than she made in months, every gadget in the world in his neat, surprisingly tidy kitchen. She hadn't dared to peek inside his bedroom. Heaven knew what she might find there. She'd hidden in the spare bedroom soon after they arrived last night and hadn't come out. He hadn't bothered her. Not if she discounted the fact that simply knowing he was there bothered her.

She heard a tap on the bedroom door, which she hadn't locked, after all, feeling foolish at the thought. Josh walked in, wearing a pair of neat brown slacks and a crisp white shirt, which he was in the process of buttoning, a gold-colored tie that matched his hair hanging loosely around his neck. His hair was damp, his jaw freshly shaven. He brought a cloud of steam and pleasing scents with him that seemed to find its way straight to her, enveloping her in a smell uniquely his.

"Hi, sleepyhead," he said. "Up and at 'em. We need to get going."

"Oh. Okay," she said, clutching the sheet to her chest, as if she thought he might come rip it away at any moment, throw her back on the bed, tear off her pajamas and have his way with her. Which was ridiculous. He wouldn't do that, and she must look ridiculous to him.

He'd scrupulously kept to his word the night before, not laying so much as a finger on her, not even when he'd courteously opened the car door for her and waited patiently for her to climb inside. A silly display of gallantry that had usually been accompanied by the play of his hands at her elbow, the small of her back or anyplace else he could manage to touch. Somehow he'd always managed to get his hands on her, and it always seemed to take on much more importance to her than it ever could to him. He probably felt next to nothing, touching her in such a simple, casual way, while she felt it right down to her toes.

It was odd and disconcerting. She put it down to inexperience and nerves and the fact that he was the most beautiful man she'd ever seen. *All* ordinary women turned to mush at the sight of a truly extraordinary man. She didn't have to beat herself up for it. And there was no way she'd let herself regret the promises she'd asked him to make. No touching. No kissing. She'd thought she was absolutely safe once she elicited those two simple promises, but she wasn't so sure anymore.

"Something wrong?" he said innocently, when she knew there wasn't an innocent bone in his body.

"No." She shook her head, trying to clear it of her traitorous thoughts, wondering how she'd gotten to the point where she was so fixated on him. His body. His touch. His taste.

Amanda looked up at him and shivered, the air suddenly different, thick and heavy. She couldn't quite breathe. There was an odd tingling to her skin, all over, a pleasant heat in the pit of her stomach that spread through her body. He stood there, casually getting dressed. He'd probably dressed in front of hundreds of women. Probably left them disheveled and pleasantly exhausted, while he got up, put on his clothes and left, never giving them a second thought.

She wasn't going to be one of those women. She was so much smarter than that. But she couldn't quite help drawing in his scent, wanting to run her fingertips along his freshly shaven jaw or press her mouth to his.

He smiled at her, that male-predator-on-the-hunt smile, the one that said he knew exactly what she was thinking, that he was willing, eager even. Amanda felt a tightness in her chest. Her breasts felt full, aching, her nipples puckering up in little knots, hard against the soft cotton pajamas she wore.

She felt it again, that odd tingling there, that urgent need to be touched. She looked at his hands, imagining them there, looked back to his full, soft lips, his mouth. She imagined his mouth on her breasts. She could picture his golden head in the vicinity of her chin, her hands at the crown of his head, buried in his beautiful hair, his face buried against her breasts.

Josh swore.

She looked at him and knew what he saw. She was aroused, just sitting there in the bed looking at him. She watched his gaze drop from her mouth to her breasts, and there was no point in hiding. He knew it all somehow. Every shameful secret. Everything she thought, everything she wanted. Somehow he just knew. She snatched up the comforter, bunching it up in front of her, as if that would be enough to shield her from harm, from sheer lunacy. She saw his hands bunched into fists at his side, saw the tightening of his jaw, the frown on his lips.

"I made you a promise," he said. "I won't touch you while you're here."

"I know," she said. Which meant everything should be fine, even if he was standing there as though he might have been carved out of stone. Then he took a breath, reminding her that he was a man—a living, breathing, dangerous man.

"Maybe you didn't realize," he said. "I didn't ask for any promise in return."

"What?"

"I said I wouldn't touch you, and I meant it. I won't. Not here. I guess I didn't realize how difficult that was going to be. But you—you aren't bound by any promises at all. You're free to do whatever you want. Start wherever you like."

"What?" she said.

He didn't come any closer, but he was crowding her with his presence, with the heat of his body, the promise of his touch. She felt like she was being stalked by a master of the game.

"You could walk over here right now and put those delicate hands of yours on me. Anywhere you like, Amanda. You could press those sweet lips of yours to mine and kiss me, and you could stop anytime you wanted. I won't do anything except cooperate."

"You can't be serious," she said, a sinking feeling warring with a shocking sense of excitement, of anticipation. "You said you'd leave me alone—"

"I said I wouldn't touch you. Have I touched you, Amanda?"

She swore at him.

He just grinned, standing there all shiny and clean and smelling wonderful.

"You promised, Josh."

"And I'm not going to break that promise."

"Then stop it. Stop looking at me like that."

"Amanda, I'd do just about anything for you, but there's no way on earth I can look at you and not want you. Seeing you here, in my apartment, in this bed…" He swore. "I couldn't look away if I had to."

"It's just a bed," she protested. "I'm just a woman, sitting in a bed."

He shook his head slowly back and forth. "I could tell you what I see when I look at you, but I doubt you'd believe me. I doubt you'd listen. Not if you're this mad at me already for doing nothing but stand here looking at you."

"It's more than that. You know it."

"I know what I think when I look at you. I know what I'd like to be doing with you right now, and even if I won't let myself, I can't help where my imagination takes me. I have a very vivid imagination." He sighed. "But that's not your problem, Amanda. It's mine. You know what your problem is?''

She groaned, thinking she really didn't want to know. But Josh never left anything alone, never stopped pushing or trying to get what he wanted.

"Your problem," he said in that silky-smooth voice of his, "is that you like looking at me, too. You liked having my hands on you, having my mouth on you, and now every time you look at me, you're going to think of that. That you liked it. That it felt so good. That I'm right here. All you have to do is reach out to me. Take that one little step, and I'm yours.''

She blushed bright red. It was one of the few times in her life she considered telling a blatant lie, feeling it was justified. He had no business invading her thoughts this way, bringing them all out in the open, tempting her and tormenting her.

"Go away, Josh," she said instead. "Please just go away.''

He stood in the doorway long enough to worry her, long enough for her to wonder what she truly wanted. Finally he turned and left.

She was relieved, she told herself. It was better this way. And she was so very stupid. She thought this would be simple, that she'd be safe here if he kept his hands off her. But she knew now that all he had to do was look at her and she wanted him.

Amanda took a shower in his bathroom. In the place where he'd stood, not moments before her, she stood naked and self-conscious and embarrassingly aroused, the scent of him seeping into her pores, being absorbed into her hair.

He had a special, scented soap—obscenely expensive, no doubt—that carried the same smell as his shampoo, his aftershave, his shaving creme. The man coordinated his scent.

She saw it as a concerted effort on his part to drive women mad, and now that scent was all over her.

He had plush, thick towels on a heated rack, waiting for her when she climbed out of a shower that was so big he could have hosted a small dinner party there. He probably had parties there, probably invited women over for dinner and ended up devouring them instead, in the shower. It had three shower heads, she found, wondering what sexual connotations she might read into that. It totally perplexed her. They were gold-tone shower heads. Surely they were just gold-tone and not the real thing. He was obviously spoiled, but she didn't think he did really ostentatious things with his money. Extravagant, but not stupid and ostentatious.

Even though he did have a sauna, a party-size shower and the biggest cedar-lined, walk-in closet she'd ever seen where his second bathroom should have been. Which meant they were sharing. His shower, his soap, his shampoo. She would smell his own scent on her hair and her skin, and it was going to drive her mad.

Dressing hastily she went off to find him in the kitchen, smiling, reminding her of the big, bad wolf of fairy tales and legends, reminding her of someone intent on devouring her whole. Because he seemed to think it was his duty to feed her, she ate what he prepared—an impossibly light, fluffy quiche and fresh fruit, fresh-squeezed juice. Nothing but the best for Josh. Apparently, the meal he'd served her last night hadn't been a fluke. He obviously knew his way around a kitchen. And he was happy in the morning, humming a bit, whistling at times, positively dancing with energy. It radiated from him, the way his scent did. And something else—an invitation. She felt as if he was deliberately trying to entice her into all sorts of wickedness, without saying a word, with nothing but the sinful promises in his eyes.

Amanda wondered how often he'd done this—sat across

the breakfast table from a woman, companionably sharing the paper and whatever he whipped up in his fancy kitchen. She wondered if this was his standard treatment. A roll in the sack, a sauna to work out the kinks, soft music, wine? Candlelight, sinfully soft sheets, him naked under the covers, that wicked twinkle in his amazing blue eyes?

She dropped her fork. It clattered onto the plate, shattering the silence.

"Something wrong?" he said innocently.

"No," she lied.

With faint amusement, he suggested, "You're not a morning person?"

"I'm not used to waking up in a strange bed," she said.

"It won't be for long, Amanda," he added, almost kindly. "I'll try not to make it too torturous for you to be here with me."

She should thank him, she supposed. She was starting to feel like a shrew, and honestly, she wasn't like that. Not with anyone. Except him. He scared her because of the way he tempted her, but there was more, too.

"I don't understand you," she complained, her voice shaky and pathetically weak sounding.

"What don't you understand?" he asked easily.

"Why you're doing this?"

"Because I'm responsible for getting you into this mess."

She'd accused him of that very thing. But honestly, he'd only been trying to help. He'd been right. She had needed someone that night after the hearing. She'd been as shaken as he feared, and he'd been kind to her in his own way. Unsettlingly kind. Lately he seemed different, too. More serious than usual. More sincere.

She believed he was basically a kind man. Arrogant when it came to women and his own effect on them, and he played at life, played harder than anyone she knew.

There had to be something wrong with enjoying life as much as he did. But despite that, everyone loved him. He positively lit up a room. He was quick with a compliment, and he made people laugh. He seemed to genuinely like people. All people. She liked him, despite the outrageous way he flirted with her and every woman he saw, despite the way he tempted her. So she couldn't reconcile liking him so much, thinking he was basically a good person, with his determined pursuit of her, despite her asking him to leave her alone.

"I'm not talking about Rudy. I'm talking about this." She waved her hands between them, to signify that unseen thing connecting them. "This thing between you and me. I don't understand why you won't back off. Especially when I've asked you to. Why do you insist on playing this game with me?"

"I told you, it's no game, Amanda." He frowned. "I want very much to hold you in my arms. I want to touch you. I want to kiss you. All over. I want you in my bed. I've wanted that for years."

"Because you can't have me," she insisted. Surely that was all it was. Still, *years?* The thought sent a little shiver down her spine. He'd wanted her for years? "I'm nothing like the women you normally chase. I'm…"

"What?" he said gently.

Damn him, he was going to make her say it. "Plain," she choked out. "Ordinary. Boring."

"I've never been bored with you, Amanda, and I don't think there's anything ordinary about you."

Amanda sighed, not wanting to have this conversation with him. They might as well live on separate planets. He was rich and dangerous and absolutely gorgeous. She'd seen him, in the society pages and in magazine layouts, photographed with some of the world's most beautiful women hanging on his arm. Beautiful, voluptuous, pampered, sophisticated women. She'd spent more time than she should have looking over those photos, wondering about his life.

Fantasizing, about him. There, she'd admitted it. At least to herself. She had fantasies starring Joshua Carter, but she had no illusions about herself. She was not the kind of woman he dated, not the kind he should even notice.

"Josh—" she began.

"Careful," he said. "I'll think you're fishing for compliments."

"I'm not. I know what kind of woman I am."

"You don't have a clue, Amanda. Did you ever stop to think that maybe you don't know me as well as you think you do, either?"

"Well—"

"Just consider it," he suggested. "Open yourself up to the possibility. Maybe there's more to me than you realize. Maybe what you see is just an image, the surface. Maybe there's some substance under my skin after all."

"Oh, Josh." She felt guilty now. "I like you. Really, I do."

He winced. "I guess that's a start."

"No. I mean it. I do. I think you're basically a nice person, and that's why I don't understand. Why won't you do as I asked? Leave me alone, Josh."

He leaned back in his chair for a moment, then carefully, slowly, he put out a hand to her, laying it palm up on the tabletop, a clear invitation. "Your choice."

It seemed churlish to refuse. Childish. Silly. She was tired of feeling like a silly woman, and she refused to consider how much she wanted this simple connection with him, why she'd come to crave his touch. Amanda put her hand in his. Just as she feared, a pleasant heat flooded her body, radiating from him to her, seeming to invade her bloodstream, infusing itself into every molecule of her being.

There was an oddly appealing tingling sensation from the point of contact. She wondered if it would happen everywhere, all over her body, if she ever let his hands roam over her at will. She wondered how so simple a touch from one man could possibly be so potent, so arousing. He was like a sweet poison, she decided, capable of making otherwise careful, cautious women forget everything they'd ever been taught about gorgeous, charming men.

"Leave me alone, Josh," she said again, desperate now. "Please."

"Amanda? Look at me." He seemed absolutely serious, no hint of the teasing quality that seemed a basic part of his nature. "Believe it or not, I care about you. I don't want to hurt you. I've promised myself I'm not going to do that ever again."

"Then stop."

"If I honestly thought you were happy, if I thought you'd be better off without me, I would. I'd walk away." He smiled gently. "So you tell me, Amanda. Are you happy?"

"What?" she asked, thinking maybe she shouldn't have started this, that she should have left it alone after all.

"You know what it means to be happy. That thing when you feel good. You wake up, and you have reason to be glad. Something to look forward to. Something in your day that's going to excite you, make you smile, make you laugh. Is there anything like that in your life right now?"

She frowned at him, felt an odd pressure at the center of her chest, an ache that radiated outward, just as the warmth from his body had only moments before. But all the pleasure was gone now. She pulled her hand from his, and he didn't try to stop her. She got to her feet and walked to the corner of the room, putting her back to him. Because she couldn't look at him anymore. Because he'd both hurt her and touched her with his words, with the idea that her happiness mattered to him.

Until that moment she hadn't realized how black a cloud she'd been living under for the past year. Tense, dark, frightening blackness. Sadness. Anger. Hurt. Grief. Guilt. She felt all of those things. It had gotten to the point where that seemed the norm for her. So it was an odd concept that he'd brought up—happiness, laughter, joy.

Amanda drew in a long, deep breath. Her chest still hurt, and when she touched her fingertips to her face, she realized tears were running down her cheeks, falling onto her blouse. She swiped them away, weakness invading her limbs. She leaned against the cabinet in front of her, suddenly too tired to even stand up straight and too weak to fight him any longer.

It was unnerving and utterly appealing—the idea that he'd been watching over her, that he cared, that in his own way he wanted to make things better for her. The idea that her happiness meant something to him amazed her.

She'd retreated into a protective shell in the last year, withdrawing from everyone around her, ashamed and embarrassed and lost. She had friends, but she'd made the mistake of pushing just about everyone away. Her parents cared, but they weren't close by and found travel difficult. So they made do with phone calls and letters, which wasn't the same as having a living, breathing person beside her, worrying over her, feeling the need to take care of her when she'd been so lost.

But Josh was here, right behind her. Still not touching her, but she knew he was there. She had radar where he was concerned. She could almost feel his desire to touch her, could feel herself giving in to that idea, her need for him growing.

''I guess this whole mess with Rob hit me harder than I

thought," she said, trying to stall, because it scared her, how fast this thing between them had surged out of control.

He didn't say anything. He was waiting with more patience than she would have believed possible. But she still needed to talk, to understand. She was still resisting all that he had to offer.

"It's only natural, don't you think? That I'd be upset? Unhappy?"

"For a while," he conceded. "But you haven't been happy for a long, long time, Amanda, and I'm damned sick and tired of standing by and watching you miserable and all alone."

"Oh," she said, her tears falling faster. She wanted him to care, she realized. She needed for someone to care enough to help her.

"Amanda." His voice was low and strained.

She knew what he was asking, just as she knew it was up to her to make the first move. She eased back a fraction of an inch, felt his big, solid body coming into contact with hers.

"It's okay," she said.

His arms slid around her. "That's it," he said. "Lean on me."

She did, finding her body cradled against his. A solid mass of man and muscle and heat behind her, wonderfully strong arms embracing her. She could collapse right now and be perfectly safe. He wouldn't let her fall. She didn't have to be so strong, didn't have to go through this alone. It was as if someone had lifted a weight off her body, as if there'd been a concrete block parked on her chest, a burden she'd carried around for a solid year, all by herself, and he'd taken it away. He was here, and he was so much stronger than she was, so much more capable. He was capable of just about anything.

She let her head fall back against his chest and shoulder,

sighing when she felt his lips brush against her temple, softly, sweetly, comfortingly. He bent his head, pressing his cheek to her temple. She relaxed completely in his embrace, never having felt so safe in her entire life. There was still the energy, the awareness, but it was banked by a disarming dose of tenderness, gentleness, kindness. She never imagined finding those qualities in such extravagant quantities in him, but there they were. There was no mistaking what he was offering at this moment. No mistaking, either, that he knew her much better than she ever imagined.

Had he been waiting, as well? To step in like this? To try to help her? Or waiting for something else? Waiting to take her to bed with him?

"You're worrying again," he murmured. "You managed to relax for a whole minute or so, and then you tensed up again. Why don't you turn around and put your arms around me and relax. Just for a little while longer."

She blew out a shaky breath, knowing she was in the danger zone now. She was totally captivated by him, totally at his mercy. "Josh—"

"Turn around. I need to see your face."

She did, wondering if she was destined to always do what he wanted eventually. He loosened his hold, and she slid around in his arms, finding him not even a breath away. Blazing blue eyes gazed down at her, his lips a heartbeat away. He held her snugly against him, one of his hands at the side of her face.

"I meant what I said that night at the beach. It's time to let it all go. Forget about that man. Forgive yourself for whatever it is you think you did wrong and get on with your life."

"It's not that simple. I don't now how I'll ever trust anyone again."

"You trust me, don't you? You know me. You know what I'm like. I'm an up-front kind of guy. I'll tell you exactly what I want in this relationship. I won't lie to you, and I won't make promises I don't intend to keep.''

"So what is this all about, Josh. What do you want?''

"You. I've always wanted you," he groaned. "You never even gave me the time of day.''

Of course not. She'd been too smart for that. At least, she thought she'd been smart. But what had she done instead? She'd been with Rob, the liar, the traitor, the man who'd used her and then left her to face the mess he'd made all by herself. There was nothing Josh could do to hurt her a fraction as much as Rob had, she realized. Josh wouldn't. He wasn't that kind of man.

Josh would leave her eventually, and that would hurt. But how did a broken sexual liaison ever compare to falling in love with a man, planning a life with him, a marriage and children and all that went along with it, then seeing it had all been a lie. Rob had never loved her, never intended to marry her. He'd used her, and she must have made it so easy for him. A man she knew died because of Rob, and other people were hurt, people she cared about.

"Ouch," Josh said. "What was that? What were you just thinking?''

"About how wrong I was thinking I was so much safer with a man like Rob than I would be with you. You'd never hurt me like that.''

"Not in a million years," he promised.

She thought he would have kissed her then, then realized he wasn't going to do that. He'd made her a promise, and he wouldn't come an inch closer without an invitation, one she felt inclined to give. But before that, there were details to discuss. She wanted to be absolutely clear about what this was.

"You want me in your bed? What else?''

"I want to see you smile again, Amanda. I want to make you happy. I can do that. I know I can.''

''For a while?'' she asked.

''For as long we both want to be with each other.''

''You have a short attention span, Josh.''

He drew in a breath. She felt his chest rise and fall, let herself lay her head against his shoulder and slide her arms around him more tightly, holding him close, to soften the criticism in her words.

''I've waited a long time for you,'' he said. ''So if this is going to happen—you and me—it's going to take some time. I want to know every inch of you. I want to please you in a way no man ever has before. I want to spoil you, take care of you. I can make you happy, Amanda. I wouldn't be doing this if I didn't think I could be good for you. But I'm not the kind of man who's going to put a ring on your finger. If that's what you want, what you honestly think you need, I'll back off. I don't want anything from you that you're not willing to give.''

''I don't know what I want, Josh.''

He backed up, cupping her chin in his hand, his exquisitely gentle hands, bringing his face in close, until they were practically nose to nose, and he gave her a little smile. ''Think about it, all right? I won't push.''

''You? Not push?''

His lips formed into a mischievous smile. ''I'll consider it a test of my willpower. I do have some, you know.''

''I'm sure you do. I just don't think it's ever been seriously tested.''

''Then this will be good for me, too,'' he said.

She laughed a bit. ''You're incorrigible.''

He nodded. ''And you're laughing. Doesn't it feel good?''

There it went again—that little zing of emotion, zipping right through her. That warm, tingly feeling. The dangerous one. She was important to him. Her happiness meant something to him.

"Oh, Josh." It was all she could manage. He'd taken her breath away.

"I do care about you. Promise."

"I'm glad," she said. "I need someone to care about me right now."

"Then it's a good thing I'm here."

She snuggled against him, thinking that she could have the right to be here, any time she wanted. He would be generous with his affection. She shivered a bit, thinking of being indulged by Josh, physically and emotionally. He'd be extravagantly attentive, lavishly attentive. He could spoil a woman like no one else.

"I like this," she confessed. "I...I don't think anyone's touched me in a long time."

She felt his chest slowly rise and fall with the force of a long, deep breath, wondered if her words had any power over him, if she could touch him, just as deeply as he touched her.

Finally, quietly, he said, "Then I'm your man, Amanda."

She buried her head in the side of his neck, finding warm, smooth, sun-browned skin and that smell she loved so much. She thought about nuzzling her cheek against the underside of his jaw or pressing the tip of her nose flat against his neck, toying with his ear, maybe even kissing him herself, all on her own.

All this time, she thought. She could have been with Josh.

It thrilled her, almost as much as it unnerved her, thinking of what he might expect from her, what he might demand. She had no doubts that he'd be a demanding lover, that he could please her in every way imaginable, and lots of doubts about whether she could please him. Lots of insecurities about all the women he'd been with and the things he'd done. There probably wasn't anything he didn't know, which made her wonder what she had to give him.

"I'm afraid if we… Well, that you'd be disappointed."

"With you?" he growled.

She nodded.

"No way," he said, sounding the way he almost always did—completely sure of himself.

"But, Josh—"

"It's not a test, Amanda. I'm not giving you a grade. It's about enjoying each other, exploring, learning, pleasing each other. I want very much to please you, and I know I can. I know I'll find the whole thing quite pleasing myself. I have no doubts about that, and you shouldn't, either."

She sighed and snuggled closer, loath to give up this spot. He had a way of making the most outrageous things sound perfectly reasonable. Reach for him, and he'd be hers. He'd take care of her. Make everything all better, for a little while. She shivered, thinking about Josh, utterly intent on pleasing her.

"I have to think about it," she said, moving it into the realm of possibility.

"And here I thought I'd rip this pretty blouse off you and have you for breakfast," he said, deadpan.

And she laughed. He was right, she hadn't laughed in a long time.

"That's better," he said, giving her a blazing smile. "Take whatever time you need. I'll be here."

"You're so sure I'll agree?"

"I usually manage to get people to come around to my way of thinking, sooner or later."

Amanda nodded, thinking maybe it was inevitable. He always got what he wanted. She used to think that was a bad thing, but maybe she'd been wrong. Maybe it wasn't.

Maybe it was time she became more like him—reaching out and taking what she wanted, taking what life had to offer her.

And at the moment she wanted only one thing. *Him.*

Chapter 6

"Ever hold one of these things in the palm of your hand?" Josh asked as he held out a gun to her, a polished, black, sinful-looking thing. She didn't even want to touch it.

"Do I have to?"

"Yes," he insisted.

He'd brought her to a private, deserted firing range in Maryland, which unnerved her. So did the way she kept forgetting the danger. Josh had a way of pushing every other thought out of her head. She wanted to let herself fall completely under his spell. She nearly had until he tried to give her his gun.

"It's an inanimate object, Amanda. It won't hurt you. It takes a person to load it, point it at you and pull the trigger to hurt you."

"I could never do that," she said.

"Maybe not, but if you ever change your mind, I might not be there to teach you how to use it first. You don't want to shoot a gun for the first time when your life is on the line.''

"I could never shoot someone," she insisted.

"I'm not going to make you. But humor me and at least learn how."

She sighed, staring at the wicked-looking thing. He was right, she supposed. Even if she didn't like it, he was right. Still... "I hate guns."

Josh said nothing. He had that "nothing is going to change my mind" look on his face, and, at the moment, nothing of the easygoing man she'd always known. Odd, how she kept finding a new side to him. Odd how utterly appealing all of them were. This one, especially, Josh her protector.

Amanda looked up at him, burnished-gold hair and bright-blue eyes and the potential for a mind-numbing grin never far away, and she complained, "You keep surprising me."

"And I won't let you change the subject. Pick up the gun, Amanda. I'm not asking you to make friends with it or to like it. Just to pick it up."

"You said you don't think anything's going to happen."

"I don't. But I don't know that for sure. We plan for what we hope will happen and anything else we can imagine that might. If everything goes wrong, and you could save yourself by using this—" he held the gun right in front of her "—I want you to know how."

She sighed, unnerved. "I don't know if I can."

"You're not getting out of this building until you do. I mean it. And it's time we got something else straight, too. We have two things going on here. A business relationship and a personal one. You're in charge of the personal one, and I'm in charge of the business one. That means you will do exactly what I say, when I say it. Now pick up the gun."

She closed her eyes and blurted out, "My mother's brother shot himself, Josh."

He waited, gun in hand, not backing down.

"It happened when I was in grade school. They said it was an accident, but…I don't think so. I think he meant to do it."

"I'm sorry," he said. "Pick up the gun."

"My mother found him," she rushed on. "I was with her. She was in front of me, so I didn't really see much. I just remembering my mother crying in the most awful way and looking so sad and so scared. I don't think I'd ever seen my mother scared before that day. She's always been a little irrational where guns are concerned, and I guess I have been, too."

"So you have a reason for the way you feel. I understand. But don't blame the weapon for what happened to your uncle," Josh said evenly. "If he hadn't had a gun, he would have used something else."

"But a gun is so fast, so easy. Move one finger a centimeter or so, and it's done. There's no time to think it over, to change your mind."

He frowned. For a second something flickered across his face, something he hid quickly, but still…something. Was it her imagination or had she touched a nerve?

"People who want to kill themselves can always find a way," he said finally.

"Josh—"

"Take the gun, Amanda."

She gave in and picked it up. It wasn't very heavy or very big. He'd told her what kind it was, but she honestly hadn't been paying attention, hadn't wanted to know. He was going to Rudy's dinner with this strapped to his ankle. Just in case.

Amanda let it rest on its side against her palm. Even knowing it wasn't loaded, she was still scared of it. Odd how anything could be so small and yet so deadly. Odd that he could be this way—immovable, so serious, so stern.

"Have you ever shot anyone?" she asked, the thought just occurring to her.

"Yes."

Amanda shivered. He sounded so matter-of-fact, his normally wonderful voice totally devoid of emotion. She found she couldn't leave the subject alone. "Have you ever killed anyone?"

"Yes."

She flinched. Even thinking she was prepared for it, she couldn't quite see it. It made her even more curious. "Have you ever been shot?"

"Yes," he said easily, with a wry smile. "Blows the playboy image all to hell, doesn't it?"

"Yes." She looked up at him, studying his features anew. He was still much too pretty to be real. She noticed now more than ever how very imposing he was. Tall, broad-shouldered, moving with such an easy grace. But obviously, there was much more to him. "I've never seen you like this."

"You've only seen a little part of me, Amanda. But I'll show you the rest, if you honestly want to know me. But not now," he said. "For now you have to load the gun."

She did. He showed her how to take off the safety, how to stand, how to aim, how to fire. So she did it again and again until he was satisfied, and she hoped he was right, that nothing would go wrong and she'd never have to do this again.

"I want her out of this," Josh told Jamie an hour and a half later. "Rudy called her last night. She's scared to death of him. I took her to the firing range this morning. I thought she was going to pass out the first time she fired a gun."

Jamie was curled up in the big chair in the corner of her

office that she liked so much. "Did you figure out why this is so important to you?"

"God, you're annoying," he complained, sitting down on the arm of her chair. "I don't know how I forgot that so quickly."

"And you're changing the subject. It's not going to work."

"Okay. You were right yesterday. She is important to me. She's way too vulnerable and impossibly naïve, and I should stay the hell away from her, too."

"But you're not going to."

"I can't," he complained. "And before you start in on me again, I've been up-front with her. We had *the talk*. She knows exactly what I want, exactly what I have to offer her. I told her it won't last."

"Josh, women don't listen to things like that."

"I said it in plain English. I looked her right in the eye. She heard me. I made sure of it."

"I'm sure you did, and I'm telling you, women don't listen when a man says something like that, because they don't want to believe it. They want to believe they can change a man's mind."

He frowned. "That makes absolutely no sense."

"And that surprises you? You're always complaining about how illogical women are."

"Amanda's not. She's careful and cautious, and she knows me. She knows what I'm like. She believed me."

"Josh, Dan told me the exact same thing last year. I didn't believe him."

"Oh, hell. You?" He had a sinking feeling deep in his gut.

She nodded.

Josh swore once again. Jamie was a smart woman. She should have known better, but still… "It worked out in the end. You changed his mind."

"Is Amanda going to change your mind?"

"No."

"Then you need to leave her alone."

"She needs me," he argued.

"She needs you to keep her safe until Rudy Olivara's gone."

"What are you? My conscience now?"

"God, no. I'm not up to that. It's a job for a dozen women at least."

"It's not funny," he complained. "There's nothing funny about this."

Jamie leaned her head against his side. "Sorry."

He slid his arm around her and complained, "I don't understand any of it."

"I could explain it to you, but you wouldn't listen. We've proven that already."

Josh frowned. "You're saying I'm being as illogical as a woman who doesn't listen when I say our relationship will be a temporary thing?"

"You got it. Did you figure out what you want from Amanda yet?"

He thought about lying through his teeth on that one, but Jamie was his friend. He was feeling curiously uneasy and frustrated and unsure of what he should do. But he was perfectly clear on all the things he'd already done wrong.

"I stayed away for a year," he said, "and before, when she was with Rob, because I thought she'd be better off without me. And I was dead wrong about that. She's gone through this all alone, and I should have been with her. I could have helped her, Jamie. I'm going to help her. I cannot leave her alone right now."

"Okay. I give up. I won't try to talk you out of it anymore. And I would talk to Dan for you about pulling Amanda out of this, but I already tried. Last night."

"He wouldn't listen to you, either?"

''He listened. I just didn't change his mind. He honestly believes it's the right thing. If Rudy or anyone else is going to try to use Amanda like this, we need to know about it and deal with it. When Dan put it to me like that, I decided he was right.'' Jamie looked thoughtful. ''He's worried about her, too. So am I.''

''Okay,'' he said. He'd have to make it work, keep her safe.

''I did volunteer to be on the mission team, if you want me.''

Jamie had worked in-house since she got pregnant, planning operations, monitoring via satellite link from the office while they were underway. They'd been shorthanded, losing three field agents already in the past year, so everyone had agreed that she would stay on at least until she had her baby. Josh liked the idea of her calling the shots from this end. There was no one he would trust more.

''Of course I want you.'' He leaned over and kissed her on the cheek, pausing for another second to rub her tummy, which he found utterly fascinating. He'd never been near a pregnant woman before. ''How's my baby this morning?''

Jamie groaned. ''Almost as annoying as you. I think it's getting too crowded in there to suit her. She's trying to bust out. Through my rib cage.''

''He,'' Josh insisted.

He got to his feet and offered her a hand, pulling her up from the deep cushion of the chair, having the nerve to laugh at the effort it took her just to stand.

''You are a truly awful man,'' she complained.

They both laughed. Josh was getting ready to say something smart, because he liked teasing her. But when he turned around, he found Amanda standing in the doorway to his office, looking from him to Jamie, then back to him with the oddest look on her face.

"I'm sorry," Amanda said. "I didn't realize you were busy."

"We're not," Jamie said, heading for the door. "I was just leaving."

Jamie slipped past Amanda. Josh grabbed her hand and pulled her into his office, closing the door behind her, wondering what she'd heard.

"Been standing there awhile?" he asked as casually as he could, hoping he wasn't going to slam any doors today. He wasn't sure his ego could take it. It couldn't take much more of her thinking he was a louse, either.

"I'm sorry," Amanda said. "I didn't mean to eavesdrop."

"Amanda?"

"Hmm?"

Josh swore. Just this morning she'd said she trusted him. Obviously, she didn't. She was also taking two steps back for every one he took toward her. She had her back against the wall, and he realized he was too close. She had her teeth over her bottom lip and was an instant away from biting down when he reached for her, barely stopping himself from touching her.

"Don't," he said instead, wondering what possessed him to make such a bargain with her. *No hands.* It was proving to be nearly impossible.

"Don't what?"

"Don't you dare tell me you would think for a minute that I'm the father of Jamie's baby," he growled. "It was a joke, Amanda."

"Okay."

Hell, no, it wasn't okay. He could see that. Sighing, he added, "Just in case you were wondering, there's absolutely no way that could be my baby."

"Okay."

"She's crazy about her husband, and as much as I adore

Jamie, we don't have that kind of relationship. She's my friend. Not my lover. She has never been my lover, has never come close to being my lover.''

"All right. I believe you."

"Are you sure?"

Amanda sighed and looked uncomfortable. "You two have always been close."

"We are. We worked together for a long time," he said, then added, without really thinking, "If anything, she reminds me of my sister."

"I didn't know you had a sister."

Josh caught the frown before it showed, used a discipline honed over the years to hide any emotion that might have surfaced in that moment. That he'd mentioned his sister at all showed how rattled he really was. But she'd been on his mind ever since Amanda had told him about her mother's brother.

"What, did you think I crawled out from under a rock one day?" he asked, as lightly as he could manage. "I have a mother and a father, too."

"I imagined you came into the world in the usual way," she said. "And I've heard about your father. The ambassador."

"What a guy," Josh quipped.

"You two don't get along?"

"No," he said, end of story. He wasn't talking about his father, either. "How did we go from talking about women to talking about my family?"

"Something about the possibility of you fathering children."

"I haven't. Not ever. Just in case you were wondering."

"Of course. You just flirt with every woman in sight. You probably never take it any further than that."

"You think I sleep with every woman I flirt with?" he asked, wondering how bad her opinion of him could possibly be. "I like women. I like to make them smile. But it doesn't mean anything, Amanda. I've flirted with every woman in this building. Do you really think I've been involved with all of them?"

"No," she admitted. "Not all of them."

"Oh, hell, I'm hardly ever here. I'm out of town more than I'm in, and I have to rest sometime. When am I supposed to have worked my way through the female population of this building?"

"You work fast?" she suggested, then honestly looked contrite. "Josh, it's none of my business what you do. If you want to throw a wild, decadent party and invite the entire female population of the fourth floor, and have them draw straws to see who gets you first, it's none of my business."

"You think I have sex parties?" he roared.

"No." She took a step back, cringing at his tone. "I guess not...I don't know, and it's none of my business anyway."

"It is now," he said, fury pouring through his veins. "I don't throw parties that turn into orgies. I don't run from one woman's bed to the next."

"Okay."

He swore once again, thinking for a sweet, quiet, unassuming woman, she had a way of making him absolutely crazy, making him yell and stomp around and want to throw things, until he felt like an absolute fool.

She made it sound as if he might as well have one of those little machines hanging from his bedroom door, the thing they used at his favorite deli that gave out numbers on little scraps of paper. So people knew when it was their turn. He could just hear it now. *No. 347, Mr. Carter will serve you now.* He could make announcements over the PA system at work. After all, he was supposedly working his way through the building.

"God," he choked out. "I don't believe this. Amanda, I want you to understand something. If you and I are going to be involved, there won't be anyone else. Not while we're together."

"You are a one-woman-at-a-time kind of guy?"

"It so happens I am." He swore, not remembering the last time he was this mad. "You think I'm a real jerk?"

"No. I think you're…busy. I think you stay…busy. With women. Which is fine with me. I mean, I don't have any right to tell you what you should or shouldn't do. That's how it works, right? Relationships. Adult relationships."

"It works however we want it to work."

"Well…that's fine. I wasn't criticizing you. I wasn't thinking I had the right to tell you what to do."

"And if I gave you that right?" he said, dead serious.

"What?"

"If I chose to give you the right?"

"I…I don't understand."

He sighed, not quite understanding himself. Just knowing he wanted her to be comfortable, to trust him, to like him. What would he have to do, he wondered, to make Amanda really like him?

"If it makes you uncomfortable to have me say things like that to other women, even as a joke, I won't do it."

She blinked up at him. "Josh, flirting to you is like breathing. As long as you're alive, you'll be flirting."

"It doesn't mean anything, Amanda. I like women. I like making them feel good. If I tell someone I think she looks gorgeous today, I mean that I sincerely like the way she looks. Is there anything wrong with telling a woman that?"

"No."

"And if I kiss a woman on the cheek? What about that?"

Puzzled, she said, "What about it?

"I don't have to do that," he offered. If it made her uneasy, seeing him touch another woman, he would stop.

"Josh, I don't understand why we're having this conversation."

"Because I want you to be comfortable with me. I want you to trust me when I tell you that right now, I don't want anyone but you. And I'm willing to do whatever it takes to convince you of that."

"You're going to change the way you act? For me?"

"I told you, I want you to be comfortable," he said, wondering why he'd made her decidedly uncomfortable by saying that.

"It's not necessary," she claimed.

"I think it is," he said, honestly baffled by the whole conversation. Was it so hard for her to believe he wanted to please her? That he was capable of showing a bit of restraint where other women were concerned? He waited, hoping she'd give him some clue as to what he should do, then suggested, "How about no hands?"

"What?"

"Same rules you and I have. No hands. No kissing. I may not be able to control what I say, because you're right, flirting is… Well, I open my mouth, and that's just what comes out. But I can keep my hands and my mouth to myself."

"You?"

"It's not exactly a hardship, Amanda. I told you, you're the only one I want right now."

She just stood there, staring up at him.

Josh waited, when all he wanted to do was take her in his arms and crush her to him. He wanted to hold her the way he'd held her this morning, and he wanted to promise her that everything would be fine, that he was going to make things all better for her, that she wasn't going to be alone, and no one was ever going to hurt her.

But he didn't do forever, and he didn't lie. All he had to offer was a good time, while it lasted, and suddenly that just didn't seem like enough for a woman like Amanda. What was he going to do if that wasn't enough for her?

Chapter 7

Amanda wanted to believe everything he told her. That he didn't have to touch another woman, didn't have to put his hands or his mouth on anyone else, because he didn't want to and because he knew it made her uncomfortable. It struck her as so odd, that he would be so concerned about her comfort, that he'd rearrange his life to accommodate her. She didn't think she'd ever been that important to anyone, and it was a heady thought that she might truly be that important to Josh.

"Hungry?" he said. "How do you feel about seafood?"

"I still can't get over the notion that you cook."

His mouth twitched. "Did you think I was helpless, Amanda?"

"No, just spoiled."

"I am. I'm a food snob, and the only way to make sure I can always get what I want was to learn to cook it myself."

"And you always find a way to get what you want."

"That remains to be seen." He gave her a slow, steamy smile.

He fed her shrimp and pasta, plied her with wine that was probably outrageously expensive, but nice. They sat at a small table in the alcove off the living room. Nerves fluttered in the pit of her stomach. He kept her smiling all the way through dinner. There was candlelight and wine and soft music, an impressive view of the Washington skyline in the background.

So this is how the other half lives, Amanda thought.

She helped him clean up, and they were standing in the kitchen when she said, "I've always been so careful. Despite this mess with Rob—"

"Let's forget all about Rob Jansen, all right? I don't blame you for anything that happened with him, and I know you've been careful, Amanda. I understand."

"Actually, I was thinking I'm getting tired of being careful," she said. "Being careful hasn't kept me safe. It hasn't kept me from getting hurt."

"I won't hurt you, Amanda. I would never deliberately hurt you."

"I know that."

And she wondered what he would do if she asked him to kiss her. Just once. Maybe twice. She wondered if she could have that and nothing more. She doubted many women held him off after just a few kisses, but he said he was in the mood to indulge her. To spoil her. She liked the idea, the sense of freedom it gave her to ask for what she wanted. Liked the idea of someone putting her wishes and needs ahead of his own.

"What are you thinking?" he asked, his voice sinfully soft and full of promise.

"That you're probably very good at spoiling a woman."

"I am," he said. "Going to let me spoil you, Amanda?"

"Maybe."

He laughed, and she laughed with him.

Amanda was thinking it was a purely magical evening and that he was obviously a magical man. It was as if he'd woven a spell around her, spun a web of pure gold. Everything seemed so much brighter. The whole world, the entire universe, when she was with him. She felt as if anything was possible. As if she could fly if she wanted to. As if the world was full of amazing and wonderful possibilities. She'd forgotten about all the possibilities, all the good things.

"I do think you could be good for me," she said.

He grinned. "This is starting to get interesting."

"You've already been good for me," she said. "For a long time all I could see were the bad things that had happened. I worried that nothing would ever get better. I was about to become a hermit in my own house, hiding away from everything and everyone, feeling sorry for myself and guilty and lost."

"Then it's a good thing we got you out of there."

She nodded, seeing the irony, too. A dangerous situation with Josh was preferable to a normal day in her orderly, solitary life. Another time she might think back on it and decide it was sad. But not now. She was with Josh, and Josh was magic. He was life and laughter and warmth, the positively sinful pursuit of happiness, of pleasure, of indulgence. She was thinking of indulging herself with him.

She went to him and placed her hand over his heart. Heat shimmered through the expensive cloth. She could feel a pulse beating rapidly and strong. She feared he might pounce on her, as he'd laughingly discussed earlier, but he didn't. He kept his word. He stood absolutely still, a dangerously intense heat in his eyes.

"Go ahead," he invited. "Whatever you want."

There were so many places on a man's body she'd longed to touch. So many places on him she'd imagined touching. Truth was, he'd always been the stuff of her fantasies, and she could hardly believe she was here with him now, touching him. Standing in his apartment after a candlelit dinner with two whole glasses of wine warming her from the inside out, his heated gaze on her.

"You make me want to do things I know are wrong," she said.

"Why are they wrong?"

"I can't remember anymore." Funny, she used to know exactly why. She sighed, her hands roaming over his chest, his shoulders, his arms. She took his hands and put them on her waist, slid a step closer to him.

"Is this a test?" he asked. "To see how much of this I can take without breaking my word."

"No," she claimed. "It's an indulgence. You said you were ready to indulge me. And I like touching you."

He grinned. "I like having you touch me."

Her hands stroked down his abdomen. She felt delicious muscles quiver beneath her fingertips, felt an answering fluttering in her. Heat unfurled deep inside, desire, need, the power of which surprised her, shocked her even.

She felt a shudder rippling through him, felt him take a breath and slowly let it out, saw a hint of surprise on his face. She absolutely loved the idea that she could make him tremble, shudder. That she could surprise him. That he would give her this kind of control over what happened between the two of them. She'd always believed if he ever pressed the point, she would be lost. That if he came at her full force, every bit of resolve in her body would simply melt away. So she'd been afraid to get near him. But not anymore.

She might well ignore every bit of common sense she possessed, for a few brief weeks, maybe even months, with him. Life had taught her she could live with regrets. What was one more to add to her already long list?

Amanda leaned her head against his shoulder, against the enticing hollow made by his neck meeting his shoulder, and she carefully moved into him, until her entire body was resting lightly against his.

"What about this?" He slid an arm around her waist, holding her more securely. "Can I do this?"

"Yes, please." She drew in a breath, drew in his scent, nuzzled her nose against the side of his neck, and she felt his chin atop her head, felt him drop a light kiss at her temple.

His chest expanded with a breath. "I don't know how it can feel this good, just to hold you."

Which struck her as odd. She backed away a bit, puzzled. "You, too? The man with a bathroom big enough to entertain an entire dance troupe?"

"I don't like dancers," he said. "They're too skinny. There's nothing to hold on to. And I told you, I take it one woman at a time."

"For how long?" she asked, her curiosity getting the best of her. "How long do they last?"

"I don't know."

"The last one? How long were you with the last one?"

"I honestly don't remember, Amanda."

"Do you remember her name?"

"What do you really want to know? How long this is going to last between you and me?"

"Yes," she said.

"You tell me—how long are you going to want to be with me?"

"I…I don't know."

"That's what I mean. It's impossible to say at this point. Do you want a time limit? A maximum and a minimum?"

"I don't know."

"You name it," he told her. "A year. A month. A week?"

"Have you ever been with one woman for a year?"

"No," he admitted. "And a week wouldn't do it. A month wouldn't do it, either. Split the difference with me. How 'bout six months?"

Six months, she thought. Would it be enough? Would he last that long? "Have you ever been with one woman for six months, Josh?"

He thought about it, thought long and hard, then admitted, "I'm not sure."

An uncomfortable silence stretched between them. She slipped away from him. He frowned, a dark flush in his cheeks. He was angry.

"I'm sorry," she said. "That's not fair of me, and you're right. It is impossible to say now how long any relationship we might have will last."

"No, I'm sorry." He sighed, cupped his hand against the side of her face. "I shouldn't have come at you that way. I'm not in the best of moods, okay? Sexual frustration isn't very becoming on me."

"Oh." She backed away.

"And you don't have to run away, either. Come back here."

She did, just for a minute, she told herself. He held her loosely, as he had before. She closed her eyes and willed herself to forget about everything that could go wrong and thought instead of simply being here with him. What it could be like. This afternoon he'd suggested going away, just the two of them. Locking themselves away from everyone. Amanda shivered with pleasure. Locked away with Josh. He'd promised her it would be good. She knew it would, once they got past that awkward first time and all her silly insecurities.

"I do want to be with you," she admitted.

He bent his head, his lips against her right ear. "Say it again."

"I want you."

She felt a rumbling deep in his chest, a wholly apprecia-
tive sound that sent an answering ripple of anticipation
through her.

"What are we going to do about that, Amanda?"

The phone rang, saving her, she supposed. She tried to
slip away.

He didn't loosen his hold. "Let it ring. The machine will
pick up."

Amanda heard the machine click on, heard his voice,
smooth and so very inviting, asking the caller to leave a
message. She shouldn't have been surprised to hear a
woman's voice broadcast from the machine, a soft feminine
laugh, a hint of a European accent making the woman
sound so worldly, so sophisticated. Everything Amanda
was not.

"Hi, it's Sunnie. I got caught up in a new piece, and
when I looked at the clock it was almost four in the morning here. I thought I'd take a chance you'd be home, but I
should have known better. Don't you ever sleep, Josh?"

Amanda just stood there, feeling foolish, thinking it was
so much easier when the other women were nameless crea-
tures, when she never had to hear the husky invitation in
their voices.

Josh brushed past her, picked up the phone. "Hi, Sun-
shine. I'm here."

Amanda didn't hear a hint of irritation or impatience in
his voice when he answered. If anything, there was genuine
warmth, genuine affection. It hurt, she found. If truly hurt.
He hit a button on the machine, so Amanda didn't hear any
more of what the woman said. But she heard his end of the
conversation. She stood right there shamelessly eavesdrop-
ping.

He laughed, then told the woman, "No, no problems at

all in Paris. And everything's fine here. The painting was waiting for me when I arrived. It's beautiful. Thank you.''

A woman who sent him paintings? Amanda glanced over the walls of the living room again, looking more closely at the artwork this time, noting a striking similarity among them. Something about the use of color and light, the style. She noted the artist's signature in the lower right corner. A decidedly feminine, elegant script. *Sunnie.*

He lived in an apartment surrounded by paintings by a woman named Sunnie.

"Look," he said. "I'm kind of in the middle of something here, and you're probably too wired to sleep just yet, anyway. Can I call you back in a few minutes?"

The woman must have agreed. Amanda wondered if she was used to calling him at night and finding someone here with him, wondered if it bothered her at all. Amanda couldn't imagine not being bothered by something like that.

"I miss you." He said, grinning. "I love you, too, angel face. I'll talk to you soon."

Amanda looked away, but not before he looked up and saw her, not before he no doubt saw the look on her face.

"You're going to feel absolutely foolish when you hear who that was."

"I wasn't going to ask," she said, already feeling foolish for thinking she had a right to know or to be upset.

He cocked his head to the right and drilled her to that spot with just a glance, steel in his eyes. "You don't even want to hear what I have to say?"

"What's the point?" she said, daring to move a step closer to him, then another. Honestly, she wanted to hit him. It shocked her a bit. She'd never hit another human being in her life. But her hands balled into fists and she imagined the satisfaction she'd get from slapping her palm against his handsome face.

"She's my sister, Amanda."

"Sister?"

"Yes."

Amanda came closer still, the urge to hit something gone entirely, the urge to simply disappear growing by leaps and bounds. Still wary, she glanced down at the counter, so she wouldn't have to look at him, her gaze falling to his answering machine. The light was blinking. Absently, she took note of the messages.

"It says you have eleven messages," she accused, feeling so childish it hurt. "How many sisters do you have, Josh?"

"Just one," he said tightly.

Amanda stood there, saying nothing, wishing she could sink into the floor. She'd been so stupid.

"Oh, for God's sake," he said, punching a button on the machine. "You want to listen to what they have to say, go ahead and listen. You choose not to believe a damned thing I say or anything I happen to feel for you, that's up to you, too."

And then he turned and stalked away as the first message started to play. A woman's voice, sultry as sin. Her name was Mitzi, and she'd just heard he was back in town. She'd love to see him, she purred.

Amanda was feeling decidedly catty herself, and foolish and downright mean. His sister? She supposed it was entirely possible. He'd already told her he had a sister, a mother and a father, too. It was reasonable to expect them to talk on the phone from time to time.

But she didn't think it was reasonable to believe he'd truly limit himself to one woman at a time. That was especially hard as she stood in his living room listening to one woman after another fussing over him and making a few suggestive invitations to him via his answering machine.

Neither could she accept the fact that Josh, beautiful and

sophisticated and spoiled as he was, truly wanted an absolutely ordinary woman like her.

Amanda felt miserable and sad and sorry for herself the next day. She hadn't even apologized to Josh. She felt foolish wanting reassurance from him about how long they'd be together. After all, it wouldn't last; he'd told her so. What did the little details even matter?

She'd also developed a shameless fascination with him and his life that by mid-morning had her in the research department, where Gwen was all too helpful, ready to show her the impressive array of information one could find on someone like Joshua Carter and his family in any public database in the country. Amanda felt guilty about invading his privacy, but still looked at what Gwen found. She was surprised to find that he was a Rhodes scholar with an undergraduate degree in international studies from Princeton. The man was no lightweight. According to the news magazines, he was close friends with the current U.S. president, who was a sort-of unofficial uncle. Josh had carried out several high-profile diplomatic missions over the years, missions she'd always suspected were cover for assignments at Division One. He also had one sister, Meredith Carter, who according to several news reports had died when she was sixteen and the family was living in Italy. She'd drowned.

Amanda couldn't make sense of that—Josh telling her the message was from his sister, when his only sister had been dead for almost ten years. It would be an incredibly callous thing to do, and he wasn't a callous man.

She was in the ladies' room, staring at the dark circles under her eyes—the telltale puffiness that said she'd been crying—when Jamie walked in.

"Bad day?" she suggested gently.

"Bad year," Amanda said.

"Josh looks like he's having a very bad day, as well. Not that I'm prying...." She hesitated, then admitted. "I guess I am."

"It's okay," Amanda said.

"I just love Josh. I always have. He's the best friend I've ever had. He's great to work with, too. He's always happy. He makes me laugh, wants to take care of me, too. He reminds me a lot of my brothers."

"He said you reminded him of his sister."

Jamie looked surprised. "He talked to you about his sister?"

"Just a little bit. Why?"

"He never talks about his sister."

"Meredith, right?"

"I don't believe I've ever heard her name."

"Do you know what happened to her?"

"I never came right out and asked, but I sensed it's something that still hurts him." Jamie hesitated. "I feel like I'm gossiping now, but just so you know, you might want to tread lightly on that subject. I heard once that she committed suicide. When she was very young."

"Oh," Amanda said.

"I know. It's hard to imagine anything bad ever happening in Josh's life, at least from what he lets people see of him. But there's a lot more to him than he ever lets anyone see."

"I know." Amanda closed her eyes, hurting for what she'd said to him the day before at the firing range about guns and suicide. She remembered what he'd said. *People who want to kill themselves can always find a way.*

Had his sister done that? Had she found a way? To drown herself?

"Josh has a big heart," Jamie added. "And he's very kind, and very good at his job. You can trust him to watch out for you."

Amanda nodded, thinking to trust him with her life, but not her heart. She almost left it at that. But there was one more thing she wanted to know. She just couldn't leave it alone.

"Have you ever heard him mention a woman named Sunnie? An artist?"

"Of course. He gave Dan and me one of her paintings as a wedding present, a beautiful, magical piece with a castle on a hill in the mountains. In Germany, I think. It has the most amazing colors, looks like something out of a fairy tale. I hung it in the nursery."

"So, they've been friends for a long time?"

"Friends?" She hedged. "Or something. But I've seen him return calls from her from halfway around the world. Women call him all the time, and if he returned all their calls, he'd never get a bit of work done. But he always seems happy to talk to her."

Amanda nodded. So he was capable of maintaining an interest in a woman over a period of time. At least in one woman. Sunnie. Josh had told the woman he loved her. Amanda thought she might hate the woman for that.

"Are you going to be okay?" Jamie said.

"Yes," she claimed. "I'm going to pull myself together. It's time."

Time she grew up a bit and accepted the man for what he was and stopped trying to make him into what she wanted him to be.

Josh slammed down the phone and swore, once again taking his anger out on an inanimate object, like some silly adolescent boy who flew off the handle at every turn. He took a bit of comfort in knowing the door was closed and there was no one to witness his little display of childish frustration. After all, he was a man who placed great value on self-control.

And he'd always possessed a great deal of it, until a
pretty little innocent, brown-eyed woman came into his life.
One who liked to snuggle against his chest and run her
hands over his body and make him absolutely crazy, and
then, in the space of a heartbeat, show him how absolutely
wrong he was in thinking she could handle the kind of
relationship he wanted or in thinking it could even be good
for her.

He heard a knock on his office door, called out a brusque,
"Come in."

Amanda stood there, hesitating on the threshold, reminding him of a scared rabbit who might bolt at any moment.
He let himself look at her more closely, as he hadn't per-
mitted himself to do this morning. Her hair was hanging
loose for a change, straight and thick and shiny, curling up
a bit at the ends near her shoulders, probably because she'd
slept so late she hadn't had time to twist it into a knot. Her
eyes looked huge and slightly scared, and he found that it
hurt just to look at her, that it was physically painful to
him to be this close to her and not allow himself to touch
her.

The night before, when he'd retreated into the dubious
comfort of a very fine bottle of scotch, he thought he heard
her crying softly in the room next to his, and he wanted to
go to her. But Amanda crying softly in the night, probably
in some prim little nightgown of the purest white, lying
amidst the rumpled sheets of a bed, was more than he could
handle. Especially when he'd already had a few drinks. He
hadn't trusted himself to go in there and try to comfort her,
and she didn't need comfort from him, anyway.

He was afraid what she needed was another man. Anybody but him.

"I can come back later if this is bad time," she said.

"No, come on in." He got to his feet and walked toward

FREE BOOKS! FREE GIFT!

PLAY BANGO!

AND CLAIM FREE BOOKS AND A FREE GIFT!

BANGO

5	19	32	54	73
6	17	41	50	
13	22	FREE	52	
5	24	44	46	
8	21	35	47	75

BANGO

9	19	44	52	71
4	20	32	50	68
11	18	FREE	53	63
7	27	36	60	72
3	28	41	47	64

★ No Cost!
★ No Obligation to Buy!
★ No Purchase Necessary!

TURN THE PAGE TO PLAY

PLAY BANGO!

AND GET THREE FREE GIFTS!

It looks like BINGO, it plays like BINGO but it's FREE

HOW TO PLAY:

1. With a coin, scratch the Caller Card to reveal your 5 lucky numbers and see whether they match your Bango Card. Then check the claim chart to discover what we have for you — up to 2 FREE BOOKS and a FREE GIFT — ALL YOURS, ALL FREE!

2. Send back the Bango card and you'll receive free Silhouette Sensation® books. These books are yours to keep absolutely free.

3. There's no catch. You're under no obligation to buy anything. We charge nothing — ZERO — for your first shipment. And you don't have to make any minimum number of purchases — not even one!

4. The fact is, thousands of readers enjoy receiving our books by post from the Reader Service™. They like the convenience of home delivery and they like getting the best new novels before they are available in the shops. And of course, postage and packing is COMPLETELY FREE!

5. We hope that after receiving your free books you'll want to remain a subscriber. But the choice is yours — to continue or cancel any time! So why not take us up on our invitation, with no risk of any kind you'll be glad you did!

YOURS FREE!

This exciting mystery gift is yours free when you play BANGO!

It's fun, and we're giving away FREE GIFTS to all players!

PLAY BANGO!

CALLER CARD

SCRATCH HERE! →

YES! Please send me the gifts for which I qualify! I understand that I am under no obligation to purchase any books as explained on the back of this card.

YOUR CARD ↴

BANGO

38	9	44	10	38
92	7	5	27	14
2	51	FREE	91	67
75	3	12	20	13
6	15	26	50	31

S1CI

CLAIM CHART!	
Match 5 numbers	2 FREE BOOKS & A MYSTERY GIFT
Match 4 numbers	1 FREE BOOK & A MYSTERY GIFT
Match 3 numbers	1 FREE BOOK

Ms/Mrs/Miss/Mr _____ Initials _____

BLOCK CAPITALS PLEASE

Surname _____

Address _____

_____

Postcode _____

Silhouette® Reader Service™ — Here's how it works:

NO STAMP NEEDED!

SILHOUETTE READER SERVICE
FREE BOOK OFFER
FREEPOST CN81
CROYDON
CR9 3WZ

NO STAMP
NECESSARY
IF POSTED IN
THE U.K. OR N.I.

her, thinking to close the door. They didn't need an audience for this.

He reached past her, and she slid to the right. He frowned, shut the door, then put a full three feet between them. Josh hated the thought of her shrinking away from his touch, hated seeing the faint, bruised look beneath her eyes, the utterly fragile quality about her. He shoved his hands into his pockets and put his back to her, staring out the window rather than looking at her.

"Sit down," he said, "please."

"I owe you an apology. For last night."

Josh closed his eyes and looked down at the floor. Something hurt deep inside of him, something he didn't understand. It was like someone planted a big ache in the pit of his chest that seemed to be growing. With each passing day, he hurt more and more, and he'd hurt her. Dammit, he'd hurt her, and he didn't think he was going to be able to make this work.

"It wasn't your fault, Amanda," he said grimly. "None of it."

"Yes, it was. You've been up-front with me about what you want, about how you live your life, and I don't know what I've been doing. Rearranging reality to suit me, I suppose. We're so different. We want very different things, and I knew that going in. In my head, I always knew. So I don't have any right to be upset with you. I'm sorry."

Josh closed his eyes, his hands balled into fists. He was still thinking about hitting something, maybe the wall. Because he was so very angry at the whole situation, angry at himself for creating it. He'd drawn her into this mess, and now it was up to him to keep her safe. Which meant he had to turn around and try to explain things to her, so she didn't feel so bad. He needed to look her in the eyes, pretty, sad, tear-filled eyes, and he wasn't supposed to touch her. He wasn't supposed to want her, either.

"You didn't do anything wrong, Amanda. It was me. I happened to think I knew what was best for both of us, and I was wrong. I'm sorry."

"I wish I could be the kind of woman you wanted."

"No. Don't do that." He did face her then, even managed to smile. "You're perfect just the way you are. Don't change because of me."

"Well, I wish things could have been different. Maybe in time…"

Josh told himself he'd let this go on too long. That he should just end it, right here. But the timing was lousy. They had business to take care of. And he didn't need to be throwing her any more curves right now. He couldn't afford to put up any barriers between them, because she needed him, and he was going to take care of her. At least in this. The personal stuff was just going to have to wait.

"Something's happened," he said. "Something I need to tell you. Rudy called. There's been a slight change in plans."

"What do you mean?"

"He says he has to go back to France sooner than he expected. So he can't make dinner Saturday night."

"Oh." She looked so relieved. "So, it's over? We're done."

"No." Josh frowned. "We're still going. Tonight."

"Tonight? Why?"

Josh nodded. "It's probably just Rudy enjoying the idea of throwing us off balance. I told you, he likes games."

"But…" She reached for him, taking his hands tightly enough to cut off his circulation. "Tonight?"

"It's probably better this way, Amanda. We'll get it over with. There's less time for you to be nervous this way."

"I'm not ready," she protested.

"You're never going to be ready. But you can do it. I know you can."

"What about you? You're not ready, are you?"

"We've had people working on this around the clock since Monday morning. We're in good shape."

"But—"

"Amanda, I wouldn't let you walk in there tonight if I thought we weren't ready. Dan Reese could go to bloody hell, but I wouldn't let you go. I wouldn't go myself if I didn't think it would be safe for both of us."

"But…if Rudy's so angry at you, and this is all about revenge, what's to keep him from just killing you right now?"

"I'm betting on good old-fashioned greed. Rudy's a middleman. He doesn't get paid unless the deal goes through. I think right now all he has are suspicions about me, and he may be toying with the idea of revenge, but he's in this for the money. To get it he needs a deal, and to make a deal, he needs me."

"Still—"

"I expect to live a long, decadent life. There are tons of women in this world I haven't even met yet. I'm going to need years," he claimed, winning a weak smile from her.

"You know, you're a very nice man."

"You're insulting me again, right?"

She shook her head back and forth. "I don't know what I'd do without you right now."

Josh took a long, slow breath. That big ache in his chest just grew about three sizes in the space of a heartbeat. If nothing else, she had learned to like him. To really like him, despite all that he was, all those ways of his she so heartily disapproved of. That was something, he supposed.

"You're going to be fine," he said. "I'll be right beside you."

"I couldn't do it without you."

She sounded sincere enough to send his heart into overdrive, and he was still trying to talk himself out of letting her go after tonight, as soon as this mess with Rudy was over.

He thought about taking her by the arms and pulling her to him, about letting her find that spot against his chest that she seemed to crave, the way he craved having her in his arms. He thought about kissing her until she wasn't afraid anymore, of anything. How many kisses would that take? he wondered.

But in the end he did what was right. Much of the time Josh honestly managed to do the right thing. He sent her on her way, to the people who would outfit her for tonight's mission, and he went back to what he'd been concentrating on before she came in here—keeping her safe. That was his job, his first responsibility to her, and he wasn't going to let her down.

Chapter 8

They took a limousine. Josh was in an expensive black suit that showed off his long, lean body to perfection. He was smiling like a man without a care in the world, and he hadn't let go of her since they walked out of the office five minutes ago for the short ride to the hotel.

She was draped in cool, elegant satin, the color the palest of grays. It followed every dip and sway of her body, the material dipping low on her shoulders and across her breasts and glittering like diamonds. Like the breathtaking ones at her throat and hanging from her ears and her wrist, the diamond pin securing her hair. There was a small fortune on her body, she calculated, nervous about that on top of everything else.

Her nerve endings were humming along, all her senses running in overdrive, the world rushing forward.

She felt totally different, oddly unlike herself, but she couldn't say she was sorry about that. She hadn't liked herself or her life in a long, long time, and now it was as though she'd entered an alternative universe, taken off on a grand adventure. She didn't understand how it could be so scary and so exhilarating at the same time.

Josh leaned toward her in the limousine and said, "You look absolutely beautiful."

"I'm so scared I'm shaking."

His arm, stretched out along the seat behind her, dropped to her shoulders, pulling her to his side. He took her hands, which were clenched in her lap, in his own. "What can I do?"

He could do anything, she thought. He was magic and light, laughter and wonder, and earlier when she'd gone into his office she had the feeling he'd been close to telling her he'd made a mistake. That any kind of personal relationship between the two of them would be a mistake. He probably didn't think she was worth the trouble. That her provincial ideas and silly insecurities were more than he cared to deal with. That he would simply move on.

And she found she was desperate to keep from losing whatever time she could have with him.

When this was over, they might never be together like this again. Her heart ached at the thought. But tonight she could ask anything, and he would give it to her.

"Kiss me," she whispered.

He groaned out her name. His head dipped down, his mouth, warm and sensual and so very wicked, settling over hers. Her lips parted at the slightest pressure from his. Before she could so much as gasp, he had his tongue in her mouth, stroking along her lips, her teeth, her tongue. His big, warm body pressed hers back into the cold leather seat, and she simply gave herself up to the feeling.

He kissed her greedily, with a staggering hunger and urgency that would have frightened her if she hadn't spent the last few hours fearing she'd lost any chance she had with him because she simply wasn't up to having a relationship on his terms. Because she wasn't adult enough for it. That heart-wrenching conversation with him earlier in his office had been the most difficult she'd ever had. She'd felt pure panic, thinking she'd never be in his arms again. Never feel so safe, so protected. Never feel this wicked, wanton need coursing through her body or his big, hard body pressed tightly against hers.

She slid her arms around him, reveled in the feel of his hot, sweet kisses and the insistent thrust of his tongue. He held her face in his hands, then buried his face in the side of her neck, dropping biting little kisses along the side of her neck. She loved the heat, the power, the thrill of anticipation, and for a moment she simply forgot everything else, until she heard him swear softly.

"What's wrong?" she murmured dreamily, shivering with sheer pleasure.

"We're here."

She blinked up at him, not sure for a minute what he could possibly be talking about. He was that good. Kissing him was that good. She'd been absolutely lost in him. She was breathing heavily, saw his gaze drop to the low-cut neckline of the gown, to the swell of her breasts, and she thought he looked every bit as distracted as she was. Which made her wonder…

"Josh?" She hesitated. "Was that—"

"I thought a distraction couldn't hurt. But no, that's not why I did it," he said, his hands still at the sides of her face. "I did it because I wanted to. I always want to touch you, and it's been hell not to let myself do it. It's going to be even worse to give up the right, once this is over."

"Oh." It would be even harder for her to give him up. "Josh—"

"Wait." He put a finger to her lips, then took one of her dangling diamond earrings between his fingers and smiled. "We just went live. And that's an open mike in these pretty earrings you're wearing and another one on my cuff links. So from here on out don't say anything you don't want a dozen different people to hear."

"Oh," she said.

She wasn't plugged in to the sound system they'd rigged on her body and his. She was transmitting all sorts of things through her specially designed jewelry but she didn't have a minuscule, all-but-invisible earpiece like the one Josh wore. Apparently it took some getting used to, to be hearing voices and instructions through an earpiece while carrying on a conversation with people around her, and they'd all agreed it was more likely to be a distraction to her than a help.

"Ready?" Josh said.

"No. Not at all."

He hesitated for a second, put his hand to the side of her face and kissed her one more time, as if he just couldn't help himself.

"Come on." He climbed out of the car first and extended a hand to her.

The hotel was ablaze with light, and she saw that they were in a long line of limousines pulled up to the entrance. Josh put his hand at her back and pulled her to his side, leading her through the lobby and into the elevator. The uniformed attendant tipped his hat to them before discreetly turning away.

"Look at me." Josh's voice took on that mesmerizing quality she liked so much. He pushed her into the corner, putting his body between her and the rest of the small elevator car, then leaned down to whisper in her ear. "We'll do it just like we talked about earlier. I'll be right beside you. I won't leave the room without you. You don't go anywhere without me, except to dance with Rudy."

She gripped the lapels of his dinner jacket, hanging on tightly. "Okay."

''He's hired a trio to play, and there's a small dance floor in the room. If he's going to talk to you in relative privacy, that's the best place. I'll be watching the whole time. You don't have to do anything except listen to him.''

His hands were on her arms, stroking lightly up and down, while she stood there shivering and hanging on to him.

''Rudy may have found out about you and Rob,'' he warned. ''Don't let that throw you, and you don't have to worry about trying to cover your nervousness. Let him see that you're nervous. It works for us in this. If he asks you to get some information for him, just listen. You don't even have to remember everything he says. The mike will pick it up. If he presses for an answer, tell him you're not sure you can get the information he wants, but that you'll try, okay? All we need to know is what he wants from you.''

She nodded, and he was so close to her now. She saw that spot on his shoulder, the one that seemed to call out to her, propelling her to him over and over again. And really there was no reason to hold back. It was understandable that she would cling to him now. He wouldn't think less of her. One more night, she told herself. One more terrifying, exhilarating night with Josh.

She moved forward, bringing her body up against his, nestling into that fragrant spot at the top of his shoulder, the side of his neck, right below his jaw. She loved this spot, loved pressing the tip of her nose against his warm skin and taking in the intoxicating scent that always clung to him, and she loved how utterly safe and secure she felt in his arms. Josh's arms closed around her in an instant, squeezing her reassuringly, before letting her go.

She moved back more slowly, pausing with her face right next to his, when they were practically cheek to cheek. Conscious of the sound equipment, she pressed her lips against the shell of his ear and said, "I think it's addictive."

"What?" he asked through a tightly clenched jaw.

"Touching you," she whispered. "Kissing you. Everything about you."

"Amanda?" he said, as if he regretted it. All of it.

But she felt his hot breath brush along the delicate skin of her ear, and until then she had no idea it could feel so good, so sexy, to have a man breathe on her. She didn't want to ever let him go.

"Josh, don't give up on me," she said. "Please."

His heated gaze fell from her eyes to her mouth. She was still so close to him, it wouldn't take anything for him to kiss her right now. An inch, she thought, a little tilt of his head. He wanted to. She could swear he did.

The elevator dinged, the attendant clearing his throat and announcing their arrival on the third floor. She'd forgotten the man even existed.

She'd even forgotten about Rudy Olivara, which was why it startled her so when Josh turned around and she looked out into the hallway and saw Rudy standing there, a speculative gleam in his eye as he took in the fact that she and Josh were standing so close together, that for a second after the elevator doors opened, they hadn't so much as moved.

She forgot to move again, taking root in that spot, in what had been a nice, private corner of the world with Josh only seconds before. He waited for her, smiling faintly and pulling her along with an arm anchored firmly around her waist. He brought her right up to the man who terrified her and stuck out his hand.

"Rudy, good to see you." The two men shook hands. Turning to her, Josh said, "You remember Amanda?"

"Of course."

Rudy bent over her hand, bringing it to his lips. She

endured the brush of his lips against the back of her hand and edged closer to Josh.

"I never forget a beautiful woman." Rudy straightened and turned to Josh. "I'm so glad you could come. Especially on such short notice."

"We wouldn't think of missing it," Josh said.

"Good," Rudy said. "Very good. Won't you come this way?"

They followed him into an elegantly decorated room: a long table set for sixteen; a string trio playing softly in the corner; three couples scattered around the room drinking and laughing; beautifully dressed women dripping in jewels; elegant men. Rudy introduced them around. Two of the women knew Josh and fussed over him, flirting outrageously. Amanda found herself glaring at one of them at one point, feeling entirely possessive when she knew she had no right to.

Josh put a drink in her hand. Wine, she realized when she took a sip.

"Slowly," he said. "You're only getting one of those."

She glared at him a bit, as well.

He grinned. "You look as if you could cheerfully claw my eyes out."

"Maria's," she admitted, referring to one of the women Rudy had introduced her to. "Didn't anyone ever tell her it's rude to proposition a man when his dinner companion is right beside him?"

"I doubt she's ever worried about being rude," he said. "How are you?"

Fighting the urge to gulp down her wine, she said, "Just don't go anywhere."

"I'm not," he said easily, flashing a smile at the lovely Maria Mendoza.

Amanda stood beside him for thirty minutes or so as he chatted with one person after another. About artwork. The

Grand Prix circuit. The prince of a small European nation and his latest escapades with an American actress. About how dull Paris could be. Rudy seemed to be circling the room in an opposite orbit from them, always watching them, never coming close enough to say anything. He was making them wait, Amanda decided. Tormenting her. Probably enjoying himself, from what Josh had told her about him.

Her stomach was in knots, so she merely picked at her dinner. Josh kept stealing her wine when anyone refilled her glass, and she had to admit she'd gotten a little buzz off the one glass he'd so magnanimously allowed her to have.

She nearly had an anxiety attack over the thought of leaving his side long enough to go to the ladies' room. The whole trip went off without a hitch, except for Maria, who happened to be inside, delicately powdering her nose.

She gave Amanda a thoroughly dismissive glance and waited until she'd almost passed to say, "So, how long have you known Josh."

"We've been friends for years," Amanda said.

"He's such a delight. I know he believes in spreading himself around, but…" The woman never finished the sentence, but Amanda knew what she meant. What in the world is he doing with you?

"Why don't you just get in line," Amanda suggested sweetly. "I'm sure he'll give you a turn. Maybe when I'm done with him."

Maria glared. If looks could kill, she'd be dead, Amanda thought.

Josh waited for her by the door. He was grinning. "Going to pass me along to her when you're done with me, huh?"

"What?"

He fingered her right earring again. The microphone. She'd forgotten.

"I never knew there was such a catty streak inside you," he said admiringly, drawing her against his side. "And I love it when a woman plays rough."

"I'll jut bet you do," she said, willing herself not to blush. It was wordplay, nothing else.

Josh threw his head back and laughed. They'd just come into the room, and she felt the gaze of every woman inside come to rest on him. Not that she could blame them. He looked absolutely magnificent, and normally a man like him would seem absolutely untouchable to her. But not tonight. He stayed right by her side, and she'd gotten to enjoy the habit of reaching over and stroking his arm, his chest, of whispering in his ear and curling against his side. He was amazingly distracting.

She'd almost forgotten to be afraid, when, from behind her and to the right, she heard Rudy Olivara say, "There you are, my dear. I've been such a poor host. I haven't had one dance with you."

Amanda gulped. Her hand tightened on Josh's forearm for a moment. She looked to his face, found some reassurance in his steady gaze.

"Just one, Rudy," Josh said, without taking his eyes off her.

"Of course," Rudy said agreeably, offering his arm to Amanda.

She took his arm and let him tug her onto the small dance floor, managed not to shudder when he put his hand at her waist. She put one of her hands in his, the other at his shoulder, finding herself just a bit too close for comfort as they began to move to the music.

"My friend seems quite taken with you, my dear." Rudy smiled down at her. "You've known each other for a long time?"

"Yes," Amanda said.

If she could get by with one-word answers, she might make it through this. Rudy turned her around, and she caught sight of Josh watching broodingly from the corner of the room. Automatically her gaze sought and found his.

"I understand you are employed by a division of the Commerce Department?" Rudy said. "As a...translator?"

Amanda faltered for a moment. "I'm just a secretary."

Rudy nodded. "And you've had a difficult year, I understand. I'm so sorry."

Amanda stiffened, but said nothing. Maybe it was smarter not to.

"I heard about your fiancé," he confided. "Such a tragedy, especially for a man so young, a woman as lovely as you."

Again she said nothing. It was all she could do to keep dancing, to keep from pulling away from him and running from the room. He knew about Rob?

"You should know, my dear, I would never condemn a man for doing what he felt he had to do," Rudy said. "A man, or a woman."

"I don't understand what you mean."

"Well, a woman such as yourself... So beautiful. I'm sure you love beautiful things as well. And, forgive me, my dear, but I understand your fiancé's unfortunate death has left you in a bit of a financial bind. His assets being frozen for so long, including the house the two of you purchased together. I'm sure it's been a strain to handle that kind of burden all by yourself."

Amanda stopped dancing altogether, nearly stumbling over his feet.

"I believe the foreclosure notice on the house will be going out in the next week?" he asked. "What a shame."

"I'm selling the house," she said. "As soon as I can. Everything will be fine."

"Of course," Rudy said, so smoothly. "I didn't mean to upset you. I hope you believe me about that. I merely wanted to offer to help, if I may?"

"Help?" she choked out.

"Yes. As I said, my friend seems quite taken with you, and I believe you and I could be quite useful to one another."

"Useful?" she repeated.

"Josh and I do business together on occasion. We even find ourselves wanting the same thing at times. And any slight advantage can work to a man's favor in business. I might find it useful, for instance, to know when he might be leaving town. Where he might be going. That sort of thing. You could tell me about those things, couldn't you, my dear?"

"I'm not sure," she said.

"Well, the two of you are living together. Surely you would know if he was leaving town. I would think he might even take you with him on occasion. It seems hard for him to part with you, even long enough for the two of us to enjoy our little dance. It's quite touching, really. In fact, he's coming this way right now. I think he's going to steal you away from me."

Good, Amanda thought, ready to turn and run.

"Think about what I've said." Rudy slipped a business card into the tiny purse clutched in her hand. "You can call me anytime. And, my dear?"

"Yes," she said.

"Unlike the other men in your life, I won't get caught."

She gaped at him. It was all she could do. She hated having him touch her, even to hold her hand in his, and she just couldn't move.

He put his free hand to the side of her face in much the same way Josh had earlier, Josh whom she adored and

Rudy Olivara who scared her to death. Rudy cupped her chin, turning her face up to his.

"You look so innocent, my dear. It's truly remarkable. I can see that a man would never suspect you of betraying anyone." He waited. "You will help me?"

She shuddered at his touch and said, "I'm not sure if I can."

Because that's what she was supposed to say, and this was what she had to do, no matter how much she hated it. This was what Rob Jansen had done to her. He'd put her in a position where people like Rudy Olivara thought they could buy her loyalty, that she would betray the people with whom she worked for money.

"Ah," Rudy smiled and turned her over to Josh. "Here she is. Safe and sound."

It was all a blur after that. She and Josh danced, and then he hustled her off to the waiting limousine. He said something to the driver about taking the long way back, and then he tucked her into the spot she liked so much, with her head against his chest, his chin by her temple, his arms wrapped snugly around her.

"He knew," she murmured, sinking into the warmth and reassurance of his embrace.

"I know. I heard. You did just fine, Amanda."

"I hated it," she complained.

Josh dropped a light kiss on her forehead. "I know, Amanda. Try not to think about it right now, okay? Just try to relax."

His hand stroked lightly up and down the middle of her back. His jacket had fallen open, so her face was against his shirt, the heat from his body radiating through it, the ends of his suit coat coming around her as well. It was like her own private cocoon. She wanted to crawl inside and hide, snuggling into that warm, safe spot.

"Everything's better when you're close," she confessed.

''Then stay right here. I don't mind.''

So she did. She stayed there huddled against him and tried to block out every bad, scary thing in her life at that moment, which was just about everything. Everything but him.

Chapter 9

Thirty minutes later, Josh and Amanda were back at the office, Amanda feeling a bit like Cinderella after the clock struck midnight. Josh had a debriefing, and Amanda had to surrender not only her jewelry—complete with the sophisticated listening devices—but was supposed to give up the shoes and the beautiful dress, as well.

The fairy godmothers of the wardrobe department at Division One had transformed her into someone else entirely tonight, a woman she hardly recognized, and while she and Josh certainly hadn't been to a ball, it had been quite different than anything she'd ever experienced in her life. A glamorous, dangerous, exciting night. As frightened as she'd been, it had all been a grand adventure, and she was sad now to think of having to go back to her real life.

She'd been living in the blackness inside her house, hiding away from the rest of the world and feeling miserable and alone for so long. Until Josh had come along and dragged her out of there.

One day soon, he'd take her back and leave her there. She panicked just a little, thinking about him leaving her in that deep, dark void her life had become. She hated the way things had always been, she realized. Even the way things had been before Rob, when she still had her illusions, had left a lot to be desired. Her normally utterly dull, safe existence, a cautiousness that had led her to draw away from life so many times she couldn't even count them all, had caused her to miss out on so many things, things she deeply regretted now.

Being cautious and careful had kept her from doing anything—from living—and she was tired of it.

Mostly she was worried about Josh. She couldn't imagine letting him go now. She felt that something vital and wonderful and impossibly right was about to slip through her fingers, that she was about to lose a chance she would never have again. That the absolute best part of her life was slipping away, right now.

She'd thought she would regret letting herself be with him, but it was just the opposite. What she would truly regret was never being with him at all, never taking this chance.

She'd already given back the jewelry, but she stared at the woman in the mirror in a dress slit to halfway up her thigh that molded itself to every inch of her body. A dress like none she'd ever worn before, like nothing she'd likely wear again, and she felt like a totally different woman. Like a woman Joshua Carter would take out on the town. A woman he'd dance with and take back to his beautiful apartment and lock the door behind them.

For days. Weeks, she thought optimistically. Maybe even months. She might well have months with him. He'd offered her six the night before.

Six months with Josh, she thought, shivering a bit.

She imagined having his undivided attention, his enthusiasm, his exuberance, his zest for life. His charm and his smile. His undeniable skill as a lover. For six months. A streak of pure sensual heat went zinging through her body. The clock hadn't struck midnight yet. Maybe she could find a way to keep this new version of herself. The woman who wasn't so very sad, so quiet, so introverted, so alone. She could reach out with both hands and grab on to Josh and everything he had to give, which would be so much more than she had now.

She walked through the all-but-deserted office, paused at the door to his office, her insides twisted into knots, and finally knocked.

"Come in." He turned around and he went absolutely still. Her heartbeat kicked up a notch. He came to stand in front of her, his gaze raking over her, a blast of heat in his beautiful, blue eyes. "What are you up to?"

There was a stillness to him, an intensity that unnerved her. She felt again that odd sensation of everything spinning out of control.

She was thinking of having an affair with one of the most beautiful men she'd ever seen. A brief, steamy, illicit affair, that was all about pleasure. All about him finding out what she liked and giving it to her. He claimed once that he wanted to spoil her. No one had ever spoiled her before, indulged her. She'd always been too down-to-earth for that. A simple woman with simple tastes, simple wishes and dreams. Not anymore. Her tastes had turned lavish. She wanted him.

Now or never, she told herself.

"I've been thinking that I've made a lot of mistakes in my life," she told him, her voice odd and tight.

"We all have, Amanda."

She nodded. He was always so accepting of that, so ready to understand and to forgive her. She needed that, she realized, needed him to understand and to forgive, and she wondered how he had known just what she needed.

"I don't want to make another mistake. All these years, I've always tried so hard to do what's right, and somehow I've messed it all up."

"But things are going to get better," he said.

"I think maybe they are. For a long time, I wasn't sure. But I have hope now. That I can change, make something good of my life. And I have you to thank for it," she said sincerely.

"You're welcome," he said. But he still hadn't touched her.

She stood there feeling suddenly foolish in her borrowed dress, all her inhibitions showing. Finally she blurted out, "Josh, would you hold me?"

He tugged her to him. She let her head fall to his shoulder, desperately aware of him, as she had been that morning, lying in the bed, with him watching her from the doorway, eating her up with his wicked gaze. It was amazing how potent a mixture he was, comfort and sexual heat, warmth and strength, patience and gentleness coupled with tender care. How was she supposed to resist all of that, all wrapped up in one disarmingly beautiful man?

"I always want this," she sighed. "It always feels so good."

He laughed, nuzzling his chin and his cheek against her forehead. "You're just feeling a little shaky now that everything's over. It's like that when all the adrenaline stops pumping and your body finally slows down."

"No, it's not just that. It's you. It always feels good to touch you."

"You're lonely, Amanda. A woman like you shouldn't be all alone. Believe me, you won't be for long."

"Maybe," she said. "Maybe not."

He frowned, looked down at her, turning all serious on her. "What's wrong?"

"I was thinking about you and all you've done for me. Honestly, Josh, I don't know which I need more—you as my friend or my lover."

He took a breath and said carefully, "It's not an all-or-nothing deal."

"No?" She thought he could either be her friend, maybe for a long time, or her lover, for a brief time. When that was over, he'd likely still flirt with her, still make her laugh. He'd find that easy blend of friendship and flirtation he adopted with all women and use it with her. But it was bound to be awkward, especially if she couldn't keep her feelings for him under control.

"I care about you, Amanda. Nothing's going to change that. Whether or not we ever become lovers, I'll still care about you. I'll still be your friend."

She held on tighter, knowing she wouldn't be able to cling to him like this, to come running to him with her problems. It would make him uncomfortable. He might feel an obligation to her, one he would come to resent in time. Which meant she had to choose. Much as she liked the gentleness with which he held her, the soft play of his hand at her back, she knew there was so much more he could give her.

"I've never been any good at risk taking," she said. "I think too much and hang back, watching and waiting. But now, I'm thinking…why bother being so careful? Or following all those silly rules?"

He backed away, just enough to look at her. "You might notice, I've been following the rules here? With great difficulty. I haven't laid a finger on you without an explicit invitation."

She smiled up at him. Getting really brave and letting her hands slide down his shoulders to the midpoint on his chest, under the soft wool suit he wore, to his shirt. She pressed her palms flat against his chest, stroking up and down, suddenly fascinated by the movement of his chest and shoulders as he breathed. He closed his eyes, bent his head toward hers, their foreheads pressed together, noses nudging against each other. She swallowed, her lips parting, their breaths mingling.

"Do you have any idea what you're doing?" he muttered.

"No," she admitted. "Did I do something wrong?"

"Not wrong. But you might want to be careful, Amanda."

"Why?"

He shifted slightly, finding the edge of the desk and leaning against it. He spread his legs wide to either side of hers. "This is why."

She let herself lean into him. The angle was different. She was much closer, and this time she felt it. He was aroused. Amanda gasped. Her eyes flew open.

"You can't be all that surprised. And you don't have to worry. I'm not going to turn into a madman."

She blushed furiously.

"Although I can't vouch for any other man you try this with," he added.

Flustered, she said, "It happened so fast."

"It happens every time I get near you."

She trembled at the point where their bodies met, at that curiously pleasing pressure. Despite how matter-of-fact he was about the whole thing, she couldn't help but be embarrassed, couldn't help but imagine all sorts of things. Like what it would feel like to be in a bed with him on top of her, skin to skin, his body pressing into hers this way. She thought about touching him, thought about her hand on his chest, on the smooth, tender skin of his abdomen, his thighs, thought about touching him in the most intimate ways of all.

Heat flooded her cheeks, her courage failing. She hadn't even kissed him, she realized. He hadn't so much as kissed her. She'd just waltzed in here and held on to him for a minute, and now that she thought about it, he'd held her a number of times.

"It hasn't happened before," she claimed. "I mean, I haven't—"

"Believe me, it's happened." He put his hands on her hips, pulling her up against him, closing his eyes and sighing with pure pleasure. "Amanda, if I'd known you'd snuggle up against me this way, I wouldn't have tried to hide it from you. But I had this odd idea it would make you uneasy, so I've been careful."

"Oh," she said. That made sense. She understood.

"What do you want, Amanda?" he groaned.

"S-six months." She stammered. "Can I still have six months?"

He went curiously still. "You'd regret it."

"I don't think so."

"You look as though you're scared to death of the whole idea."

"No," she claimed. "Just a little nervous."

Josh blinked down at her, as if she'd lost her mind. She thought for a minute he was going to push her away, that she would lose all the delicious heat and strength and need, that she would never have it, never have him.

"It would be a mistake," he said, as if he was considering it, anyway.

"Then it wouldn't be the first one I've made, and I don't think it would be the worst, either."

Her heart threatened to pound its way right out of her body if it beat any harder. She was suddenly hot and cold all over and clinging to him, wanting this so much, yet nervous. But she knew him; she trusted him; and she couldn't imagine doing this with anyone but him.

"I'm tired of being careful, Josh. I'm tired of being cautious and scared. I'm tired of pushing people away. I'm tired of waiting. I always used to think I'd wait and be so good and so careful, and someday, I'd have everything I wanted. I thought I'd find a man, a good man, who wanted to marry me and have children with me and build a life with me. I thought that's when my life would begin."

"It will," he insisted.

"I don't know if that man's ever coming, and even if he is, I'm tired of waiting for him. I'm tired of waiting for my life to start. I want now. With you."

He stared down at her, a hard stamp of satisfaction on his face. "I'm not husband material. I told you that. This is not going to end in marriage."

"I know."

"And the other bargain? It's finished? I get to put my hands on you, my mouth, anytime I want?"

"Yes. I lasted almost two whole days," she said, laughing, feeling a bit wicked and incredibly free. She wondered if she could wait until tonight, wondered if he would make her wait and just how awkward it might be.

"I know it's a mistake, but I don't think that's going to be enough to stop me. Not tonight," he said, as his mouth finally settled over hers. She parted her lips, eagerly, greedily, letting him inside. Loving the slow, sweet thrust of his tongue inside her mouth, the answering thrust of his hips against hers, the heat and the need and the anticipation.

He took her so far, so fast, she was dizzy from it. Almost in an instant, her whole body was one big, empty ache. She wanted his hands everywhere, wanted them on her bare skin, wanted his sinfully soft lips and his wicked tongue, and she wanted to see him. All of him. As much as she feared she would be embarrassed to have him staring at her in full light, she knew she wanted to see him, just that way. She wanted to indulge him, as well. Spoil him. He could teach her how. He could teach her everything.

She kissed him back greedily, mimicking the movement he made with his tongue, surprised to find that somehow in the midst of this, long steamy kiss, his hands had been busy. Her dress was unzipped, and if she hadn't been holding it up with one hand, it would have fallen at least to her waist by now. He had his hands on her bare back, sliding down to cup her bottom, his hands so smooth and hot, her skin so cool, so sensitive.

She shivered, and he buried his face against the side of her neck, his mouth weaving a sensual trail to the top of her shoulder, the skin more sensitive than she would have believed possible. She gasped, shuddered and clung to him. His hands were still busy, pushing down the bodice of her dress, sliding beneath it to cup her breasts, one in each hand.

"Josh," she protested, the need intensifying to a burning sensation, deep in her belly. She could feel her nipples puckered up against his palms. His mouth was still doing wicked things to her neck, but she could imagine now what his mouth would feel like on her breasts.

He brushed the pad of his thumbs across her nipples, teasing them. It sent a jolt of sensation straight through her, a mysterious line that seemed to be running from that point on her neck where his mouth was busy, to her breasts, to that aching, empty spot between her legs. She'd never been so conscious of her own body, of the urgency to have a man's body on top of hers, inside of hers. She shuddered yet again, felt an answering ripple of awareness shoot through him.

He swore softly. "We'll stop. I don't want to rush you. Not the first time."

"Okay," she said, though honestly she would have let him do anything to her, absolutely anything.

"In a minute," he muttered, arching her against him, the dress falling free.

He drank in the sight of her with his eyes, and she fought the urge to grab at the fallen bodice of her shimmering dress, to cover herself. Instead, she stood there in front of him, her breasts feeling swollen and aching for more of his touch. She couldn't quite believe she was standing here in his office half-undressed. She'd grown absolutely shameless in the course of a day with him.

"This is crazy," he said, touching her again, his fingertips tracing the contour of her mouth, her breasts.

"I know," she said. "I like it."

He laughed. "Me, too."

And then she got her wish. She watched as his golden head filled her vision, as he nuzzled his nose against her collarbone, then put his mouth over the delicate bone, taking a leisurely path to the spot she was dying to have him touch. She put her hands on his head and pulled his mouth to her breast, gasped when she felt him take her nipple inside his mouth and tease at it with his tongue, drawing it deep into his mouth. She clutched at his hair, holding her to him. She wriggled her hips against his and moaned. It felt so good. So impossibly good.

"Josh," she said urgently.

"Maybe slow isn't such a good idea. Sometimes fast is good. Very, very good. We can go slow next time," he said, lifting his head, pulling her to him and proceeding to kiss her senseless. "The office is practically empty, and the door has a lock. I'm not sure I could make it back to my apartment, anyway." He stared down at her again in what could only be described as awe. "You're beautiful, Amanda. You're soft and warm and so responsive. I knew it would be like this. Just like this."

Before she knew it, he had his hands on her bottom. He'd locked the door. The dress was around her ankles, and his hands were inside her panties, tugging them down. She was half sitting, half lying on the love seat in his office, and he was kneeling on the floor, his mouth on her breasts, his hands so busy, so quick, arousing her until her body absolutely ached and then moving on, finding another sensitive area and doing the same thing to it. She was getting just a bit nervous.

"Am I the only one who's going to be naked here?"

"No," he promised. "I plan on joining you. In just a minute. But first—"

His mouth fell to her rib cage, to the vicinity of her belly button.

"Oh," she said, sensation piling on top of sensation, that unnerving rushing feeling coming over her. Her whole life was rushing forward.

His wicked mouth was on her thigh. He was nibbling at the skin along her thigh, pushing her legs apart, and she couldn't help but be a bit embarrassed at the position in which she found herself.

Her body was wet, and that embarrassed her, too. It seemed so wanton, so eager, to think of him touching her there for the first time and finding her so very wet. And whatever he was doing to her with his mouth was making her feel odd. She couldn't be still. She had her hand in his hair, urging him on, and at the same time, she feared where they were going and what she was going to do, feared that loss of control, that rushing, hurtling-through-time-and-space feeling.

"Josh," she said urgently.

"I know," he said. "Believe me, I know."

"Know what?" she said, needing to understand and needing some reassurance at the moment.

"How you feel," he said.

His mouth was dangerously close to that embarrassingly damp place on her body. He bit gently on the delicate skin on the inside of her thigh. She pushed her legs together, pushing him away. He laughed, his mouth coming back to hers, his body moving over hers, the hard, reassuring weight of him settling over her.

"You're shy," he said. Not as a complaint. As if she'd surprised him, but not unpleasantly.

"I can't help it."

"It's okay," he said, his hand slipping between their bodies. "I want to kiss you. Here…"

His hand was there before she knew it. She gasped.

"You like it when I touch you?" he said, weaving that spell again with his voice and the play of his hands.

"Yes."

"When I kiss you?"

"Yes."

"It'll be just like that. Only better." She hesitated, tensed. "But I can wait. We can do that another time, if it makes you uncomfortable."

"Yes," she said, thinking she could get over being uncomfortable and embarrassed and shy. She could get over anything with him.

He stroked her with his fingers, delightfully skillful, wicked fingers. She forgot to be embarrassed, forgot to be quiet. She gasped again, the sound absurdly loud in the quiet room, when he took two fingers and rubbed at the opening of her body.

"Oh, that's nice. That's so nice, Amanda. You want me, too. I like the way your body tells me that, the way you show me."

And she forgot to be embarrassed about that, too. She forgot about everything except the heat and the need. The whole world had gone speeding out of control, careering forward, and she wasn't sure where they were going, didn't care, as long as he took her there.

His finger slid inside that tight, slick opening. She wriggled away at first, at the unfamiliar sensation. But then he was stroking her again, in and out. Her body was damp and swollen down there, where his fingers were so busy. And then she clung to him, her nails digging into his arms and shoulders, her hips picking up the rhythm that he'd set, moving against him.

"Josh, please."

"It's okay," he said. "You first."

"Me?"

"Yes," he said, his hand moving faster, stroking, demanding. "Just like this."

The way she responded to him left no room to hold back, to resist. He urged her up and over that invisible barrier. She saw it coming, right at the very end, went hurtling over the edge, into a dark, mysterious void where there was nothing but him and a pleasure so intense she cried out again. He took her mouth in a searing, demanding kiss. Her whole body convulsed around his in rhythmic waves. It went on and on and on, and he kept kissing her, stroking, laughing a bit there at the end.

She was gasping for breath by the time it was over. They were curled up on the love seat together in his office, the lights still blazing. She didn't have on a stitch, and he was fully clothed with his hand still stroking lazily between her legs. Her body was utterly relaxed, spent, her limbs trembling, her heart pounding, the sensations still overwhelming. She couldn't quite believe it had happened right here. That he'd pulled off her clothes and in minutes had her naked and literally screaming in his office at ten o'clock on a Wednesday evening. Not that she minded in the least. She was just surprised.

"It was so good," she said. "Thank you."

He put a hand on her chin, urging her mouth up to his, kissing her deeply, lingering over her mouth. She could feel the smile across his lips, heard him laugh.

"You're so polite. Even in bed. Or I assume you will be, if I ever make it to a bed with you."

She would have asked if that was a bad thing, a foolish thing, being polite. She would have asked if he'd rather finish this in a bed. Any bed. Anytime. Preferably very, very soon. But his mouth came down to hers one more time. She became aware of the insistent pressure of his arousal against her hips and shuddered at the idea of him being inside of her when she went over the edge the next time. She wanted to know if it was like that for him, that out-of-control edginess, the empty, aching need. She wanted to know if he felt every bit as greedy as she did. If she'd pleased him. She wanted to give him the same pleasure he'd given her.

"Tell me what to do," she said. "Tell me what you want."

"Everything," he said, a hard, exciting edge to his voice. "I want us to do everything."

"Me, too," she agreed, just like that, ready for anything he wanted. "I can't believe I waited this long, but now I'm glad that I did. I'm glad I waited for you. I can't imagine being here like this with anyone but you."

Chapter 10

Josh knew he wasn't thinking too clearly, but it sounded a lot like she said, *I'm glad I waited for you.* He lifted his mouth from hers. "What?"

"You," she said, heat bringing a pretty blush to her cheeks. "I'm glad I waited. For you."

He blinked down at her, having trouble thinking straight. "What do you mean, you waited?"

She pulled away from him a little. He forgot for a minute that she wasn't wearing anything, forgot that he intended to be inside of her by now, even forgot that constant throbbing in his groin.

"You know I've never done this before," she said.

"What?" He was starting to sound like a damned parrot who only spoke one word. And he wondered if his hearing was going at the ripe old age of thirty.

"Josh, you know that. I was interrogated for three days after Rob died, and you were there the whole time. Lucky me, I got to tell a bunch of total strangers and you that I was a virgin."

"No," he insisted. "No way."

"It's not something I'm likely to forget," she said.

Which he couldn't argue. She was the one most likely to know about her own sexual history. "But—"

It was one of the oddest moments of his life. Like that morning in the coffee shop when he realized Rudy saw him with Amanda and was going to make something of it. It was a like the first time he'd kissed her and known...known he was in serious trouble. Or the time after Rob died, when he realized he hadn't been with another woman in months because he couldn't stop thinking about her, because he didn't want anyone but her. For a while, after all of those moments, nothing in the world made sense. Now it was happening all over again.

"You knew," she said. "You heard me say it."

He had, of course. He hadn't left her alone the entire time she was questioned. He remembered someone asking her how often she spent the night at Rob Jansen's apartment and how often he stayed with her at the house they'd just bought together. Which had led to an awkward exchange in which she claimed neither of those things had happened, followed by an even more awkward and detailed question with Amanda answering, in a voice that dared anyone to challenge her, that she'd never had sex with her fiancé or anyone else.

"I thought you were lying," he said. "I thought it was the only thing you lied about the whole time."

Amanda stared at him for a moment, then scrambled off his lap and got all flustered when she realized she didn't have any clothes on. He took off his suit coat, wrapped her up in it and sat her back down, beside him this time, not on his lap. He tried not to look at her, her hair all mussed, finally free of that damned knot she twisted it into every day, her cheeks flushed, her skin...all of that bare skin. *Damn.*

"I don't lie," she said. "Not about anything."

Josh sat there with his mouth hanging open, not sure how he'd possibly gone from having an incredible, mind-altering sexual encounter with her one minute to having this impossible-to-believe conversation the next. He normally handled women so well. He made a habit of being very careful with them.

"I thought," he said slowly, deliberately, "that you were simply refusing to discuss that part of your life with anyone."

"You thought I lied?" she repeated.

"Oh, hell, I admired you for standing up to them. I didn't think it was any of their business, and I certainly didn't want to sit there and listen to little details about your sex life with Rob."

"We didn't have a sex life. We never had sex."

"That's crazy. How can you be engaged to a man and not have sex with him?"

"How can you have sex with perfect strangers, Josh? With every woman you meet."

"I don't have sex with every woman I meet," he insisted.

"Okay. Fine. I don't have sex at all. Or, I didn't. Not until now."

"We didn't actually have sex," he said, needing to be clear on that. "And we're not going to."

It was for the best, he told himself. It would have been better if he'd known maybe thirty minutes ago. Two weeks ago. Two years ago. But if this was all the warning he got, he would take it.

"You're kidding," she said.

"Do I look like I'm kidding?"

She stared up at him, clutching the ends of his coat around her. Her smooth, soft thighs visible beneath the bottom of the it. Josh willed himself to look away, to forget what almost happened, to simply put it out of his mind.

He could do that. He had to.

"The fact that I've never had sex with anyone before means that much to you?"

"Obviously it's very important to you, or you wouldn't have waited this long." He scratched his head, still hardly able to believe it. "How in the world did you wait this long?"

"I don't know. I just did." She colored profusely. "It's not that unusual, is it? I mean, it's not like I'm the only virgin on the planet."

"You're the only one I've ever met," he said.

She crossed her arms in front of her, no longer worrying about the coat. It gaped open in the middle, giving him a distracting view of the inside curve of her breasts. She had truly luscious breasts. Creamy, satiny-soft skin and— Josh groaned, jerking his head to the right so he couldn't see her. Someday soon he would forget the way she felt in his arms, the way she tasted, the satisfied little sounds she made. He'd forget it all.

"Josh, you're being ridiculous. Do you take a sexual history on all your women before hopping into bed with them?"

"No."

"You think you have some right to pass judgment on their sex lives before they met you?"

"No." She was twisting everything around.

"So why would it be any different with me?"

"I'm not going to hurt you," he said. "I swore I wouldn't hurt you."

"Emotionally, right? Because physically, I really don't expect it to be that difficult—"

"Amanda."

"You're yelling," she said.

"I never yell," he insisted, doing just that. Damn. "I'm sorry. All right? I'm rattled."

"I noticed."

"And I never get rattled."

"I didn't think you did."

"Except when you're around," he complained, shaking his head. "I can't believe this."

"Neither can I, and I really want to understand. If I were to go out and find some man—any man—to relieve me of my virginity, and meet you back at your apartment in an hour or so, we could pick up where we left off?"

"Don't even joke about that," he growled.

"I'm just trying to understand."

"It's not going to happen. Not with me." He groaned. "Wait for someone you love, Amanda. For a man you'll marry."

"I was going to marry Rob. But he didn't love me, and he didn't really want to marry me. He just used me. Are you telling me you wish I'd slept with him—a liar and a traitor—first? That I would have been better off with him?"

"I'm telling you that you've been through a lot of things—"

"A year ago. It happened a year ago," she pointed out.

"And I don't believe you're thinking clearly right now—"

"Because I want to be your lover?"

"Yes."

"So you've decided you know what's best for me."

"Right now I do. I'm not putting a hand on you," he claimed, wondering how in the world he was going to manage that little miracle.

By remembering she was a virgin, he told himself.

God, how could she be a virgin at twenty-four?

"Josh, this makes no sense."

"It does to me."

He shoved his hand into his pockets, thinking they might be safe there. She was fuming, and he was…well, he was feeling decidedly uneasy, like a man in over his head. Or as if he'd gone wading in a nice shallow pond and his next step had him in water up to his neck, and he couldn't imagine where the next step might take him.

She took a step toward him, and he had the ridiculous urge to take an answering step back. He'd never run from a woman in his life. She smiled as she came closer, and he stupidly held his ground. She'd already sent him fleeing from his own office once; he wasn't going to do it again. She had him clumsy, burning his hand, slamming doors and now he was shouting at women. At her.

"You know something else?" she said, when they were nearly nose to nose.

"What?" he said, his gaze drawn to that alluring strip of bare skin left visible between the lapels of his jacket, which she wasn't even trying to cover.

"I don't think this is over. Not by a long shot," she claimed. "Because I think you still want me. And I don't think you're going to be able to resist, not after what just happened here. I think you'll be the one to come to your senses, and sooner or later we'll finish this."

Josh was still smarting the next morning from her parting shot. He was tired and cranky from lack of sleep, slightly hungover, because he'd had too much to drink, trying to drown out the memory of having her naked in his arms.

He couldn't believe he'd turned noble all of a sudden. He'd waited so long for her, had all but convinced himself he would never have her, and then to have that too-brief taste of her, that glimpse of what it would be like, and then to find out once and for all that it would never, ever happen…

He still couldn't believe she'd never done it, that no other man had ever done the things he'd done to her. No one had

seen her that way, touched her that way. No one had
brought her that kind of pleasure. He could be the one to
introduce her to it all.

Josh swore. No way he was going to be the one.

Then he imagined her actually doing what she'd threatened—finding someone else. She wouldn't, he told himself.
Even as he said it, the idea of Amanda with another man
was enough to have him slamming doors and storming from
room to room like a madman. Thank goodness he was in
his own apartment. There was no one but her to witness
his little fit of temper.

It wasn't helping that she had invaded his space so thoroughly. That he had to bring her back here last night and
know she was curled up asleep in the next room while he
reached for a bottle of scotch again. She'd been in his
shower before that, and he'd wanted to be in there with
her. He wanted to see her with the water streaming down
her body. He wanted to taste her, everywhere, wanted desperately to be inside her, all the way, in a place where no
man had ever been before. Josh groaned. Why in the world
that would ever appeal to him, he couldn't understand. The
idea that there had never been anyone who'd touched her
the way he had? That she would be his and his alone?

She hadn't come out of the bedroom this morning, which
meant he had to go get her. Josh poured himself a cup of
coffee, then one for her, and knocked on the door. She
called out for him to come in, and his frown intensified.
He didn't need to see her in a bed, not after last night.

He needed to find a way to forget the way she looked
here, in the middle of all his things. How well she seemed
to fit in and how unusually empty he feared it might be
when she was gone. Josh never brought a woman here if
he could help it. The ones he wanted to hustle out the door
the next morning were always the ones who developed the
annoying habit of wanting to stay.

But he'd enjoyed having her here, as crazy as it had made him, as difficult as it had been to keep his hands off her. There was something oddly cheerful about imagining coming back here and finding her here, about sitting across the breakfast table from her, drinking a strong cup of coffee and cooking something for her. He liked feeding her, he realized. He liked watching her eat, seeing her all warm and rumpled and sleepy. She looked absolutely adorable in the morning, and so sexy. He liked every damned thing about her except for the fact that he couldn't have her.

Gritting his teeth, he walked into the bedroom. Damned if she wasn't still lying in bed, three dented pillows around her, the sheet pulled up to her waist. She looked a bit lost and sad and so damned beautiful, wearing a delicate-looking, white pajama top, and, he hoped, a matching pair of pajama pants. Her hair was loose and spread out across the pillow. She stretched her arms and yawned, then she blinked up at him, oh, so innocently. Most of the women he knew would have run for the bathroom, for the shower and their makeup, rather than let him see them like this. Of course, most of them weren't nearly as beautiful as Amanda.

"I brought you some coffee," he said. "We need to go."

"All right." Her lashes came down. A faint blush rose in her cheeks.

He couldn't help it. He thought about diving onto the bed, thought about waking up beside her, bringing her coffee in bed and then lingering there. He thought about a dozen different ways to take her, slowly, sweetly.

"I don't suppose you've changed your mind..." she said tentatively.

"No," he insisted.

She might want him on a physical level. She might need someone right now, but not him. She wasn't the kind of woman who could have a physical relationship without her heart getting involved, as well. It just wasn't in her nature. The two of them were as different as night and day, and nothing was going to change that. He thought he could take care of her for a while, make her happy again. But it wasn't going to work in the long run. It was going to take a better man than he was.

"This is my fault," he said. "All of it. I got you into this whole mess and then used it as an opportunity to get you into bed with me. And I convinced myself and nearly convinced you that it would be good for you."

"I think it would," she said sadly, all her bravado fading away.

Maybe because she knew what he was going to say. That it was over. Women always knew. Some of them cried, too. He couldn't stand it when Amanda cried. And he wasn't going to let himself touch her. Not again. He'd wanted her all these years and somehow done without her. He could do it again.

"I know what you need, Amanda. I've always known," he said. "You know it, too. You said it last night. You were meant to be some lucky man's wife, someone who's going to come home to you every night and give you children, and spend the next fifty years with you. I knew all along I wouldn't be that man."

"I never thought you would be," she insisted. "But it would be enough, Josh. Whatever we had together would be enough."

"Not for a woman like you. You don't need a lover right now, anyway. You were right about that. You just need a friend. You need someone to hold you in his arms and comfort you, while you put your life back together. You need someone who makes you feel safe, who can make you smile again."

"I suppose I do." She sighed. "Because it's felt so good

to have these last few days. The problem is, I can't imagine that with anyone but you."

Josh stood his ground. He'd made his choice, and he knew it was the right one. He wanted to be that man, the kind she needed, but he wasn't.

Still, he found he could barely breathe, could barely speak. Deep inside, pain blossomed, spilling over into his chest, hot and pulsing and angry. But the bottom line was clear. Amanda and all of her feelings and her tender, bruised heart were much more important to him than anything he wanted or needed right now. Which meant he couldn't waver on this.

"It wouldn't be right," he said. "I was kidding myself thinking this might be an even exchange. In thinking that anything I had to give you would be equally as important as what I want from you."

"I never thought it would be equal, Josh. I always thought you'd give me so much more than I could give you."

"Amanda," he said, feeling his self-control slipping another notch at her generosity, at the faith she seemed to have in him. He didn't need a woman putting her faith in him. "You and me... It's not going to happen. And I'm sorry. I'm sorry I took advantage of you, especially while you were going through such a hard time."

"You didn't, Josh. You helped me so much, and I'm grateful for that. For everything you've done."

"And I appreciate everything about you," he said. "I wish I could be the kind of man you need. I wish I could give you what you need."

She stared up at him, tears flooding her eyes, running down her cheeks.

"Oh, hell," he muttered, thinking this was goodbye. Surely he could put his hands on her one more time as he told her goodbye. He sat on the bed, cupped her chin in his hand and wiped away those tears. "It's better this way."

"Are you sure? Because it feels just awful."

"That'll go away in time." He bent his head down to hers, his forehead against her brow, his hands cupping her cheeks. He was so close, heartbreakingly close. He had her soft, delicate skin beneath his hands, her tears wetting his fingers, her hands clutching at his arms, holding on to him. God, he just wanted to hold her, to make it all better, and there was so little he could do, so little he had to offer.

"Amanda, all we have to do is make it through another day or so, and this whole mess will be over. You can go back home, back to your regular job. You can put all of this behind you. Everything will be just the way it was before. You'll see."

"I didn't like things the way they were," she said, as if her heart was breaking, too. "And I'll miss you, Josh."

"I'll still be your friend." He dipped his head another inch, quickly covered her mouth with his, tasting her tears and all the sadness. "I'll always be that. If you need me, I'll be right here."

"But it won't be the same. I know it won't."

And then he got a little scared about how alone she seemed to be, how sad.

"Promise me something." He was still holding her face in his hands. "If you ever need me, you call me. Anytime, okay?"

"If I need you to be my friend, right?"

Grimly, he nodded. "That's the way it has to be."

She frowned, hesitated, then asked, "Did you like being with me last night?"

"God, yes," he muttered.

"I didn't do anything…wrong?"

"You just picked the wrong man for the wrong reasons. That's all."

"Men seem to find it awfully easy to resist me. It's not as though I've ever taken a vow of celibacy or anything. I mean, you were right, I always thought I would wait for the man I married. I always thought it would be something special. But I'm twenty-four years old. I've been engaged twice—"

"Twice?"

She nodded. "The first time to a boy I dated all through college. He decided a couple of weeks before our wedding that the woman he couldn't keep his hands off was one of my best friends... Imagine that? I probably would have slept with him, if he'd ever really pushed the issue. But he didn't, and neither did Rob, and I'm starting to think there's something really wrong with me—"

"No." He swore. "There's absolutely nothing wrong with you. You're beautiful and delicate and you taste so sweet. You're soft and warm and generous, and I think very easily I could become addicted to the way you feel in my arms."

"But you still don't want me," she said.

"No, I just won't let myself have you. Believe me, there's a difference."

She nodded, tears filling her eyes, a brave smile on her face. God, she was killing him here.

"I can't believe I'm being noble. I'm never noble when it comes to sex," he said, self-deprecatingly. "This is one of the hardest things I've ever had to do, but I'd be awful for you in the long run. I've always known that. Marriage is just not something I'm ever going to do. Can you understand that?"

"No, I can't. I've always believed I'll get married someday. That I'll have children. I can't imagine my life without that."

"Which is why we're absolutely wrong for each other. Amanda, I would do anything in the world for you..."

"Except be my lover. Or my husband."

He nodded. "Anything but that."

"You can just forget? You can walk away and forget me. Just like all the others?"

He took a breath and forced himself to look into her eyes as he said, "I've done it a hundred times before."

She flinched. "Of course."

He looked at those tear-rimmed eyes of hers and cursed the day he ever went after her, the day he decided she needed him, too, which somehow justified him having her. He wondered if she would regret her relationship with him as much as she regretted her relationship with Rob Jansen.

"Dammit," Josh said. "I really didn't want to hurt you."

Her chin came up. She forced a smile. "Don't worry. I'll be fine."

Josh wasn't at all convinced. He would have someone watch over her, he told himself. Before he left for Europe, he would find the right person. He'd leave detailed instructions, make a few threats, as well. He certainly didn't want anyone else taking advantage of her the way he had. She was vulnerable right now, needy. It would be so easy for some other man to take advantage of her. He would take care of it. He'd make sure she was okay.

She took a breath, let it out slowly and looked so damned fragile he thought a stiff wind could totally destroy her. *Damn.*

"So," she said. "What's going to happen next? With Rudy, I mean."

"Rudy took an overnight flight to Paris last night. He should be there by now, and I'll probably be there myself by this time tomorrow." It was probably his only shot at sanity, the fact that they'd be thousands of miles apart by morning.

"Why would you follow him? He's dangerous, Josh. You said so—"

"He's the best connection we've got to the people out there peddling plutonium. We've got to find them, Amanda. We can't leave that stuff on the open market."

"Oh," she said quietly. "What about me?"

"We'll have someone watch out for you until I get what I need from Rudy. But with both of us in Europe, you shouldn't have anything to worry about. You're done, Amanda," he said. "If anybody from Dan Reese on down tries to talk you into doing anything else like this, you just flat-out refuse. And I'll back you up."

"You think they'll ask me to do something else?"

"No, I just want you to be prepared."

"For the best and the worst, right?"

"Yes." And this was the best. Forcing her to get on with her life without him. It might be easier if she didn't look so lost, so uncertain. If he didn't have those nagging doubts about just how depressed she was about everything that had happened in the last year. If he still didn't know quite how bad things had gotten before he came and dragged her out of her house and turned her life upside down.

She was all right, he told himself. He'd misjudged the situation completely. She'd never been in danger, not from herself. Still, he had to fight the urge to get a little closer, to reassure her.

Instead, he settled for saying simply, "You're going to be fine."

"Of course," she said, brushing her tears away, sitting there miserably in the middle of the rumpled bed.

He had to look away then, just had to. She'd gotten inside his skin, as if there was a spot in his arms made just for her, where she fit as no one else ever had. He itched to touch her one more time. To take what she'd so generously offered. Sex with no strings. It was supposed to be a man's dream, not a nightmare.

Sex with Amanda. Something no one else had ever had. It blew his mind just thinking about it.

Just a few more hours, and he'd be safely on a plane to Paris. By the time he got back, he'd have found a way to deal with this, a way to stay away. She might have even found someone else by then. So what if he felt absolutely murderous at the thought? He'd get over it, just like he'd get over her.

Josh rushed through the day—strategy sessions, intelligence reports, phone calls. He didn't stop for a minute, because he already missed Amanda. He missed her like crazy, and if he'd had a second to spare, he would have gone to find her. By evening, he was on an overnight plane to Paris, with a connecting flight to Nice to take care of Rudy Olivara.

All he needed was for Rudy to think he was brokering a deal for Josh to buy the plutonium, which would lead Josh to whoever had it. From there, Division One would do whatever it had to do to confiscate it. That Rudy had come back to France worried Josh. He thought Rudy must have another potential buyer here, or that Rudy wanted Josh for some reason. Josh worried that this might be a trap, but at this point, he had no choice but to follow Rudy.

If he was lucky, it would take weeks to sort out the whole mess. By the time he was back in D.C., Amanda would be fine again, normal, happy.

He desperately needed for her to be happy, and in the end she wouldn't be happy with him. He knew it. Which meant he'd done the right thing for once.

He settled into his seat in first class. Ten minutes after takeoff someone sat down next to him. A woman he supposed, trying to work up some inkling of enthusiasm for the prospect of meeting a new woman. He just couldn't do it.

So he sat there with his eyes closed, his head resting in the corner against the window, and he must have had it bad for Amanda because he thought he could smell the perfume she normally used, something light and sweet that tended to curl up inside his head and linger long after she left a room.

Which meant he was losing it. He was about to absolutely lose his mind over a woman, something he'd never done before.

Curiosity got the better of him. He opened his eyes, glanced at the woman sitting next to him and thought for a minute his pathetically muddled brain had simply short-circuited altogether. He hadn't had much sleep in the past few days, thanks to Amanda. Stress and prolonged lack of sleep could do just about anything to the human body, including bring on hallucinations. It was either that, or she was sitting right next to him. Looking quite pleased with herself.

"Hi," she said tentatively.

"Hi?" he roared.

She flinched. "I really don't remember you yelling before."

"Hell, no, I didn't yell." He'd had a perfectly sane, manageable life before she came along. He'd been a perfectly reasonable man. Calm, rational, methodical, careful, despite the image he projected. "What in God's name are you doing here?"

"Going to the South of France."

"No," he said. "No way."

"I have a ticket." She held it up, dared to smile a bit.

"No," he repeated.

"You know, I said the same thing when you wanted to

move in with me, and you didn't listen to me then. I'm not listening to you now. I'm going."

"You just decided to hop on a place and follow me to France?"

"No, Dan decided I should."

Dumbfounded, Josh stared at her. "He wouldn't."

"He did. Right after you left the office, in fact. I guess he didn't want to argue with you any more than I did."

"Well that's just too bad. Because he's going to have to deal with me. I'm going to kill him."

"Not now," Amanda said. "It looks like Jamie's going into labor. He's not going to be talking to anyone but her for a while."

Josh swore once again. "Is she okay?"

"Just a little uncertain. She's not sure if this is the real thing. I guess it can be hard to tell with labor, especially with first babies. And it's a little early."

"A month early. That can't be normal."

"Unless the doctor miscalculated her due date. It happens, she said. She was actually pretty calm, but I wouldn't want to get in Dan's way right now."

Josh stared at her as if he didn't even know her. As if another woman had taken over her body and was impersonating her, just to drive him insane.

She dared to smile. "Everything's going to be fine, Josh. I promise."

"No, it's not. You can't be here."

"Dan's orders. Rudy called me," she said. "He bought the mortgage on my house. No one's going to foreclose now. At least, not as long as I do as he asks."

"Dammit, you should have said something to me about that before."

"What? Josh, please pay off my house? I think that goes a little beyond friendship."

He glared at her, hating the thought of her being at anyone's mercy, especially because of Rob Jansen. Josh had just learned yesterday, because of what Rudy said, that she'd been stuck with a house she could scarcely afford on her own, but was unable to sell it because Rob owned half of it, and his assets had been frozen. She'd been struggling with this on her own for a year and hadn't said a word to anyone.

"You should have come to me," he said. Money was nothing to him. He had more than he'd ever spend in his lifetime.

"It's going to be fine. The investigation's officially over. I should be able to sell it soon. After we're done with Rudy, I suppose. In the meantime, he's put me in his debt, and he intends to collect. He strongly suggested I get on a plane and come with you. So, here I am."

"I don't give a damn what he wants you to do—"

"Dan thought it was a good idea, too. He got some news right after you left. He said to tell you that when you check in tomorrow morning, he'll have some information from you about— I can't remember the name. Chyr—"

Chyrnen was trouble. A particularly nasty agent for a particularly aggressive little country in the Far East with too much money and too many enemies.

"Chyrnen?" he guessed.

"Yes. He seems to be much closer than you thought to finding…the material," she said, looking around to make sure no one was listening. "Dan said you don't have much time, maybe just a couple of days, before Chyrnen has it. Which means you have to move quickly with Rudy, and you need me."

"Why? To tell Rudy about my travel plans? He'll know that soon enough. I plan on seeing him tomorrow."

"He already knows. Dan had me call him before I got on the plane."

Fuming, Josh said, "So you're going to tell him my

every move? In hopes that we get some inside information on what he's up to? Do you really think he'd tell you anything of value?''

''No. I'm going to tell him you know Chyrnen's closer than anyone realized, which will hopefully make him more anxious to put you in touch with his suppliers, so you can get there first.''

Josh swore yet again. The stewardess was starting to look worried, as if she thought he was going to throw a fit anytime now. He bet if he tried to get a drink from her, the woman would refuse to serve him.

''All I have to do is talk to Rudy,'' Amanda said. ''I'm capable of having a conversation with the man. I've already proved that.''

''I can't believe you're in the middle of this. That you're here.''

''I can hardly believe it myself. I've never been to France.''

''Amanda, this is not some grand adventure. It's dangerous. It scares you, remember?''

''Not so much when you're here with me.''

Blind faith, he thought. God save him from innocent women and their blind faith in him. ''And if I'm not with you? What happens if I'm not there when you really need me?''

She must be braver than he thought, because she dared to reach out and touch him. She put one of those delicate hands of hers on the sleeve of his jacket and smiled up at him.

''You've always been there when I needed you. I think you're the only one who even noticed how bad the last year's been, the only one who cared enough to try to help me,'' she said. ''So I'm not worried at all, Josh.''

And with that she proceeded to push the armrest between their seats out of the way. She snuggled against his chest, her head in that spot she loved, right under his chin, as if she were turning in for the night.

"I'm really tired, Josh. Can we talk about this in the morning?"

"In the morning you're getting on a plane and going right back to the States."

"Want to bet?"

"No," he said, sounding all surly and mean. "I don't want to bet."

"Good." She said agreeably, then kissed him softly right above his heart, her lips searing through his shirt. "Can I sleep here? Do you mind?"

Josh shook his head and couldn't quite stop his arms from encircling her, from locking around her and anchoring her to him in a near death grip.

"You're trying to make me crazy, aren't you?"

"Could I?" she said hopefully.

"Yes," he admitted. "Dammit, yes. This is a plot, right? You and every other woman on earth, ganging up on me. Trying to punish me for every woman I ever walked away from."

She eased away from him, just enough that she could look him in the eye. He thought for a minute she was going to lean down and kiss him, and then he would be lost for sure. It didn't sound so bad now, he realized, to be utterly lost in Amanda. But she didn't kiss him.

"You think I'm here to torment you?" She looked up at him with those soulful brown eyes of hers and gave him one of the most serenely beautiful smiles he'd ever seen.

"Yes," he admitted.

"And here I thought you'd come into my life to save me," she said, slaying him. Absolutely slaying him.

He wanted to save her, from everything in this world that could hurt her, including himself. She had to know that he was the worst man in the world for her, the absolute wrong man.

Obviously, she didn't. Because she snuggled back into that spot that must have been made for her, draped her gorgeous body against his and went to sleep in his arms.

Chapter 11

Josh woke the next afternoon to the delicious sensation of a warm, willing woman draped across his chest, a silky feminine thigh tucked between his own, an insistent ache in his groin. He was seconds away from rolling her over and nudging apart her thighs and slipping inside her, when something registered in his pitifully muddled brain. Something that said, much as he hated it, he had to open his eyes and think about this.

Oh, no, he thought without opening his eyes. *Please, no.*

But what he said was, "Amanda?"

"Hmm?"

He added something vile. Lately it seemed every other word that came out of his mouth was a curse of some kind. She frowned, then moved sensually against him, her thigh slipping between his, nudging against the hardness there.

"Do you always wake up like this?" she asked ever so innocently.

"When there's a woman with her hands all over me, I do."

"Any woman?"

"Any woman," he lied.

"You knew exactly who I was," she chastised him.

He swore yet again, grabbed her roving hands and held on to them. "What do you think you're doing?"

"I've decided I like sleeping in the same bed with you, too."

"You certainly don't know how to stay on your side of it," he grumbled.

It was a big bed. He thought that might save him somehow, after it became obvious they'd share a room—and a bed—at Rudy Olivara's rented villa in Nice. Josh couldn't let her stay alone, and Rudy thought they were lovers. There was no way to ask for separate rooms, just as there hadn't been any way to talk anyone out of having Amanda along on this trip with him. He'd been livid when they'd walked in here and the full reality of sharing this space with her started to sink in. Although the room had been bugged, he'd disabled those. But he hadn't been able to leave her side. Every time he rolled over, there she was, her body draped over his, behind his, in front of his, and she very nearly ended up beneath him, just moments ago.

"Sorry." Little Miss Innocent blinked up at him. "I'm not used to sharing a bed. There must be an etiquette to this. Maybe you could explain it to me."

"I couldn't begin to. I don't normally share. I get up and go home."

"You don't like sleeping with a woman?"

"Sleeping?" he grumbled. "No. Not particularly."

"So if you and I were lovers, we wouldn't sleep in the same bed? You wouldn't want to wake up beside me every morning."

She smiled up at him. The thin strap of her silk nightgown drifted down her shoulder. She didn't look at all concerned. He gaped at her, thinking she couldn't possibly be the same sweet, shy woman he'd always known.

"What are you doing, Amanda?"

"Taking advantage of the situation?" she suggested. "You would. You take advantage of every situation. Which makes me think it's so odd that you won't take advantage of me. Even when I ask nicely. Why is that, Josh?"

"Because I care about you," he groaned.

"What are you scared of?"

"I'm not scared of anything, Amanda. I just don't want all the complications that would come from having sex with you," he said, deliberately trying to put it on a purely physical level. He could have sex with her, and it would feel good. His body would like hers a great deal, but that would be it. And afterward, he would feel very, very guilty, and she would have all sorts of regrets. He knew that.

"Go for the promises, Amanda," he said softly. "For someone who can give you everything."

Still, he couldn't help but think of the things he'd like to give her, to show her. He imagined seeing her face when he slid inside of her, imagined all the pleasure he wanted to give her. Not just sexual. Everything. There were places he'd love to show her, a million different ways he'd like to spoil her. There was a whole world out there that she'd barely begun to explore. He wanted to show it to her, wanted to see it all again through her eyes. But he couldn't.

"I'm sorry. I just don't have it to give. Can you understand that? I don't have it inside of me to give."

"What's not inside of you?" she asked. "Love? You've never loved anyone? Not in your whole life?"

"I like women. I enjoy them, but I don't stay with them and I don't love them."

"Never?" she asked. "Not once in your whole life?"

"The only one I ever loved..." He closed his eyes, groaned. What the hell, he'd gone this far. A careful mix of truth and innuendo might work. To end this, he could do it. "I let her down, Amanda. I wasn't there when she really needed me."

"You made a mistake, you mean?"

"A man doesn't get to make a mistake like that. Not with a woman he loves."

"So, what happened? She couldn't forgive you?"

"No. She forgave me. I couldn't forgive myself."

"So you walked away from her?"

"No. I took care of her, as best I could. But it was too late. The damage was done."

"So…you're still in love with her?"

He looked her right in the eyes and said, "Yes."

"Oh."

It was one of the saddest sounds he'd ever heard. He could feel her withdrawal from him completely, even though she didn't move at all. He could feel the tension come into her limbs, feel the way she was bracing herself, too late, for the hurt he'd inflicted upon her.

Dammit, he thought. He had hurt her. He'd known, despite every time he'd sworn otherwise, that in the end he would hurt her.

"I'm sorry," he said, knowing it was totally inadequate, fighting the urge to take her in his arms and comfort her, when he'd been the one to hurt her so badly. It made no sense, to deliberately hurt a woman like this and then want to try to take all that hurt away. He couldn't. He'd have to leave that delicate task to some other man. That's what he wanted for her, after all. An eminently more-suitable man.

This was the way to show her he wasn't going to turn into Prince Charming and give her some ridiculous, happily-ever-after ending. Everyone knew there was no such thing as living happily ever after. Everyone knew that heartache was sure to follow. He thought he'd have to find another woman, flaunt the relationship right in front of

Amanda. But it seemed the words would do it. It would end this once and for all, before things got any more complicated.

She'd be fine, Josh told himself as he stared up at the ceiling. They'd never even made love, and he wouldn't touch her again. She'd get over him. In time, she would be glad it ended this way. She'd find someone else, and he would handle it.

Hopefully better than he was handling seeing her hurt this way. Because hurting her was the lowest thing he'd ever done.

"We've got work to do," he said, because concentrating on work might well save him. "We're going to find Rudy. You're going to give him your little message, and then you're done."

"I understand," she said.

"You're going to find a public place to have your conversation. Don't let him take you anyplace. And then you're done. You're getting on a plane out of here."

"Okay."

"It's better this way, Amanda," he insisted, simply unable to keep things from turning personal for more than a minute.

"Better for whom?"

"You," he said.

"No it's not," she insisted. "Maybe it's safer. Maybe it's going to keep me from getting my heart broken, because you're right. I do have a hard time keeping my silly, little heart out of this. But my heart's been broken before, and I survived. I think my heart could even survive you and whatever it is you think you're going to do to me."

"I'm not willing to take that chance," he said. Not with her delicate, battered heart. And then he couldn't stop there. He couldn't let it go. He found himself compelled to add, "And I'm sorry."

"Don't be. It's not your fault. And I'm not sorry about anything, except that you're done with me, when we barely got started. And I'm going to take your advice. I'm going to learn to forgive myself for all those things I've done wrong, and I'm going to stop being so cautious and so careful. I'm going to take some chances. There are all these things I've always wanted to do, all these places I've wanted to see. My first trip to Paris, and we were there for all of an hour and a half. I've never even been out of the States. You probably can't even imagine that."

"No," he said. He couldn't. He'd been around the world several times before he was ten.

"I'll be fine, Josh," she insisted.

He wondered what it would take for him to believe she would be, wondered if he'd ever stop worrying about her or wanting her.

"So," she said, "this woman? The one you still love so much. What happened to her? Do you still see her?"

He frowned, then admitted, "Not as often as I'd like."

"She never married?"

His jaw tightened. He didn't like misleading her like this. "No."

"And there's no one special in her life?"

"No."

"So, why aren't you with her? Why are you letting something that happened so long ago still stand in your way? Particularly if she's forgiven you?"

"It's not that simple," he insisted, thinking he never should have started this. He should have found another way.

"Why not? If she's what you want? I know you, Josh. You never let anything stand in the way of what you really want."

"I couldn't explain it to you if I had to."

"Is it all the other women? Are you saying that you've

found someone you love, and you can't be with her? Because you can't keep your hands off all the other women? Is that what she couldn't forgive you for?''

''No. It's nothing like that,'' he said, digging himself in deeper, then he swore softly. Even if he wanted to come clean now, he couldn't.

''It's the woman who was on the phone the other night, isn't it?'' she guessed. ''I heard you tell her that you love her.''

''Amanda, just leave it alone.''

''Her paintings are in your apartment. You live surrounded by her work, but you won't let yourself go to her? I can't make sense of that, Josh. I didn't think you were afraid of anything.''

''I'm not afraid of her.''

''You're not going to tell me you think she's better off without you? Just like you've decided I'm better off without you?'' Amanda frowned. ''Because I can't help but thinking we're somehow connected inside your head. I can't help but think there's something else going on here. Some subtext that's gone totally over my head. What is it, Josh? Just tell me.''

He got the hell off the bed, got to his feet, started pacing the confines of the room, rumbling around like a caged animal. She was worse than he was when it came to refusing to give up on something. She might look like a sweet, docile, innocent woman, but there was much more to her than that.

''That's it, isn't it?'' Amanda asked. ''You've somehow connected us in your mind? You loved her and you ended up hurting her. For some reason, you're convinced you'll end up hurting me, too.''

''I did, didn't I?'' he said bitterly. ''I did exactly what I told myself I wasn't going to do. I hurt you. And I hurt her.''

"Intentionally?"

"What do intentions have to do with it?" he said through gritted teeth. "Whether I intended it or not, you were hurt. She was hurt, too."

"But you didn't mean to hurt me. Rob didn't care in the least, and the two of you are nothing alike. Don't try to tell me that you are," she argued. "As far as you and this other woman, I can't imagine anything you could have done to deserve to be without her for the rest of your life. Particularly if you love her."

"Amanda, please—"

"And none of that has anything to do with you and me. Unless you're punishing yourself?"

"I'm trying to do what's best for you," he insisted.

"I don't think so. I think deep down the problem is with you, and that's so odd coming from you. You're the one who told me to forgive myself for Rob. You were so generous to me. You said I just made a mistake and that everyone makes mistakes, so I don't understand. I'm allowed to make mistakes, but you're not?"

"I'm not going to talk about this with you, Amanda. I don't talk about it with anyone. I haven't for years."

"Maybe it's time you did."

"Talking doesn't change anything," he said. "It doesn't do any good."

"Has keeping it bottled up inside of you helped at all?"

"Nothing helps, all right?" The words exploded out of him. "Nothing."

"So you think you're going to live your whole life without ever loving anyone else? Without ever being important to anyone? So you won't hurt anyone else? So you won't let any other woman down?"

"If you say so."

"You're going to be all alone? Forever?" she asked.

"I'm not alone."

"Even with a different woman every day of the week, you can still be alone, Josh."

"It's my life," he said. "I live it just the way I want to."

"Do you? Or are you doing the same thing I've been doing? Living in a way I hope won't leave me hurting in the end, which isn't really living at all."

"I'm not unhappy with my life," he insisted. "It suits me."

"Which makes me what? A temporary diversion? Someone you thought you wanted, who just turned out to be too much trouble? Is that what you would have me believe?"

"God, Amanda. I don't care what you believe as long as we can be done with this, all right?"

There, he thought desperately. He'd done it. She flinched. Visibly. Seemed to crumple before him.

He closed his eyes, so he couldn't see her any longer. He couldn't believe how far she'd pushed him, how deeply she'd dug inside of him or how much it still hurt. Even now. And he didn't even want to think about whether she might be right. He didn't want to think about Sunnie and how much she'd been hurt. And he couldn't let himself think of how much he'd hurt Amanda just now.

"Josh…"

She dared to put her hand on his arm. He shoved it away, breathing hard and feeling absolutely out of control, feeling trapped in a way he never had in his life.

"Josh, just tell me. Tell me."

"You remind me of her, all right?" he said, finding that his vision had gone blurry, his eyes taking on an unfamiliar heaviness, the weight on his chest blossoming and making it hard for him to breathe normally, to do anything but let the words spill out. "You've always reminded me of her."

"How? Why?"

He turned his head away, his tears spilling over and

streaming down his cheeks. He swore softly and put his fist against the windowsill, wishing he could smash the window into a million pieces. Amanda just got to him on a gut-deep level. On every level that mattered. And she was right—she and Sunnie were hopelessly entangled in his head.

"How am I like her?" Amanda asked.

"In every way," he said, pushing his hand back through his hair and keeping his back to her, though it was actually a relief to tell her this part of it. To tell her what he saw in her. "You're so delicate. So fragile and vulnerable and good, right down to the core. There's kindness and gentleness in every pore in your body, in every corner of your heart. And there's absolutely no pretense to you, Amanda. I know it. Everything about you is real and genuine."

He paused and grabbed a breath. She put her hand on his back, a comforting, delicate hand. Even now she was trying to comfort him.

"You expect the best of everyone," he said, "that everyone's heart is as pure as yours, and the world doesn't work that way, Amanda. All those things I admire about you leave you so damned vulnerable. You were bound to get hurt, and dammit, I didn't want to be the one who did it. I knew I should have stayed away."

"Why didn't you?" she said.

"After what happened with Rob, I just couldn't. I was worried about you. I was afraid…"

Amanda stood behind him, her hand on his back, feeling the tension inside of him, hearing the raw emotion in his beautiful voice. He cared about her. She knew it. But there was something else. Something she didn't think she was going to like.

"What were you afraid of, Josh?"

"You were so sad," he said. "Every time I came back to town, you seemed to have withdrawn a little more. I was asking about you. I knew you'd become even more isolated, and I was worried. I didn't know how bad things were for you. I didn't know if you had anyone to turn to. I couldn't stand the idea that there was no one to help you, and I decided I would be better for you than no one at all.''

''You're much better than no one. Better than anyone I can imagine,'' she said. ''I did need you. I needed you desperately, and you were there. I'm grateful for that, Josh. But what did you think I was going to do?''

He finally turned around and looked at her. His eyes were a brilliant blue and glittered in the light, his brow knotted, pain and wariness stamped on his handsome features. She'd never seen him look sad, she realized. Never seen him in pain. And she was afraid…afraid she'd stumbled onto the only thing that had ever hurt him, and afraid she finally understood, that she'd finally figured out the connection.

''Is this about your sister?''

He flinched. ''What do you know about my sister?''

''I'm sorry. I had no right to do it.'' She felt so ashamed of it now. She had shown so little faith in him, about something so silly as another woman calling him. ''I looked through some old magazine articles. I'm sorry. I shouldn't have done it. But…Josh, is your sister the one you loved so much? The one you won't forgive yourself for hurting?''

He said nothing for the longest time. Neither did she. She couldn't. She felt so bad for him and for whatever happened so long ago. And she was starting to make the connection between herself and his sister, the reason he'd been so insistent on nosing his way into her life.

''Josh, were you afraid I was depressed? That I was going to do something to myself? That I might hurt myself?''

''I wasn't sure,'' he said carefully.

Amanda closed her eyes tightly, squeezed them shut against the pain, both for him and for her and for his lost sister. Selfishly she thought of herself first, just for a moment. He'd come to her because he was afraid she was going to hurt herself, because he'd somehow tied the two of them together in his mind—her and his sister. Which meant he'd done all of this out of fear or concern or a mistaken sense of obligation toward her, maybe in an effort to right a wrong he thought he'd done so long ago to another woman, a woman he loved.

Oh, she hated that thought. Absolutely hated it. And it hurt. More than anything Rob Jansen had ever done to her, it hurt. Because Josh meant more to her than Rob ever had, she realized. Josh who was so full of life, who'd come barging into her world and dragging her out of that hole she'd sunk into. Josh who was so determined she had to forgive herself and start living again.

Well, he'd done it. She was ready to live every moment to the fullest. But she couldn't imagine doing that without him. But that thought was for later, when he wasn't here to see how hard it was, when he didn't need her so much.

It was good in a way—that he needed her. That she had something to give back to him—a man who'd been kind and warm and gentle and so determined to help her. If nothing else, he'd shaken her out of that odd despondency that had hung over her since Rob died. He'd shown her a whole, wide world, and she wouldn't make the mistake of retreating from it again.

For now it was her turn to help him.

"I want you to know that I appreciate everything you did, and I think I'm very lucky to be able to consider you one of my very best friends. You'll still be my friend, won't you?" she said, desperate to have just that. "You promised."

"I remember. I meant it."

"And I'm sorry about your sister, Josh." Then she realized something else, something that didn't fit. "You said the woman on the phone the other night was your sister."

"Yes," he said.

"But…she didn't commit suicide?"

"She tried," he said bleakly. "She didn't quite succeed."

Amanda started to ask exactly what happened, then decided now wasn't the time. Because she'd hurt him, just by asking. He was obviously still punishing himself for whatever happened, for whatever he thought he'd done wrong. She knew what that was like, and she didn't want him doing that, didn't want him hurting like that.

"I can't imagine you did anything so bad that you should still be paying for it now," she said. "I can't believe your sister would want that from you. I wish I could find a way to help you, the way you've helped me."

He cupped her face in both hands and brushed away her tears. His eyes were wet, too, she saw, and he looked as if every molecule in his body absolutely ached, as if someone had beaten him to within an inch of his life.

"Josh, I won't ever forget what you did for me," she said, unable to keep herself from adding, "And I'll probably always love you, just a little bit."

He winced and looked away for a moment. She'd made it worse.

"But I'm going to be fine," she rushed on. "I promise. You don't have to worry anymore, okay?"

Still, he said nothing. The bleakness hadn't left his face. If anything it had intensified. She had tears streaming down her face. She just let them fall, and it was all too much, too much for her to handle anymore.

"Dammit, there's no place to go," she said, looking around the room, desperate to get away. She couldn't talk about this anymore. It was too hard. "This is awful. People shouldn't have conversations like this when they're stuck together."

She closed her eyes, then thought of the bathroom.

"I'm going to get in the shower," she decided. That was one place she could avoid the bleak look in his eyes. "I just...I have to go."

She was shaking badly when she tried to turn on the shower. And the water never seemed to get warm enough, but she didn't have the luxury of caring. She was weeping by then, big, heaving sobs that shook her whole body, and the last thing in the world she wanted was for him to hear. So she got into the shower and sank down to the floor, folding her legs in front of her and wrapping her arms around them, curling into one big aching lump under the tepid water and wept.

Chapter 12

Amanda couldn't look him in the eye. She felt raw and exposed—every need, every hope she'd ever had. He looked nothing like the man she'd always known. He looked tired and guarded, no hint of a smile on his handsome face.

She felt guilty for every secret she'd dragged out of him, every wound she'd exposed. As if she had the right to pick his life apart that way. He'd been much kinder to her when he'd been so intent on getting her to talk to him, and he'd obviously loved his sister in a way she'd never loved the man who'd betrayed her. She would forget about Rob Jansen long before he ever forgot his sister.

Amanda wished there was something she could say, something she could do to help him now. Obviously, he'd been motivated the whole time by genuine concern, coupled with a bit of cold, hard fear, she supposed. When he said he worried about her, it was a bone-deep kind of worry, the kind that could only come from a man who'd loved someone dearly and nearly lost her.

He didn't love Amanda, but he cared for her. He was honestly concerned about her, and she was touched. Deeply touched. Men had said they cared about her before, that they loved her, but their actions had said something completely different. Josh's actions spoke loud and clear. He'd treated her like a man who cared about her, like one who was determined to put her welfare above his own. No man had ever shown her that kind of consideration before.

She was still trying to assimilate the things she'd learned about him in the past few days. He wasn't the man she'd thought. He was so much more. There was substance to him, a seriousness, a sense of responsibility, a genuine kindness, a world of hurt inside him that he carefully hid away from the rest of the world. Amanda wanted to help him. She wanted to do for him what he'd done for her. She wanted him to forgive himself.

Maybe when this was over. Maybe he wouldn't push her away instantly. Maybe they would have a little time. Maybe she could be good for him, too.

"Time to go," he said quietly, coming to stand beside her next to the door of the room they shared. "Ready?"

She nodded. "Stick close."

"I will."

And if Josh said he'd do something, he would. She trusted him completely. He opened the door. Rudy was right there waiting for them. He took Amanda's hand and kissed it with a flourish.

"I was just coming to check on the two of you."

"We slept in," Josh growled.

Rudy arched a brow and smiled speculatively at her. "I can certainly understand that, but I was hoping you'd join us for cocktails."

He led them to a small salon, where a half dozen people were milling around and sipping drinks. Amanda needed to have her talk with Rudy, so she allowed him to draw her away from Josh, to the opposite corner of the room. She was nervous, but she could do this. She knew it. And Josh was right there, watching her, watching everyone, she saw.

Rudy asked her quite politely how she enjoyed his dinner party the other night, how the flight from the States had been, how she liked Nice, and he seemed to be watching Josh as closely as she was.

Something was happening, Amanda realized, too late. Something bad.

She saw Rudy nod to a man who'd just walked into the room, and then Rudy slipped his hand around her elbow and drew her to him. "I need to speak to someone. Just for a minute, if you don't mind?"

"Of course. Go right ahead," Amanda said, thinking he would leave her alone for a minute.

"Come with me," he said. "And don't worry. Wherever you go, Josh is sure to follow. We've already established that."

Amanda looked over at Josh, who was indeed watching her. She nodded toward the door Rudy was leading her to, and Josh indeed followed them. Rudy picked up a drink at the bar set up in the corner and handed it to her.

"Try it, please. My family has a vineyard. This is one of our best."

Amanda took the wine glass and sipped politely. "It's lovely."

"No, my dear. You are lovely."

He drew her into the room, urged her to take another sip and started asking her things she simply didn't understand about wine. About undertones and nuances that totally escaped her.

Amanda thought she must have turned her head too fast when she went to look for Josh because suddenly she felt a bit dizzy. Too late, she remembered Rudy had a nasty habit of poisoning people. Josh has warned her of that. The room tilted alarmingly. Rudy's hands were on her arm, holding her up, and she opened her mouth to cry out to Josh for help. But it was too late. Dizzy as she was, she could still see him. The second he walked into the room, a man reached out and struck him on the back of the head, and he crumpled to the floor, a moment before Amanda collapsed into Rudy's waiting arms.

Josh woke to a thick, oppressive blackness. There was an incessant roaring in his ears, and the surface on which he lay—which felt suspiciously like a bed—was pitching and rolling. He was on a boat, he realized, blinking, trying to flex his hands and his feet with mixed results. He was blindfolded, tied up and on a boat. He swore softly at the predicament, sheer panic, the kind he'd never known, setting in as he thought of one thing, one person.

"Amanda?" he whispered urgently.

No response.

He turned his head to the right, sensing the presence of someone else in the room. He inched along the soft, giving mattress, and once he got close enough, she rolled against him, deadweight, not making a sound. But it was her; he knew by the way she smelled. He nudged her head with his shoulder, inched down until he had his face against hers, until he could feel the breath coming out of her mouth.

"God," he said harshly. She was breathing, and she was with him. Now he wanted her to wake up. He needed to know she was okay. "Amanda?"

Nothing.

The last thing he remembered was the sickening smile on Rudy's face, and then everything went black. He'd been hit, he decided. On the head. It hurt. So did his arms and his wrists. His ankles were bound, too, but he could deal with that.

He listened for a moment to Amanda's breathing. He

listened to the boat. They were running full throttle, in the dark, he suspected. He had an uncanny ability to track the time of day in his head, and he was seldom wrong by more than a few minutes. He thought it was about two in the morning, and from the way no light at all penetrated the blackness under his blindfold, he was likely right. He hoped to hell the person who was driving knew what he was doing.

Josh suspected they were in the Mediterranean. It would be the easiest thing—to toss them on a private boat and take off. But to where? And how long had they been traveling like this? How long did he have before they reached their destination? He had to get himself loose from the ropes, had to get rid of the blindfold. He desperately needed Amanda to wake up and tell him she was okay. He'd promised to keep her safe. He couldn't let her down.

By his estimation it was nearly an hour later—the longest hour of his life—before she began to stir.

"Shh." He kissed her softly on the lips.

"Josh?"

"I'm here. I'm right beside you. And we need to be quiet. We don't want anyone to know we're awake." He stayed there, with his face next to hers, nuzzling his nose against hers, his cheek, his relief staggering in its intensity. She was awake.

"Where are we?" she whispered.

"On a boat." He knew from the rocking motion.

"I can't see," she said, panicked.

"You're blindfolded. Lift your head up a bit, and I'll get it off." He caught it in his teeth and tugged awkwardly until it slid off her head. Her eyelids fluttered open, a movement he felt more than saw.

"It's pitch-black in here," she complained.

"I think it's the middle of the night."

"I can't move my arms. Or my hands. They're numb."

"We're both tied up, but I can fix that. Are you okay, other than that? Does anything else hurt?"

"My head," she said.

"He hit you? I want to tear the man apart with my bare hands—"

"No. I just remember getting dizzy. He gave me some wine, and I got dizzy."

"Drugged you, the bastard," Josh said. "You're sure nothing else hurts?"

"I'm just scared," she confessed.

"I know, Amanda. I know. Let's work on the ropes first, and then we'll figure out the rest of it."

They wriggled around on the bed, until he could get his hands on the ropes binding her hands. Whoever had tied them up must have had some qualms about treating a woman that way, because hers weren't that tight. Josh had her free quickly, and not long after he was free himself.

"Told you I'm good with knots," he bragged.

He took a few precious moments to haul her into his arms, telling himself it was to reassure her, but maybe it was to reassure himself, too. She was okay for the moment. He searched the cabin, checking windows, the door, checking for anything that might be helpful to them as they tried to get out of this mess and finding little.

Looking out the cabin windows, he saw there were at least four armed men on the boat. Three were wandering the deck, talking quietly, laughing at times, and there had to be one man piloting the craft. They were speaking Italian, Josh thought, but he had trouble making out the words. He jammed the lock on the door. No one was getting in without him knowing about it first.

Then he slipped back onto the bed. Amanda rolled into his arms, as if she were meant to be there. As if they were two halves of a whole. Josh would have said it was the stuff of bad romantic lines until this moment, until he felt the rightness of it. The two of them lying on their sides facing each other, her snuggling against him, his arms wrapped tightly around her.

"I'm sorry about this," he said.

"It's not your fault," she insisted.

"I told you I'd keep you safe. I promised—"

"This is not your doing, Josh. It's Rudy's and whoever's working with him." She shivered. "What happened?"

"Bad luck, I suppose. Or maybe Rudy's suspicious mind. I caught a glimpse of a man I know from Rome. Someone I did business with years ago. Someone who has as much reason to hate me as Rudy. And I know who has the uranium now."

"Oh. But Rudy knows for sure who you really are? What you do?"

"Looks like it."

"What do you think they'll do to us?"

"I don't know."

He heard an odd hitch in her voice as she asked, "What are we going to do?"

"Get ourselves rescued, I hope."

"You hope?"

"We had two agents in Nice. They were hanging back, but they were there. I've got to believe they're tracking us—"

"How?"

"One of the guards outside is wearing my Breitling."

"A Breitling?"

"It's a watch." Josh smiled. "A rather extravagant one. He probably filched it when he tied us up. The watch has a very sophisticated tracking device inside it. It's saved me more than once. So Division One knows where we are."

"And they'll come get us?"

"Someone will," he said.

"What do you mean, someone?"

"A situation like this calls for more military might than Division One normally uses. A big, military helicopter, lots of ammunition, a small team of soldiers trained in hostage rescue. I'd guess Dan will call in a Navy Seal team."

"You guess?" She sounded skeptical.

"Yes. We threw this thing together pretty quickly, without as many contingencies in place as I would have liked. But things happen that way sometimes. You just have to move." He hesitated. "I'm a good guesser, did I mention that?"

"No. When do you guess they'll come for us?"

"About an hour before dawn, the most dangerous hour of the day. People get tired. Their senses aren't as sharp. Their bodies crave sleep. They don't react as quickly. You can only keep running on adrenaline for so long. Pretty soon it shuts down. Fatigue takes over. And then boom, that's when they come at you."

"So what do we do?"

"Wait and be ready," he said.

"You have a lot of faith in these people, in the system."

"It's not the first time the system or the people have come through for me," he said, but he could still feel her doubts. "There are too many armed men outside, Amanda. If it was just me, I'd take my chances. But you're with me, and that changes things. I won't take that risk with you. We'll wait. If no one's come to get us by dawn, we'll try something else."

"Oh. Okay."

She still was tense. He could feel it. He rolled over onto his back and pulled her along with him, hauling her on top of him. Her head fell to that spot on his shoulder she seemed to crave. One of her hands was pressed flat against his chest, over his heart, and she brushed her other hand across his chest. He rubbed at the tension at the base of her spine, tried to ignore the way one of her thighs had slipped between his.

"I'm so scared," she confessed.

He tugged on the ends of her hair with one hand, until she lifted her head, and then he pressed his mouth to hers, kissing her softly, leisurely, not looking for heat or passion or anything like that, but finding it anyway. She kissed him back greedily, hungrily, and her body relaxed totally against his. It was as if she'd been turned into liquid and poured over him, molding herself to him. Her breasts were firm and heavy against his chest, her mouth was hot and eager, and in seconds there was an incessant pressure in his groin, which was nothing new. He was always aroused when she was close, and he was used to ignoring that fact. He broke off the kiss. She didn't move, her face right above his, her dewy soft lips mere inches away.

"I forget to be scared when you do that," she said. "I forget everything else in the world but you, when you touch me."

He laughed a bit and slid his hand along the side of her face, into her hair, holding her there. "Are you trying to take advantage of the situation again? Take advantage of me?"

"Have you ever been taken advantage of?"

"Now that you mention it, I don't think I have."

"I want to be the first," she said.

He let himself kiss her again, didn't try to fight the heat that was thundering through his veins. They had hours until dawn, and she needed to be in his arms. They were alone. The door wasn't coming open without a good bit of warning; he'd seen to that. He could chase away her fears. A few slow, hot kisses would do it. It didn't have to lead to anything else. He could keep all this under control.

Long, hot moments later, she pulled her mouth from his.

"You're still intent on saving me for some man who might never show up, aren't you."

"Let me do the right thing, Amanda. For once in my life—"

"I don't buy it, Josh. Not anymore. I know you, and it just so happens you're a very nice man. One of the nicest men I've ever known."

"Nice?" He groaned.

"Kind, thoughtful, generous, patient, incredibly protective of me. I don't know where you've been all your life not to notice, but believe me, most men aren't nearly as good to a woman as you are."

"Amanda," he groaned. He hadn't been nice to her. He'd taken advantage of her and hurt her, and he wasn't going to do that anymore.

But he could kiss her, so he did. They sank down into the bed. It was like sinking into air. The mattress pillowed up around them. It was still dark, and the roar of the engine drowned out nearly every other sound. They were in their own little cocoon, locked away from the rest of the world.

He thought of the places he'd imagined taking her. Far, far away, where it was just the two of them. He wanted to be in that place with her, wanted weeks, months, wanted a long, long time to make love to her with no holding back.

"Please," she said.

"It's not going to happen, Amanda."

"You're so sure I'd be better off with someone else? You're so sure that the next man will be so much better for me than you are? So much more considerate and patient and kind?" she said. "We may not even make it off this boat alive."

"So this is a dying wish now?"

"Would that work?"

"No. We're not going to die."

But he went right on kissing her. He was getting used to

this, he told himself. Sexual frustration and need like he'd never known. He figured he could deny himself just about anything if he could get off this boat without making love to her—which he was determined to do. But he could also give himself just a little bit more of her, could give her more, as well. He told himself not to, but his hand went to work at the buttons on her blouse, pushing her clothes aside until he had one bare breast in his hand. One delicate, soft, full breast.

"Kiss me." She sucked in a breath. "Right there."

"This is not what I had in mind," he argued, even as he shifted her, until she had a thigh on either side of his hips, until there was an even snugger fit of her body against his. He lifted his head and found her nipple, drawing it into his mouth and laving it with his tongue. He loved the taste of her skin, the exquisite delicateness of her body, the softness. Those sweet, shy hands, spread against his chest, her head falling against his until her mouth was nibbling on the rim of his ear.

"It's so good," she whispered to him. "I can't believe how good it is when you touch me."

He indulged himself with the taste of her and by letting his hands run over her body, arousing her to a fever pitch. He stripped off her pants and her underwear and laid her on her back. She made quick work of the buttons of his shirt and he threw it off and lowered his body to hers, skin to hot, sweat-slick skin. She gasped when his chest came into contact with hers. He backed off a bit and rubbed his body against hers, teasing her. He'd forgotten just how good it could feel, nothing but the slide of naked flesh against naked flesh.

Her breasts were surprisingly full and her nipples little pebbly points that pressed into his chest. He stroked a hand down the side of her body. Her thighs parted willingly for him. He stroked her there, slid one finger inside of her, finding her slick and swollen and ready for him.

Kissing her hungrily, he stroked her to satisfaction, barely managing to smother her cry with his mouth. She responded to him completely, without holding anything back, and he let himself lie heavily on top of her as he kissed her again, easing her down slowly, the throbbing ache in his groin nearly blinding him to everything else. He fought it, fought to think, to find a shred of control.

But her hands were on his chest, stroking him, dipping lower. One delicate hand closed over the bulge at the front of his pants. He arched deeper into the mattress, away from her, and sucked in a breath, perilously close to coming apart right then, just from the delicate touch of her hand through his clothes. Josh thought about just letting it happen. It would solve the worst problem of his shrinking sense of self-control. He could let her take him between those delicate hands of hers and be done with it.

"Hell," he muttered. He'd be hard again in seconds. He knew it.

"I want it to be you," she said. "Isn't it enough that I want it to be you?"

"Amanda." He pulled her hands away, settling his body against hers, pinning her down with all his weight and imagining the incredible luxury of sinking inside of her, of all that liquid heat, that tight, slick passage. "I want to. God, I want to."

"Then do it," she said.

"I don't even have a condom. I haven't done it without a condom since I was sixteen and too stupid for words."

"I won't get pregnant," she claimed. "I know my own body. It's the absolute wrong time."

"Not enough," he argued.

But he kissed her some more, trying to soothe her, trying to ease her frustrations and his rather than heighten them.

It wasn't working. He knew he would never forget the delicious feel of her in his arms, the way she smelled, the way she tasted, the sweet sounds she made. Just for him, he thought. All of this, all of her, could be his and no one else's.

Suddenly, from outside the cabin, seemingly right on the other side of the wall, came shouting. An angry burst of Italian. Startled, Amanda cried out herself, and he pressed his hand over her mouth and urged her to be still. He'd heard faint rumblings of voices all along; he hadn't so entirely forgotten himself and his responsibilities that he was oblivious to what had been going on around him. But this was different. An argument of some kind. It scared her, scared him, too.

He pulled the covers off the bed, wrapped her in them and then he sat with his ear against the outer wall of the cabin, trying to make out what they were saying. His Italian wasn't bad, but the words were muffled, distorted by the angry tone.

It was about Amanda. He got chills when he figured out what they were saying. They were arguing about her. About what they intended to do to her. It seemed both men had ideas. Very similar ideas. That sickened him.

Josh waited there until the argument was over, until everything quieted down and he was satisfied that nothing was going to happen anytime soon. It was a little after four, he calculated, and from what he'd heard, they still had some time.

He walked back over to the bed, and she reached for him. He took her hand in his and held on to it, thought about those delicate, soft hands of hers trying to fight off a man intent on hurting her.

That's what they intended, and he would stop them or die trying.

He honestly believed he could stop them. Still...

"What is it?" she whispered.

"Nothing," he lied. "They just had a little argument. It's done now."

He couldn't imagine a woman's first sexual experience being anything like that. A frightening, hurtful, show of force, of rage, of violence. He couldn't see how she would ever get past an experience like that, if that was all she'd ever known of sex. Which meant he was trying once again to justify what he wanted so desperately. He wanted to make love to her. He was dying to find a reason, And he might not be able to protect her.

Josh closed his eyes. He wasn't invincible, but he didn't think he was about to die. He had so much more to do and see and experience. He didn't think she was about to die, either, would never forgive himself if she did. But he couldn't be sure this thing wouldn't turn very ugly before it was over. He couldn't be sure she wouldn't be hurt, maybe by those men outside arguing over who could have her first. He got sick just thinking about it.

"Josh?" she said. "Come back to bed."

He thought about what she'd said earlier, about the next man. There were no guarantees of what the next man she found would be like, even if it was someone she gave herself to freely and willingly. She'd had lousy luck with men, after all. But Josh would be exquisitely careful with her. He would make sure she thoroughly enjoyed it, and he wanted her first time to be good for her. He wanted every time to be good, wanted nothing but the best for her, always.

She put her hand on his thigh. All that heat was right there, ready to explode. All the awful, aching need. He heard a faint, crude laugh from outside the cabin once again, and then it faded away. He felt her tremble.

"Ahh, damn," he whispered, wishing he could see her,

wishing he could take all the fear away and save her. He desperately wanted to save her.

Amanda lay there in the plush softness of the bed, naked and, until a moment ago, very aroused. But the voices outside had scared her. Something bad was going to happen. Josh knew it, and he was keeping it from her. She looked up at him, able to see just a bit of him now that her eyes had adjusted to the darkness. "What is it?"

She heard him undoing his zipper, heard a rustle of fabric, what she thought was him shoving his pants down. He slid into the bed beside her. Surprised, not wanting to think about what he'd heard, what changed his mind, she rolled into his arms, a thousand new, delicious sensations bombarding her. His thighs were more muscular than she would have expected, and she felt the slight abrasiveness of the fine hair on his calves and thighs as he slid one leg between hers, then another.

"I think maybe you're right," he said. "I think it's going to have to be me."

"You mean it?" she asked, her heart thudding all of a sudden.

He nudged her thighs apart even farther, settled himself more fully against her. She gasped, feeling something she'd never felt before. She wanted to touch him, wanted to hold him in her hands. She wanted to kiss him and explore his body at will, wanted to know everything there was to know about him, everything he could teach her.

But it wasn't going to be like that, she realized. They had precious little time—maybe something he'd overheard just then had told him that. Maybe this was all the time they would have left. She pushed the thought aside. If this was it, she'd gladly spend it just like this with him.

He kissed her deeply, urgently, teasing her with the big, blunt tip of his erection stroking at the opening of her body. "You feel so good," he said. "So amazingly good."

The urgency was new. It had always been inside of her. She'd always wanted more, but now it was in him. She could feel it. Maybe it had always been there, and he'd only now given in to it. Which meant she was about to get what she so desperately wanted. Him. Deep inside of her. She couldn't imagine how he'd fit down there, but trusted him to know exactly what he was doing.

He kissed her breasts, quickly, ruthlessly, stroking and sucking and taking that tension inside of her body and sending it spiraling higher and tighter. She clutched at his hair, not sure if she was trying to make him stop or make sure he never did. She moved restlessly against him, letting her legs fall apart, letting him find his way right there, right to that throbbing, empty place inside of her. She was wet, she realized. Down there. Embarrassingly wet, like her body was crying out for him. He didn't seem to mind. If anything, he liked it, teasing her with a hand he slipped between their bodies, a finger he slipped inside of her. Oh, yes, she was wet.

"It's supposed to be this way," he said. "Just like this. You're supposed to want me, just like this."

"I do."

"Good."

He stroked her some more, until she was clutching at him, tugging at him, begging him. "Josh!"

"Shh." He brought his mouth down to hers and left it there, so they were face-to-face, cheek to cheek, mouth to mouth, until he was her whole world. And then he settled his body heavily over hers once again. "You're so delicate. So small. I don't want to hurt you."

He pushed gently at the opening. She gasped as he slipped inside, just the tip of him. He was so very big. She put her hands on his hips, to hold him there. She couldn't breathe, couldn't move, but she wasn't letting him get away now.

He kissed her lightly, rubbed his cheek against hers. "I wish I could see your face right now."

"Next time," she said, thinking, please let there be a next time.

He thrust gently, sinking a bit deeper, and groaned, his forehead resting against hers, his lips right there, hers for the taking. She did, kissing him softy, amazed at the intimacy of the act. He was everything to her now. Everything in her world. Everything she could see and hear and taste and touch. Every inch of her body pressed tightly against his. She loved how big and broad and heavy he was as he lay on top of her. She could feel the straining muscles in his arms and shoulders and back, could feel the tightly sheathed control inside of him.

"Try to relax," he said, so tender, so gentle with her. "This will work. I'll be so deep inside of you, in just a minute. All you have to do is relax."

And she was, she realized. All those little muscles inside of her, ones she didn't even know she had, were shuddering, stretching, giving, making room for him. He rocked his hips against hers, going a little bit deeper each time, until he hit a place where there was no give left.

"That's it?" she said.

"Not quite." He grinned.

"But—"

"Amanda? I've never done this before, either, okay?" He thrust against her again, easily, not going any farther. "I'm figuring this out as we go."

She laughed a bit, as well. Because it was deliciously intimate and way too personal and she couldn't imagine being like this with anyone but him.

She loved him impossibly, loved him too much for words, with too much emotion for her heart to contain. He was a one-in-a-million man. There'd never be another one like him. Silly little tears sprang up in her eyes. She closed them tightly, and held on to him and urged him forward.

He went, pushing past the barrier and sliding so deep, so very deep, until he was buried inside of her. It was a bit of a shock. It didn't hurt—not exactly. But he was so big, so long and hard and he filled her so exquisitely. Her body was struggling to adjust, to make room, and she'd clasped him so tightly. It was amazing really, how all of this worked. She hadn't quite believed him when he claimed it would. But it did. She should have known he would find a way.

"Are you okay?" He'd gone still inside of her, above her, all around her. He'd propped himself up on his forearms and dipped his head and nuzzled his nose against her cheek and found those silly tears, she supposed.

"Yes," she said, finding his mouth, giving him a salty tear-wet kiss.

"I hurt you." He said it as if it hurt him, the thought of hurting her.

"No," she said. "I'm fine. I'm just being silly."

He moved back. She thought he was done, that he was going to pull away from her. But he didn't. He backed up only to slide deep inside her once again.

"You like that?" he said, a hint of wickedness coming back into his voice.

"Yes."

He did it again. Harder. Deeper. She felt a pulse throbbing inside of him, of her. Suddenly she was aware of every place on her body that was touching him, every pore. It was as though her skin had been supercharged into awareness. There was heat and sweat-slick skin, and all those delicious muscles of his, working so diligently for her pleasure and his.

"Do it again," she said. "And again."

Josh laughed softly against her mouth. She absolutely

loved his laughter, and she had tears seeping out of the corner of her eyes. He was everything, she realized. Everything she'd ever wanted and more. He was strong and brave and good. Deep in his heart there was a goodness that she reveled in. And he was too beautiful for words and so sexy she could hardly breathe.

"Hold on to me," he said, as he moved more urgently against her, thrusting strongly, smoothly.

She did, her nails digging into his back. She felt him throbbing inside of her, hotly, powerfully, felt a shuddering deep inside, her body gripping his so tightly, in strong, rhythmic waves.

She almost screamed, buried her face against his shoulder instead. Her entire body was strung so tightly, all her muscles clenching uncontrollably. She felt so out of control. The feelings he'd brought up in her were so powerful, so undeniable. He'd sent her flying, and now she was just hanging in the air, suspended in time and space. Just her and him. She didn't think she could ever be this close to another human being, wouldn't believe she'd ever want to be.

It was just so good. So heartbreakingly good.

Sensations flooded through her, her body starting to relax, feeling utterly spent, utterly satisfied. He was fussing over her, kissing her, asking if she was okay.

"Okay doesn't begin to cover it," she said finally.

A moment later he thrust against her once more, experimenting it seemed. "Sore?"

"No," she said. "There's more?"

"Just a bit," he claimed.

Then she felt so foolish. Of course, there was more. He hadn't... Well, he was still there, inside of her. He was still holding back, still waiting for her, still intent on nothing but her pleasure.

"What can I do?" she said, wriggling her hips and arching against him.

"Not that," he growled.

"Why not?" He seemed to like it, if she was any judge. He muttered something that sounded like a plea, for someone to save him from an innocent woman. She did it again, because she liked the way he shuddered and gripped her more tightly.

"Amanda? I don't have a condom, remember?"

"Oh." She forgot. "So, what are you going to do."

"Something really stupid," he confessed. "But honest to God, I can't leave it like this."

And then he was moving against her, all restraint gone. She moved with him, arching her hips against his, taking him deeper, feeling herself spiraling up toward yet another climax. It wasn't fair, she thought. He'd given her so much. She wanted him to have the same thing. More even. She desperately wanted to please him.

The pleasure gripped her yet again, rolling through her. He thrust one more time, so impossibly deep. She felt him shudder, deeply, heard him swear and withdraw completely from her. She didn't understand at first. He pressed against the softness of her belly, thrusting softly, groaning. She felt him shudder once again, felt a new wetness between them, on her belly. He gasped, pressing his mouth against hers and pushing inside with his tongue, when he wouldn't let himself be inside of her in any other way.

It wasn't nearly enough for him, she thought. Not nearly enough. But it was delicious in its own way, cradling his body in hers and feeling those ripples of satisfaction tear through him, feeling all his muscles clench and feeling him fall heavily on top of her, spent. Satisfied, she hoped. Happy.

He'd made her so very happy.

More silly tears seeped out of the corners of her eyes,

and she clutched at him with her arms around his shoulders. There was a fine sheen of perspiration on his broad back, a fine trembling rippling through him, and he was heavy. She liked how big and heavy he was, sprawled on top of her like this.

Amanda took stock of the situation, languid heat, exhaustion that had her feeling like she'd run for miles, a faint soreness between her legs, the dampness there, their naked bodies pressed together so intimately. He raised his head and she could sense him studying her. She wished she could see him more clearly, wished she could imprint the memory of him and the way he looked right now in her mind forever. But she would never forget the moment. Not one moment of this. Of him.

"Are you all right?" he said huskily.

"Yes." She smiled. "Thank you."

"You're so polite. Like I did you a favor." He laughed a bit, kissed her once again. "I wanted you. So badly. It seems like I've wanted you forever."

"Which is why you made me beg, I suppose?" she said, trying to keep this light, trying not to blurt out something silly, something sentimental and monumental, like the fact that she loved him, desperately and completely loved him.

"You're too innocent to even know how much I wanted you. Or how hard it was to keep my hands off you for this long."

"And that's bad?"

"No," he said, serious himself now. "Not bad at all. Just…different. Very different. For me."

She nodded, honestly not sure if he was trying to pay her a compliment or let her down easy right now.

"I'll never forget you," he said. "I'll never forget this."

"Don't regret it," she said, worried that he would. "Promise me."

"I couldn't. Not completely. No matter how hard I

tried.'' He paused, considered. ''You're an amazing woman. A beautiful, delicious—'' He kissed the side of her neck, took a little bite of her. ''Sexy, amazing woman.''

Which sounded a lot like goodbye to her.

''The only thing I regret,'' he said, ''is that we don't have time to do this again. Right now.''

''Me, too,'' she said.

He rolled onto his side and tugged at the sheet, finding a corner and wiping off her belly, which was sticky and warm. ''Sorry. It was the best I could do, under the circumstances.''

''It's all right,'' she said.

''It's also about the worst method of birth control known to man. You know that, don't you?''

''Yes,'' she admitted.

He cleaned himself up and rolled onto his side, pulling her onto her side, holding her close again, sliding a hand against the side of her face and kissing her softly. ''You might be pregnant.''

A torrent of emotion flickered through her—that she couldn't imagine anything more satisfying than having his child. That he didn't want anything from her, save a few months in her bed. That she had to hope she wouldn't get pregnant. That she truly had no right to hope for anything else from him except maybe a few months spent just like this, if they got out of this mess.

She struggled for sanity, to choke back emotion. ''I don't think you have to worry. Not about that. It really is the wrong time.''

''Amanda? If it happens? We'll deal with it, all right? You'd come to me, right? You wouldn't try to keep something like that from me?''

''No, I wouldn't.''

''Promise me.''

She did. He sighed and kissed her again, sounding like a man full of regrets.

"You promised you wouldn't regret this," she reminded him. "I begged you. Don't start developing a selective memory of it now."

He paused. "Okay, I won't."

"Honestly, we have other things to worry about right now."

"I'm going to get you out of here," he promised.

"I'm counting on that."

Chapter 13

Josh got dressed and then he dressed her, the invisible clock inside his head urging him on. He put her in the corner behind a heavy bureau—as much protection as the room afforded—and made her swear to stay right there until he said otherwise. Though Josh knew it was only about twenty minutes or so, it seemed like hours before the boat veered right. That was their first warning. Then it veered left. Then the engines died down. He pushed Amanda down behind the bureau and kissed her hard and fast, one last time.

"Wait for me," he ordered.

With effort, he blanked his mind of everything else—of her, of what they'd shared, how it had felt, the risks they'd taken, of what might happen if he failed her now—and concentrated on getting her out of here.

He stood with his back pressed to the wall. When the door opened, he would be ready. He had no weapon, but he was good with his hands, fast and strong. He could take someone out in seconds with his bare hands.

He heard the thrumming of a helicopter all of a sudden, as the boat engines cut out completely, heard shouts of anger and fear in Italian, gunshots. He waited, not wanting to think about how thin the walls of a boat were, about bullets ripping through them and tearing into flesh. Deliciously soft, delicate flesh.

He heard the pounding of feet, heard someone on the other side of the door, fumbling with the lock. A shot came through the door. Josh winced, knowing the bullet had to have come close to the bureau. Amanda screamed.

She was scared, he told himself. That was all. Not hurt. Just scared.

The door swung open, and then he didn't have time to think at all. He just reacted. The man came through gun first. Josh grabbed it, tugging the man inside and hurling him against the wall. He bashed the man's hand against the wall three times before he had the gun in his hand, and then—much as he'd like to use it on the man—knocked him over the head instead and left him to crumple to the floor.

Josh was by Amanda's side two seconds later. He grabbed her and held her so tightly he would probably leave bruises. "You okay?"

"Yes. What next?"

He pushed her behind the bureau, then crowded in beside her, shielding her with his body. It went against his nature to hang back at a time like this, but he would do it. For her. Because that was the safest thing.

"We wait," he said. "I'll shoot the next person who comes through that door. Unless it's an American soldier."

The door had been left open. They could hear a scuffle, the occasional burst of gunfire, and there was some light to see by. He knew someone was coming through the door. Instincts honed over the years told him so. Someone was standing on the other side of that door, thinking, listening, carefully considering his options. Josh hadn't heard a sound, which reassured him. He was counting on the fact that the soldiers coming to their rescue were much better trained than Rudy's thugs.

Like a flash, two men were in the room, barrels of their weapons coming first, night goggles on their faces. "Out," one of the men ordered. "Now."

And they surrendered willingly to a crew of U.S. Navy SEALs.

Minutes later the boat was secure, the helicopter hovering overhead. Josh stood on the bow with Amanda, the boat rocking on the choppy seas, the wind blowing steadily but not too fast, the sun just starting to come up. It was a surreal scene. Two of Rudy's men dead, two injured, a crew of black-clad soldiers with weapons standing on either side of him and Amanda, lest some unknown trouble come out of nowhere to threaten them. Amanda's face was buried against his chest, her hair fluttering on the wind. He had her wrapped in a blanket, because she was trembling so badly, and it was cold in the heavy sea breeze.

He just held her tightly. He didn't want to let her go, even though they had to get out of here. "Hey?" He took her face in his hands, and he forced himself to smile. "It's all over. Time for us to take a little ride."

She looked up at the helicopter. "In that?"

Josh nodded. "You'll love it. They're so fast."

She didn't look convinced. "How are we going to get on the helicopter?"

"That's the really fun part," he insisted, as the helicopter lowered a harness. "You want off the boat. This is the quickest way."

She threw her arms around him and groaned.

"You first," Josh said to her. "I'll be right behind you."

Which was how he ended up standing on the rocking bow of a boat watching her dangling from the end of the cable. He literally held his breath until she was swallowed up by the aircraft. Josh stood there, his face tilted up into the sky, waiting for that knot in the pit of his stomach to dissolve away. That was it as far as she was concerned. She was done with this operation. He didn't have to be afraid for her anymore.

He also had to let her go.

He closed his eyes, refusing to think about that, about what he'd let himself do and how amazing it had felt. But it had been wrong. There were damned few things in his life he regretted, but he had no right to touch her that way.

Josh closed his eyes a moment later as he hung in midair. Blown this way and that by the wind, he felt like a man at war with himself. No matter what she said to the contrary, she would get ideas. All sorts of ideas about the two of them being together forever, and he had nothing to offer her. His life was crazy. He was seldom in the same place for any length of time, and he put his neck on the line regularly. It was no life for a woman like her.

He would forget her, he told himself. Eventually his life would get back to normal, and he would forget all about her.

So it wasn't panic surging up inside of him from the minute she'd disappeared from his sight. It wasn't desperation that, once he was aboard, had him brushing aside any attempts anyone made to communicate with him, except to ask where she was. It couldn't have been jealousy that had him, when he found her surrounded by two very solicitous Navy SEALs, shoving them aside—not something he'd recommend to any man who wasn't looking for a serious fight—in order to get to her.

But the next thing—he couldn't lie to himself about the next thing—it was definitely fear. A desperate, cloying, paralyzing fear, that grabbed him by the throat when he saw her, wrapped in a thick blanket, looking pale and a bit lost as she lay on a stretcher, blood on the sleeve of her blouse, which had been cut away to reveal blood on her arm, as well.

It was fear that nearly sent him to his knees whispering, "Amanda?"

Her eyes focused clearly on his face. She gave him a faint, weak smile. "Hi."

"What happened?" he growled.

"She got nicked," the medic said calmly.

"Nicked?"

The aircraft started spinning. The whole world did. He could swear the chopper was going to spin into the sea at any moment, and he wondered why he was the only one who realized it. Because no one else was moving. No one reacted in any way except to stare at him.

"Sir?" the medic said. "You okay? Are you hit? Do you need to sit down?"

Josh gaped at him. Hell, he was already on his knees. Sitting wouldn't help, he realized, just as he realized the chopper was just fine. The world wasn't spinning out of control. It was just Amanda. Suddenly everything in his whole life was Amanda, and she was bleeding.

"I'm all right," he claimed. "How is she?"

"Nicked," the man repeated. "Probably not even by the bullet. She said she was behind a piece of furniture when a bullet came zipping by. I think the wood must have splintered and a few slivers ended up in her arm."

"I didn't even feel it," she added. "I didn't know anything was wrong until we saw the blood."

They both looked at him. He thought all eyes in the helicopter were on him, that he'd made a fool of himself over a few slivers of wood and a bit of blood.

But it was her blood.

"You're sure she's okay?" he said again, needing to hear that.

The medic smiled patiently. "There's no entry wound. No exit wound. No bullet. She just has some slivers of wood in her arm. I promise, I can handle that. But if you like, I can have a doctor tell you that, once we get her on the ground."

Which was when Josh knew without a doubt that he'd made a fool of himself. He still didn't care. He thanked the medic and turned back to Amanda.

She reached out and touched his forehead. "You bumped your head."

He caught her hand and kissed it, oblivious to the audience they had. "I'm fine," he said, thinking this was the kind of conversation they should have with her in his arms, with her face tucked into that spot against his chest she liked so much.

"Mr. Carter?" He heard an annoyingly insistent voice coming from behind him, one he thought he must not have acknowledged the first two or three times the man said his name. Josh didn't take his eyes off her, maybe because he knew what was coming. "Skipper'd like to see you up front, sir. And we have an urgent communication coming in for you on a secure channel."

Oh, yeah, he thought. He had to go. "Would you tell your skipper I'll be there in just a moment?"

"Turn around. You can tell him yourself," a man's voice said.

Josh turned, because he recognized the voice. Relieved, he had a genuine smile for the man standing in front of him. "I didn't think they let you out from behind your desk much anymore. Little rusty, aren't you?"

"Hey, show some respect. I was flying this thing."

"You?" Josh asked, surprised.

"I have to check out the boys every now and then. See if they haven't gotten too lax since I left," the man said. "I was in the area. When I heard you'd gotten yourself into another mess, I thought I'd straighten it out for you. And these guys—'' he looked around the chopper with an obvious mixture of pride and regret ''—are my old SEAL team. I talked them into letting me tag along, for old time's sake.''

Josh wondered again exactly what the man standing in front of him did these days. Because nobody sat in on a mission with a SEAL team. Even an ex-SEAL, turned Pentagon desk jockey. What the hell kind of pull did that take?

The SEALs must have caught some invisible signal from their former leader, because they scattered, leaving the three of them in relative privacy. Josh turned to Amanda and said, "This is Jamie's brother, Sean."

"Leave it to Josh," Sean said. "He never goes anywhere without a good-looking woman."

"Not if he can help it," Amanda said.

"Sean Patrick Douglass." He moved in to shake her hand. "Glad to have you aboard, Miss Wainwright."

She shook his hand and looked puzzled. "Have we met?"

"At Jamie's wedding?" Josh suggested.

"No," she said. "I wasn't there."

Oh, hell. Josh knew where they'd met. He thought to spare her, but Sean jumped in first.

"I work at the Pentagon. They keep me chained to a desk most of the time. But I was at your house," he said softly, matter-of-factly. "The day Rob Jansen died. I was…one of the men questioning you afterward."

Amanda stiffened, a look of surprise frozen on her pretty face. "Oh."

"I'm sorry. I know that was a difficult time for you."

"Yes." She managed a smile nonetheless. A delicate, soft, Amanda smile.

"Oh, hell, I forgot for a minute," Sean said to Josh. "I just got word. Congratulate me. I'm an uncle."

Josh grinned. "Jamie's all right?"

"Just fine."

"And the baby?" Amanda asked.

"Great. It's a boy." He turned to Josh. "And no, they didn't name him after you."

"The next one," he suggested, having a hard time thinking of Jamie with a baby, of Amanda and the incredible risk they'd taken. She might be carrying his child.

"They named the baby after Rich," Sean said. "Richard Douglass Reese. Soon as I clear up the worst of this mess you made, I'm flying home to see him."

"Rich? I can't argue with that." Sean and Jamie had a brother named Rich who died in the Gulf War. "Give Jamie my love."

"Mine, too," Amanda said.

And then there was no time left for anything but work.

"Somebody from your office is dying to talk to you," Sean said. "They're ready to patch you through down front."

Josh didn't want to leave Amanda. But the moment was fast approaching when he had to send her home, send her off to that life he was so certain was so much better for her than anything he could offer her. And he would hate it.

"I'll be right back," Josh told her.

"And your father wants to talk to you," Sean called out. "He was in Nice. I figured we could use all the diplomatic help we could get to smooth this thing over. He's going to meet us when we land."

Josh swore. He would rather stick a needle in his eye than see his father.

"Sorry," Sean said. "We need the help."

Amanda sat there watching as Josh waved it off, as if it were nothing, and disappeared into the front of the aircraft, leaving her with Sean Douglass.

"He and his father aren't exactly best buddies," Sean offered.

Amanda warily brought her gaze up to the big, broad-shouldered ex-Navy SEAL. She remembered him now, remembered a quiet, serious, intense, intimidating-looking man.

"I'm really sorry about everything that happened last year," Sean said. "I know it must have been rough for you."

She nodded.

"You should know, Josh fought us all the way, on everything we wanted to do concerning you. He never believed you had anything to do with it."

Amanda smiled faintly, that ache in her heart intensifying, thinking about the faith he had had in her even then. He really was the most amazing man.

"And don't worry. There's no way off the helicopter, at least not at this altitude. It's too low to parachute out, and we're too high for him to jump without one. Now, my guys could do it. But not Josh. He's not nearly as tough as they are."

"What?" Amanda said.

"You looked a little nervous." Sean laughed. "I just wanted to reassure you that Josh is coming back. Not that I think he'd ever leave voluntarily. He looked as if he was about to spit nails when he found my guys huddled around you, even working on your arm."

He thought Josh was jealous, she realized. Which was silly. Silly, too, to think he'd stay. "You must know him very well," she said. "He leaves everybody eventually, and someday soon, he'll leave me."

Even saying it out loud, even knowing it was true, Amanda never expected it to happen so fast. In minutes it seemed, they were on the ground. She was standing on the tarmac, still wrapped in a woolen blanket, her knees threatening to buckle. There was a limousine waiting. A tall, distinguished man in his late fifties, maybe his sixties, stepped out, his bearing positively regal, and waited imperiously by the car. Josh's father, she realized.

Josh swore. "I have to talk to him, okay?"

Amanda watched the tense, stilted exchange, seeing no signs of affection whatsoever. Then Josh turned and walked back to her. Something in his eyes gave her a clue about the seriousness of what was coming, giving her a split second to prepare. Still, it was a shock when he said, "I have to go buy some uranium."

God, she'd forgotten about that. She couldn't even breathe at first, thinking about him going back into the midst of this mess that had blown up in their faces.

"No," she protested. "They know who you are, Josh. Rudy grabbed us. If he knew, the people he was working with have to know, too."

"Not necessarily. Rudy's more of a middleman."

"Even if they're not the best of friends…"

"The situation's under control, Amanda."

"And if it's not? If you're wrong?"

"I have to do this. It's my job. My responsibility."

"Send someone else," she begged. God, she was ready to beg. "Or don't send anyone. You know where they are. Why can't someone just grab them? Take the helicopter and blast them away?"

"I know them, Amanda. They don't have what we want *with* them. They have to be willing to lead me to it, and I've done business with them before. They'll take me to it."

"It's too dangerous."

"It's a calculated risk, and I'll take it."

"No." She grabbed on to him, thinking she just wouldn't let go. She felt the world speeding up again, leaving her dizzy and feeling as if she truly didn't know him at all. He was so calm, so determined, and she'd been so wrong when she thought he played at life. This was his life. It was what he did. All the time. She never saw the whole of it, the danger, until now, and it terrified her.

"Amanda, listen to me. We left two people dead on that boat, two hurt. The French authorities may come looking for an explanation of what happened, and my father can offer you some protection from them. I want you to go with him. He promised me he'd take care of you. I hope this will be over in forty-eight hours or so." Josh pulled her into his arms and tucked her head against his chest, squeezing the breath out of her. "Try not to worry."

She snuggled closer, with mere seconds to imprint the feel and smell of him upon her memory one more time. "Please don't go."

"It's the last thing in the world I want to do."

"I'm afraid you won't come back," she cried.

"Amanda?" He loosened his hold on her, had to take her hands and pull them from his sides, then looked her right in the eye. "Listen to me. If anything happens to me, go to my sister, all right? She uses the name Sunnie Carter. She's a jewelry designer with a small shop in Paris called the Treasure Chest. I talked to her from the helicopter. I told her, just in case—"

"No," she cut in. "Don't say that. Don't you dare tell me one minute you'll be fine and the next—"

"You could be carrying my child. So you have to listen to me now. If anything happens to me, go to Sunnie. She'll take good care of you."

"Josh."

"Babies are expensive. I'm a wealthy man, Amanda, and you'd need the money. And Sunnie…she's every bit as kind and generous as you are. She would take good care of you. You'd need that, too. Tell me you would go to her. Promise me."

Amanda couldn't speak by then. She was crying too hard, was afraid she was going to collapse into a puddle at his feet. Or wrap her arms around him and make him pry her hands loose in order to get away. But she finally gave in to the insistence in his voice and nodded. She would go to his sister.

"One more thing... Damn this is awkward. You're getting the Carter family history in a ten-second blitz. You don't want to mention Sunnie's name to my father."

"Why?"

"Who do you think put out the story that she died all those years ago?"

Stunned, Amanda gaped at him. His own father? Let the world think his sister was dead? "Why?"

"I suppose he decided it was inconvenient—having a daughter with a thing for razor blades. It was easier to have no daughter at all, which is why he came up with that little story about her drowning."

"And you let him?"

"I don't give a damn about him, but when I thought about it from Sunnie's point of view, being dead to a man like that didn't sound like such a bad thing. It's kept him out of her life. I happen to think she's better off without him and without all the pressure that comes with being his daughter."

Amanda stared at him, thinking he'd taken on that worn-down expression once again. Thinking she really had no idea what his childhood was like, that there were so many things she didn't know about him, and now he was going. She was losing him, losing absolutely everything, just as she always knew she would. She knew it could never last with him.

"Josh?" She just grabbed him and choked out, "What I said before? About loving you a little bit? I do. I love you. Not just a little bit, either. I love every bit of you, with every bit of me. I love you. I just couldn't help it.''

He stared at her, that bleak look on his face. She thought she might die, right there. He didn't love her, and she'd done the one thing she promised herself not to do. She'd fallen for him, totally and completely. She never stood a chance, and he'd known it, right from the start. He'd known it would end just like this.

"Don't say anything, okay?" She groaned and leaned forward and pressed a quick kiss to his lips, a kiss wet and salty with tears. "It's all right. I'll be all right. I just needed to say it to you. We could just pretend I didn't, okay? We don't even have to talk about it. Not ever. Just know that I do—I love you. And I'll always be your friend, too. So if you ever need me, I'll be here. I want you to have whatever you want, Josh, everything you need. Even if it's not me.''

He said nothing, just reached for her. But she was at her limit, past it; she couldn't take any more. He might as well have ripped out her heart and torn it to shreds, as to stand there and say nothing to her now, except that he had to go.

She found the strength to back away from him, even to lie, "I'll be fine. We'll get through this, and we'll go home and everything will be fine.''

"Sure it will," he said hoarsely.

"I meant what I said. Every word of it. You don't have to worry. I know it's not what you want from me, so I won't say it again. I just… I had to tell you.''

"I'm sorry." He swore softly, turning his head away, then faced her once again, that bleak, lost look in his eyes. "I'm sorry about everything. I don't want to leave you, but dammit, I've got to go. Right now.''

He kissed her one last time and then wrenched free, walking her to the limousine and pushing her inside, leaving her alone with a man who looked oddly like him. Josh, but not Josh. Older, nearly as handsome, but with none of the warmth, none of the laughter, none of the joy. None of the things that made her love desperately the man who'd just walked away from her.

Chapter 14

"What do you mean she's not there?" Josh roared into the phone ten days later.

"Well, hello to you, too," Sunnie said sweetly. "It's so good to talk to you."

"Oh, hell. You know I'm always happy to talk to you. Now where's Amanda?"

"I'm not sure," she said.

Josh thought his heart might have stopped for a minute. "Where did she go, Sunnie?"

"Probably just for a walk. Or out to do some touristy thing. And to think…"

"Thank God," he said.

"…about leaving before you come back," she added.

"She doesn't want to see me?"

"She's worried herself half to death over you, but she also thinks that all you ever felt for her is a misplaced sense of obligation—the same kind of misplaced obligation you have for me."

He frowned, finding it hard to move from one subject to the other, then decided to deal first with his sister. "There's nothing misplaced or obligatory about my feelings for you. I love you."

"And I love you, too, Josh. I've just about stopped beating myself up over what I did nine years ago, and that's because of you. So I find it particularly hurtful that you're still beating yourself up over it."

"Sunnie—"

"I would never have survived it if it hadn't been for you. I didn't even want to survive, but you wouldn't let me go. And I felt the pull of every bit of love you had for me. I saw how much it would hurt you if I didn't find a way out of my depression. Before I ever wanted to succeed for myself, I wanted to do it for you. Because the last thing I wanted to do was hurt you anymore. I don't think I would have had the strength to fight without you beside me." She paused, catching her breath. "You're the best, Josh."

He took a breath and held it, wondering why all the women in his life had turned weepy lately. "And you just thought I might need to hear this?"

"Amanda did. She has an incredibly kind heart."

"I know."

"And I think you love her."

Josh shook his head, all of his excuses right on the tip of his tongue. He just wanted her. He needed her. It was the novelty of it. The newness. He and Amanda, together, intoxicatingly sweet and overwhelming and new.

"She makes me crazy," he confessed. "She got a scratch in that mess on the boat. Honestly, that was it. But I saw blood on her blouse, and I nearly lost it."

"So you've got it bad for her, too," Sunnie said.

"I suppose you're trying to be helpful?" He groaned, and wished he was close enough to grab her and haul her up against him for a quick hug. He really didn't see nearly enough of her. She was trying to be helpful, and Lord knew, he needed help. "Amanda has a way of pushing past all my defenses. She even got me to talk about you."

"She's good for you, Josh."

"Maybe," he admitted grudgingly.

A part of him wanted to stand up and scream, *She loves me!* Women had said that to him before, of course. He just hadn't believed it, hadn't placed any value on that most-mistaken and misunderstood of all emotions. It had no staying power, after all. It was so fleeting, so unreliable, how could it matter in the least? But Amanda had staying power. She was real. Her feelings for him seemed painfully real. He knew, because he'd seen her looking so sad it seemed to have broken his own cynical heart. So sad that it made him hurt inside, a physical ache that spread through his entire body and nearly had him on his knees begging her to forgive him.

She was a generous woman, he knew. She would have forgiven him for making her love him and then walking away from her, for saying nothing when she cried and told him she loved him. She would forgive him. But he had to ask himself, what was he going to do with his life? What did he have to offer a woman like her?

"I hurt her," he confessed.

"And I hurt you," Sunnie said.

"No—"

"How could I not, Josh? You loved me, and I ignored all of that. I discounted it, as something that wasn't an important enough reason for me to try to go on, and I was wrong about that. I was so wrong, Josh. But you didn't stop loving me."

"I could never stop loving you," he said, the words torn from the depths of his heart.

"But you've decided to keep yourself from loving anyone else?"

He stopped, feeling as if he'd slammed into a wall. As if Sunnie and Amanda had taken him to this point and hurled him up against a solid concrete barrier. What was he so afraid of?

"I'll hurt her," he said. "I'll let her down. Just like—"

"I love you, Josh," she cut in. "Don't you ever think you let me down. You're the reason I survived. You're the one constant source of encouragement and love in my life. You're kind and generous and incredibly loving, when you let yourself be, and it's time you stopped running away from who you really are."

"You think I've been running? All this time?"

"I think you don't want to get hurt, either, as much as you don't want to hurt anyone else. Either that or you don't want to take the responsibility for guarding anyone else's heart, the way you always tried to guard mine."

He thought of Amanda's heart. Her fragile, battered heart.

"Sometimes love hurts," Sunnie said. "But not all the time. It can be really good, too."

"I never thought I could be good for Amanda."

"You've already been good for Amanda. She told me so."

"She's not like anyone else I've ever been with."

"Thank God for that," Sunnie said.

He sighed, wanting so badly to see Amanda, to hold her in his arms again and reassure himself that she was okay. He wanted so damned much for her, wanted everything. Absolutely everything.

"She won't wait much longer," Sunnie warned.

"I know."

Four days later the doorbell rang at Josh's sister's flat in Paris. Amanda jumped, as she did every time it rang.

"It's not him," Sunnie said. "He picks the lock and

comes right in. I usually don't even know he's here until he grabs me and kisses me.''

"He picked the lock at my house once, too," Amanda said sadly.

"It's a hobby of his." Sunnie gave her a quick hug. "He's fine. I have a sixth sense where he's concerned. I'd know if he was hurt."

The bell rang again. Amanda watched as Sunnie, a pale, thin, fragile-looking blonde went to answer it. She was beautiful in a totally eccentric way. She lived in loose, white, gauzy things, tied at her tiny waist with elaborate, jeweled belts she made herself and sold in her boutique. She almost always wore at least three necklaces made of colored crystals, earrings to match and a series of wide bracelets on each wrist, and she looked delicate, like a fairy creature. Her hair was startlingly blond, a bit curly and long, her eyes the same blue as Josh's, and she had his smile, as well. Sometimes it was hard just to look at her, she reminded Amanda so much of Josh.

She'd rescued Amanda from the ambassador's winter retreat in Nice nine days ago. It had been a revelation, seeing what Josh's life must have been like. It told her so clearly that they came from totally different worlds. The ambassador's house was as elegant as a palace, with polished marble floors and oriental rugs, priceless sculptures and paintings, glittering crystal. Amanda had been afraid to touch anything. There were antiques and decorator-perfect rooms, an astonishingly beautiful view of the Mediterranean and a highly efficient staff at her beck and call.

Amanda had felt insulated, physically safe, but emotionally brittle. There was no warmth there, no genuine laughter, no emotion whatsoever. Josh's father treated her with the quiet, if hurried, politeness she supposed he would offer any stranger foisted off on him. He'd asked her exactly two questions about his son—whether he was doing well in his work and whether Amanda knew when to expect him back. If he was at all worried about Josh, it didn't show in anything he said or in anything she could read on his handsome yet oddly blank face. She dared to ask how long it had been since he'd spent any time with Josh, and the man looked puzzled, as if it hadn't occurred to him to keep track. Two years, possibly? Three? They were all so busy, of course.

She met Josh's mother on the evening of the second day, found her a suitable match for her husband. Beautiful, obviously used to the best money could buy, she made cold, scarcely polite inquiries about her son for all of two minutes and then excused herself to get ready for a party she was scheduled to attend. Amanda caught the tail end of what she thought must have been a nasty argument between the couple when she came downstairs to breakfast the next day, startling them and embarrassing herself.

Josh had grown up in the midst of this, she thought. Was it any wonder he didn't believe in love or that he didn't want anything to do with marriage?

He regretted making love to her on the boat. He'd only done it because she had begged him. She'd been totally unfair to him, pushing for a more intimate relationship than he wanted with her. All along she'd taken kindness and concern and a misplaced sense of responsibility on his part and tried to make it into something else entirely. Into love.

And he didn't love her.

Amanda leaned forward, resting her forehead in the palm of her hand. Now he was gone. She was starting to think he wasn't coming back. Which might be for the best. If he came back, she had to pull herself together and face him, thank him for all that he'd done and try not to make a fool of herself.

If there was any way for her to get out of here, she would. But there was this odd little matter of her passport, her identification, her credit card, her cash, all left at Rudy's villa and never returned to her. She was at the mercy of the French authorities and the U.S. Embassy. Otherwise, she'd have been gone by now.

Sunnie walked in carrying a huge, flat, rectangular box tied with a fancy bow and held it out to her. "Special delivery. For you."

Amanda started trembling all of a sudden.

"Someone has very good taste, and I bet I know who," Sunnie said.

Josh.

After an excruciating week and a half, *Josh*.

Amanda gave a slight tug on the ribbon. It fell apart in her hands. She pulled the top off the box and found a card with her name on it in a familiar, nearly indecipherable scrawl. A bit scared of what it might contain, she set it aside and dug into the box, finding a silver, shimmering dress inside, much like the one she wore to Rudy Olivara's dinner in Washington.

"Seems a bit elaborate for a man bent on saying goodbye. Even for my brother," Sunnie said. "Read the card."

Amanda pulled open the flap. The card read: "Have dinner with me. Please. 9 p.m."

He named a Paris hotel and scrawled a big *J* at the end. That was it. Dinner.

"I don't know if I can do this," Amanda said shakily. "I'm no good at goodbyes."

"How do you know it's goodbye?"

"What else would it be? He'll never stay with one woman. He told me so. Just like that. Right from the beginning he told me it wouldn't last. I didn't listen to him. So it's not his fault. None of this is." Amanda took a breath, tried to steady herself. "He really is the most amazing man."

"I know," Sunnie said.

"I'll never, ever forget him. It's a sad commentary on what my life is normally like, but I have a feeling that getting my heart broken by Josh will be the best thing that ever happens to me," she admitted. "I felt so alive with him, Sunnie. The whole world was full of possibilities. There were no limits to what might happen. Good things. Impossibly good."

"He has a gift."

"Yes." That was it. *A gift.* Feeling foolishly sentimental at the moment, she admitted, "I look at him and think of fairy tales, of endings with happily ever afters, even when it's obvious there's no way things could work out."

"Nothing's impossible," Sunnie insisted.

"He's the prince. He's every man I ever dreamed about when I was a little girl, before any man had ever lied to me or broken my heart."

"Josh has a truly kind heart."

"Yes, he does. Which is why I don't think I can face him again. I'll do something really stupid, like tell him again that I love him."

Sunnie smiled. "I knew all along that you loved him."

"What woman doesn't? I might as well get in line."

Unbidden came the memory of his voice, of one tantalizing promise. *There's no line, Amanda. There are no other women in my life right now. There haven't been for a while now.*

"Amanda?" Sunnie took her hands, bringing her back to the present. "I haven't set foot inside one of my father's houses in nine years. Josh knows that, and he loves me. For him to ask me to go there and get you... He would never ask that of me if you weren't very important to him."

"He feels responsible for me, that's all."

"He's never asked me to watch over one of his women before. He sounded as if he was afraid that by the time he got back, you'd be gone.'' Sunnie sighed. ''I want him to be happy. If anyone deserves that, it's Josh.''

''I want him to be happy, too.''

''So go to him. Give him a chance to tell you how he feels.''

Amanda gave in. That night she donned the dazzling, shimmering dress. Cinderella once again, off to see her prince. Sunnie wanted to put her hair up, but Amanda politely refused. Because Josh liked it down. She did let Sunnie adorn her with pretty colored stones and do her makeup. Sunnie even drove her to the hotel, giving her a kiss for luck before she got out of the car.

''Ms. Wainwright?'' The doorman came up to her right away. ''Mr. Carter's waiting for you in his suite. Would you follow me, please?''

She let him put her in an elevator and give the elevator operator instructions on delivering her to Josh's door. She'd counted on being in a restaurant, with people all around, not alone. The elevator whisked her to the top of the hotel, and the attendant walked her to the door. He even knocked, as if he'd known she might not have had the nerve to knock herself.

Josh opened it before she had time to even catch her breath. Even if she had, she would have promptly lost it once again. He was beautiful, dressed all in black, a tuxedo this time, his hair gleaming like gold in the dim light of what must be two dozen candles. His mouth was stretched into a tight, thin line; his gaze raked over her. He didn't say a word, merely extended a hand. She laid her palm across his. He pulled her inside, closing the door behind her, leaving them well and truly alone.

Vaguely she noted the table in the corner by the windows, set for two with crystal and china and silver, the fresh flowers, the candlelight, the elegance of the room, the soft music. So this was how Joshua Carter romanced a woman, she thought. Was she getting the standard treatment now?

Despite that, a little lick of heat unfurled inside of her.

She'd missed him desperately. Josh, her lover. Her one and only lover, and their one, too-brief night together. She remembered the fevered way he'd moved inside her, the husky need in his voice when he'd told her, "I want to see you," when there'd been nothing but near blackness inside the locked cabin on the boat. She'd wished to see him, as well. To see that powerful, exquisitely beautiful body of his bared for her to see, to touch, to taste.

She dared to look back up at him, her breathing fast and shallow, her head spinning. He looked just as affected as she did when he hauled her into his arms.

"I really meant to feed you first," he said, a second before his mouth closed over hers in a stormy, demanding kiss that left her limp and feeling like putty in his arms, like a woman he could do with what he wanted, without one squeak of protest from her.

When he lifted his head, she was glad to see that he was breathless, as well, and his eyes were positively smoldering. "We had a deal," he said. "Six months. You promised. Six months for me to have my fill of you. Which means you owe me five months, one week, six days, three hours and some change."

"That's what you want?" she said carefully. "Five months?"

"If that's all I get, then, yes, I want it," he said, pushing her against the wall and pinning her there with his body, with his big, hard, heavy, aroused body.

She felt an answering awareness in hers, that tightness to her breasts, swelling and puckering and begging for his touch. She felt heat in her stomach, between her thighs, the weakness in her knees.

"Josh, please," she said.

"Please, what?"

Tears seeped out of the corners of her eyes. She closed them tightly and hung on to him. He had his face buried in the sensitive curve of her neck, his hands running all over her body. Hers were busy, too, pushing against his chest, trying for just enough room to undo his tie and the studs on his shirt, so she could touch him. She desperately needed to touch him. She'd never been so greedy in her entire life.

He undressed her with lightning speed and stealth. She was hardly aware of it until the cool air hit her skin, her dress somewhere around her ankles.

He carried her to the bed, lowered her to the cool sheets and started yanking at his own clothes. Her mouth went dry. He was a man made for candlelight, she decided, drinking in the sight of him. She was on her knees on the mattress in front of him, touching him, stroking him.

"Later," he said, swearing softly, pushing her back onto the mattress, following her down. "Believe me, I want you to touch me. But later. For now—"

He pinned her to the mattress, kissing her deeply. A moment later he rolled onto his back, bringing her with him, settling her on top of him, palming her hips and pulling her against him. He felt so hot, so big. She leaned down against him, draping her body across his. He kissed her greedily, thrusting inside of her with his tongue. She lost all track of time and space, her world nothing but him, his big, hard body, his wicked fingers, his hot, soft mouth.

"Open your eyes," he said, tugging on her hair, bringing her head up. "I want to see you this time."

She looked down into his fevered eyes. She felt his hands between their bodies, and a minute later, with one subtle little shift in pressure, she felt him, pushing at the opening of her body, stretching. He thrust inside of her, smoothly and deeply. Her eyes flew open. She gasped, watching him, his jaw tight, his eyes locked on hers, the rippling muscles of his chest, all that golden skin.

She decided she liked having him inside of her, buried to the hilt. Liked wriggling her hips and making him groan. Liked that control he gave over to her in this position. Liked the fact that she could do whatever she wanted with him, that she could make him cry out. She liked thinking that one day she would know his body and play it with every bit of skill he used on hers, liked the idea of making him limp and spent and exhausted by what she would do to him, one day.

But for right now, she was his. Utterly his. Her body spasmed out of control and she cried out, collapsing on top of him, her head finding that spot on his shoulder and hanging on. He moved even more urgently than before. She loved the urgency, the edge of desperation. Loved feeling the hot, pulsing of his release, the dig of his fingertips into her hips, the strain showing in every muscle in his body. She loved being able to see him, to watch him, to lean over and kiss him softly on his mouth, easing him down, as he'd eased her down that first night.

It didn't stop for a long time, she found. That slow, gentle slide into exhaustion, satiation, utter relaxation. Their bodies were damp with sweat, their breathing finally slow and deep. He had his arms locked around her, and she lay heavily on top of him, her head in the crook of his shoulder.

"I like this spot," she said.

"I thought you would," he murmured, turning his head, kissing her sweetly. "I missed you."

"I missed you, too," she said cautiously.

"So why were you trying your best to leave before I got back here?" he said carefully.

"I was just trying to get my passport back," she said.

"I know. I went to considerable effort to make sure you didn't."

She took a breath, seeing the determined side of him. The man who always got what he wanted. And she tried not to think of what he meant by that. She tried not to think about how very good it was to be with him, even for a little while, how it seemed like forever when it had been less than two weeks. If two weeks had felt like an eternity without him, what would a month be like? A year? A lifetime?

She eased off him, rolling onto her back, pulling the covers up around her, and admitted, ''I didn't want you to have to ask me to go.''

He swore again, threw back the covers and walked into the bathroom. She stared up at the ceiling, waiting. He was back a minute later, slipping into the bed beside her, staring at her for a long time, then said, ''Who said anything about asking you to go?''

''You would, eventually,'' she said. It would be one more thing he would regret, and she didn't want him to have any more regrets about the time they'd spent together. And then she thought of one more regret—one of her own. ''I'm not pregnant. At least, I wasn't, before this.''

If anything, his expression seemed more stern than before. ''You think that's the only reason I'm here? To find out if you're pregnant?''

''It… I just thought you should know…that you don't have to worry about that. Or, you didn't. Before this time.''

''I used a condom,'' he said. ''I managed to grab one in time.''

''Oh.'' She'd scarcely realized.

The scowl across his handsome face intensified. She had the sensation of rattling a tiger's cage, without realizing how dangerous he truly was.

''Do you think I have so little regard for you?'' he asked.

''I know you care about me.'' Just as she knew caring would never be enough for her.

''Care about you?'' He frowned, moistened his lips and

backed off a little, not crowding her so much. "I'm not handling this well. I haven't handled this well right from the beginning. I thought about it last week and realized we've never even been out on a date. It sounds ridiculous to say it, but I've never even taken you out."

She looked around the candlelit room, the scene set for seduction. "This is your idea of a date, I suppose?"

He frowned. "Believe it or not, I used to know how to make a woman feel special. I want you to feel that way."

"You don't have to do that." Amanda closed her eyes, hurting. She didn't want him to treat her like all the others. "You didn't have to go to all this trouble."

"I wanted to," he said. "Don't you know? Don't you have any idea? I am absolutely lost without you. I can't quite figure out what I'm supposed to do without you."

She curled her bottom lip over her teeth and bit down, trying not to make a sound. All the breath rushed out of her, and silly little tears flooded her eyes.

"Amanda, I just spent the last three days rearranging my whole life for you."

"What do you mean, rearranging your whole life?"

"My father's resigning," he said. "There are people looking for someone to take his place, and my name's come up."

"You?" She gaped at him. "An ambassador?"

He nodded, never once taking his gaze off her face.

"Why?"

"It seemed to make sense, once I thought about it. My father's pushing for it, for his own sake. He likes the idea of being succeeded by his son, even if he does happen to barely tolerate me."

"I didn't think you cared what your father wants."

"I don't. But he has a good bit of influence. If he wants this, he could make it happen. And the job has its advantages. It would keep me in one place most of the time. I wouldn't be flying off to this country or that one. It wouldn't be quite as dangerous—''

"It's dangerous? Being an ambassador?"

"Not much, not under normal circumstances. But one of the reasons certain people are interested in seeing me in this job—one of the reasons I'm interested in it—is that it would put me in a good position to do some discreet work for Division One from time to time.''

"Oh," she said.

"Not a lot," he rushed on. "And probably more behind-the-scenes stuff than I do now. Not as dangerous.''

She sat there thinking. Obviously, she was missing something. "So your father wants it, and it wouldn't be as dangerous and it would keep you in one place?''

"Yes. That doesn't mean we couldn't travel. Paris is a good starting point to see all of Europe, Asia, Africa, the Far East. Whatever you wanted.''

"Me? You're doing this for me? You'd change your whole life for me?''

"And for me," he said soberly, quietly. "For us.''

"You don't love me," she said. "You don't want to ever get married, and even if you did—''

"Don't tell me it wouldn't be you," he said tightly. "Don't you dare tell me that.''

"Josh—''

"I just never understood this part of it, Amanda. Jamie and I talked about marriage a couple of weeks ago, and she said something I hadn't considered before, something that didn't sink in for me until a few days ago. I always looked at the limitations that come with marriage. I saw it narrowing all the possibilities about how I would live my life—''

"You mean the women," she said. "Narrowing the possibilities with all the women.''

"No," he said, then backtracked. "I mean, I am talking about that. About limiting myself to one woman. I'll do that gladly. I'm not expecting it to be any hardship. I don't happen to want any other woman but you.''

She just stared at him, wanting so badly to believe him.

''Amanda, before that night on the boat, I hadn't been with another woman in almost a year. Not since right after Rob died. Not since I decided I couldn't stay away from you any longer, that we were finally going to have a chance together.'' He grinned. ''I knew I was in trouble when I realized how long it had been and I still didn't want to do anything about it. Except get back to the States, back to you.''

She lay back against the plush pillows, struggling for air. He leaned over her again, looking particularly god-like, his golden hair and his bare skin glittering in the candlelight.

''You've gotten under my skin,'' he said. ''Inside my pores. Sometimes I feel you've got my heart in the palm of one of those delicate hands of yours and that my heart is yours to do with what you will. Lately it feels like you're crushing it. Right now, looking as if you hardly believe a word I'm saying… you're breaking my heart, Amanda.''

''You're breaking mine,'' she cried.

''Oh, Amanda.'' He kissed away her tears. ''Don't.''

He kissed her softly, sweetly. She was dizzy by the time he pulled away.

''My parents despise each other,'' he told her. ''The whole time they've been married, it seems. It is so ugly. I don't think I've ever known two people who were honestly happy with each other and married. At least not until very recently. I thought of marriage and imagined fights and power plays and people inventing hundreds of little ways to hurt each other, as if it was a game of one-upmanship. I thought of love, and all I saw was disappointment and hurt.''

''It doesn't have to be like that,'' she said.

''No, I don't suppose it does.'' He put his hand to the

side of her face, staring down at her. "Because I look at you, and I imagine all the things you bring to my life. You're so generous. So open. So sweet. You have so much to give. And there's so much I want to give you. What do you think about that?"

"I don't know if I can do this halfway," she said. "I know I said I could take whatever time we have together and then walk away. I thought I could, but—"

"I know." His gaze was steady, sure. "I've always known that about you. You're the kind of woman a man marries."

"So, you're saying what? That you've thought about it?"

"Yes." He groaned.

"But—"

"What am I supposed to do without you, Amanda? Tell me that, because I don't even know," he confessed. "I've been walking around for two weeks with a knot in my stomach the size of a baseball and just about as heavy, trying to figure out how to make this work, and most of the time all I could think about was that I don't even know what to do with my life without you in it."

"Oh." She started to cry in earnest.

"I can't go back to the way things were before. You were right. I was hiding. I was running away, and I was lonely. I need you."

"And I can't go back to the way things were before, either," she said. "I decided I've got to get out. I've got make something different of my life. I promised myself I was going to see the whole world somehow."

"I want to show it to you," he said. "I want to give it to you. I want to give you everything. I can make you happy. I know how to do that."

"I stopped believing in fairy tales a long time ago," she

admitted. "I stopped believing in just about every good thing in this world."

He grinned at her. "I will make you believe."

Amanda was dizzy. The room was spinning. "You're saying you want to marry me?"

"I'm saying I want to bind you to me, in every way possible," he said. "I want to spend the rest of my life with you. I want to give you children. I want to protect you and cherish you and give you absolutely everything. I don't think marriage demands any stronger commitment than that from a man."

"No," she said carefully. "I don't think it does."

"I won't lie to you. It makes me uneasy. I've never seen a marriage that worked."

"We can make it whatever we want, Josh. Marriage isn't a piece of paper. It's the promises we make to each other. It's what's in our hearts."

"I want every little piece of your heart. I'll guard it with my life. I will treasure it," he vowed. "I'll make you happy."

"You already have."

"I can make you happier, Amanda."

"That would be really hard to do," she said, smiling through her tears.

He reached into his pocket, took out a tiny box. A treasure box from Sunnie's shop. He pulled off the lid. Winking back at her was a diamond, a round, glittering stone set amidst an ornate, medieval-like setting of intricately carved silver.

She stared down at the ring. "Okay, maybe I could get happier."

Grinning, he slipped it onto her trembling hand.

"It's beautiful," she said.

"Just so happens, it's part of a matched set." He held up his right thumb. Around the end of it were two silver bands in a design that matched the ring. "I'll wear the ring. I'll keep the vows."

"It's what you want?"

"More than anything in this world," he said. "Put me out of my misery, Amanda. Say you'll do it. Say you'll marry me."

"You forgot something," she reminded him gently.

He took her face between his hands, looking her right in the eye. "I love you," he groaned. "Nothing in my life works without you."

"In that case," she said. "Yes. I will. I'll marry you."

* * * * *

*Sean Patrick Douglass takes centre stage
in Sally Tyler Hayes's next book*
HER SECRET GUARDIAN,
*coming only to Silhouette Sensation®
in May 2001.*

Silhouette Stars

Born this month

Gayle Hunnicut, Ronald Reagan, Bob Marley, Holly Johnson, John Travolta, Prince Andrew, Lee Marvin, Teddy Kennedy, Alain Prost, Sir David Puttman.

Star of the Month

Pisces.

As the year unfolds life will become calmer and more stable, so you can at last relax and plan for a happier future. Romance is well starred, relationships become stronger and you will feel able to enjoy the new opportunities on offer.

SILH/HR/0301a

Aries.

Spring heralds new beginnings and you will feel ready to take control of your life in a positive way. A special friend lets you know just how much they care.

Taurus.

Career moves are on the cards, but you must take care to understand all the implications. Finances are improving and you may feel able to commit to a group holiday later on in the year.

 Gemini

Others seem to be relying on you to organise their lives but you need the time to focus on your own. A day out late in the month brings a smile to your face.

Cancer

This month should prove to be a lucky period and you can achieve some of your long held ambitions. A friend seeks advice but they could surprise you with their reaction to your thoughts.

 Leo

Life is certainly improving. You have been through a very trying period but your resilience has paid off. A new friendship continues to blossom and keeps your spirits high.

Virgo

You know what you want and now is the moment to take it. Others will be amazed at your determination. Late in the month news from abroad could start you planning a trip.

SILH/HR/0301c

 Libra

There may be some conflict to overcome in order to get relationships back on track. A social event late in the month brings an old face back into your life.

Scorpio

The hard work of the last few months pays off and you should be able to relax and enjoy the rewards. Romance is well starred with loved ones in a very receptive mood.

 Sagittarius

You may have to keep your thoughts to yourself if you don't want to upset the balance in your personal life. Career moves, however, are well aspected with your talents being noted.

Capricorn

Spring heralds changes all of which you will welcome as you have been stuck in a rut for far to long . A chance of a welcome break should not be missed.

 Aquarius

Holidays occupy your thoughts. It seems that everyone is going away and, although you may be included, you need to think carefully about what you want. A gift comes as a pleasant surprise.

Look out for more
Silhouette Stars next month

▼™ SILHOUETTE
SENSATION®

AVAILABLE FROM 16TH MARCH 2001

THE DADDY TRAP Kayla Daniels

Kristen Monroe would do anything to save her nephew, but even she hesitated at Luke Hollister's door—for despite Kristen's adolescent crush on him, he'd been in love with her late sister and he wouldn't be expecting the bombshell Kristen was about to deliver...

THE WILDES OF WYOMING—HAZARD Ruth Langan

Desire gripped millionaire rancher Hazard Wilde when doe-eyed Dr Erin Ryan came to unravel the mystery surrounding his herd. But as passion engulfed them, danger crept closer and threatened Erin next!

GABRIEL'S HONOUR Barbara McCauley

When Gabriel Sinclair discovered Melanie Hart and her young son hiding in an abandoned house, he felt an unusual need to protect and succour them. But Melanie didn't want to divulge her secrets to her strong, attractive rescuer...

EGAN CASSIDY'S KID Beverly Barton

The Protectors

Years ago, rock-solid mercenary Egan Cassidy had spent a night of sensual ecstasy with Maggie Douglas. Now their son—a child he never knew existed—had been kidnapped!

THE RANCHER'S SURRENDER Jill Shalvis

Ty Jackson wanted the land Zoe Martin had inherited, but although his smooth charm and strong good-looks brought most women to their knees, Zoe didn't trust him. Could the sexy rancher fulfil her secret desire for a home, kids and a husband?

THE COMEBACK OF CON MACNEILL Virginia Kantra

Con MacNeill was determined to reclaim his high-powered career, but first he had to rescue Val Cutler from her business problems. He'd always sworn against emotional involvement with his clients—but Val was impossible to resist...

AVAILABLE FROM 16TH MARCH 2001

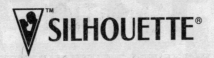

Intrigue

Danger, deception and suspense

LANDRY'S LAW Kelsey Roberts
CAPTURED BY A SHEIKH Jacqueline Diamond
A RANCHER'S VOW Patricia Rosemoor
BLACK RAVEN'S PRIDE Aimée Thurlo

Special Edition

*Vivid, satisfying romances
full of family, life and love*

WHEN BABY WAS BORN Jodi O'Donnell
MAN OF PASSION Lindsay McKenna
DYLAN AND THE BABY DOCTOR Sherryl Woods
THE MILLIONAIRE SHE MARRIED Christine Rimmer
MARRIED BY HIGH NOON Leigh Greenwood
SUMMER HAWK Peggy Webb

Desire

Intense, sensual love stories

DR IRRESISTIBLE Elizabeth Bevarly
A WHOLE LOT OF LOVE Justine Davis
EXPECTING HIS CHILD Leanne Banks
BLOOD BROTHERS Anne McAllister and Lucy Gordon
THE PREGNANT VIRGIN Anne Eames
A ROYAL MASQUERADE Arlene James

2 BOOKS
AND A SURPRISE GIFT!

We would like to take this opportunity to thank you for reading this Silhouette® book by offering you the chance to take TWO more specially selected titles from the Sensation™ series absolutely FREE! We're also making this offer to introduce you to the benefits of the Reader Service™—

★ FREE home delivery   ★ FREE gifts and competitions
★ FREE monthly Newsletter   ★ Exclusive Reader Service discounts
★ Books available before they're in the shops

Accepting these FREE books and gift places you under no obligation to buy; you may cancel at any time, even after receiving your free shipment. Simply complete your details below and return the entire page to the address below. **You don't even need a stamp!**

YES! Please send me 2 free Sensation books and a surprise gift. I understand that unless you hear from me, I will receive 4 superb new titles every month for just £2.80 each, postage and packing free. I am under no obligation to purchase any books and may cancel my subscription at any time. The free books and gift will be mine to keep in any case.

SIZEC

Ms/Mrs/Miss/Mr ....Initials.................................
BLOCK CAPITALS PLEASE

Surname...

Address...

....

....Postcode ....

Send this whole page to:
UK: FREEPOST CN81, Croydon, CR9 3WZ
EIRE: PO Box 4546, Kilcock, County Kildare (stamp required)

Offer valid in UK and Eire only and not available to current Reader Service subscribers to this series. We reserve the right to refuse an application and applicants must be aged 18 years or over. Only one application per household. Terms and prices subject to change without notice. Offer expires 30th September 2001. As a result of this application, you may receive further offers from Harlequin Mills & Boon Limited and other carefully selected companies. If you would prefer not to share in this opportunity please write to The Data Manager at the address above.

Silhouette® is a registered trademark used under license.
Sensation™ is being used as a trademark.